"Are you okay?"

"The change in position made my head throb and the room spin, but I'll live."

As he positioned himself, Dave's body heat and his soap and leather scent enveloped her, and the occasional brush of his thigh against hers or his chest at her back sent a tingling sensation to her belly. With her wrists taped together, her range of motion was seriously restricted as she felt blindly for his pocket. Her fingers found the soft cotton of his T-shirt over the taut plain of his belly, and he hissed.

Lilly jerked her hand back. "What? Did I hurt you?"

"No. I'm...ticklish." Was that embarrassment she detected in his tone?

He grunted. "Ignore me. Just...try again. Lower." His body skimmed along hers as he moved to better align her hands with their target.

An awkward awareness shot through her, along with a ripple of something she refused to call pleasure. She was not, not, not attracted to her late sister's boyfriend...

* * *

Dear Reader,

As I write, a book's characters become very real to me. They are my friends, my family, my children. It's truly rewarding for me to give my heroes and heroines happily-ever-afters. But my empathy is not only for the main characters. Every now and then, a secondary character will stand out to me, whether because of their bold personality or because they were innocents, left without their own happy ending. The hero of this book, Dave Giblan, was one of those characters. I knew he needed closure, a happy ending...and maybe a bit of redemption along the way.

Who better to match him with than the one person who shared his grief over a certain loved one's death? I hope you will enjoy *Rancher's Hostage Rescue*, and Dave and Lilly's second chance for a brighter future.

By the way, as in all my books, *Rancher's Hostage Rescue* includes a cat. But this is no ordinary cat. I'm pleased to introduce you to Maddie, my grandcat! My son, who grew up surrounded by my felines, learned to love cats and all their eccentricities almost as much as I do. I was thrilled for him when he adopted a skittish long-haired cat during his first year of graduate school. Maddie has overcome her scary pre-adoption beginnings (mostly) and is now an attention-hungry, lovable fluff ball. Thanks, Jeffery, for sharing Maddiecakes for this story! You can find pictures of our family's cats on my website, bethcornelison.com.

Happy reading,

Beth

RANCHER'S HOSTAGE RESCUE

———

Beth Cornelison

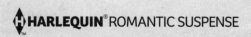
HARLEQUIN® ROMANTIC SUSPENSE

Recycling programs
for this product may
not exist in your area.

ISBN-13: 978-1-335-66208-8

Rancher's Hostage Rescue

Copyright © 2019 by Beth Cornelison

Printed in U.S.A.

Beth Cornelison began working in public relations before pursuing her love of writing romance. She has won numerous honors for her work, including a nomination for the RWA RITA® Award for *The Christmas Stranger*. She enjoys featuring her cats (or friends' pets) in her stories and always has another book in the pipeline! She currently lives in Louisiana with her husband, one son and three spoiled cats. Contact her via her website, bethcornelison.com.

Books by Beth Cornelison

Harlequin Romantic Suspense

The McCall Adventure Ranch

The Mansfield Brothers

Black Ops Rescues

Visit the Author Profile page at Harlequin.com for more titles.

To Paul and Jeffery—all my love

Prologue

The plan was ready. His weapon cleaned, primed, loaded. His target identified and surveilled. His escape mapped out. Contingencies decided. The time had come.

He stashed his gun in an accessible place on his person, then covered it with his long shirt, his jacket. By this time tomorrow, he'd be out of state, on his way to his next small-town target as he made his way to the Mexican border. To freedom.

Wayne Moore strapped on his grandfather's watch, the only thing he had left of his grampa's. His father had given it to him just days before he'd died. Wayne acknowledged the familiar tangle of regret, longing and disgust he experienced when remembering his father. A complicated legacy. A love-hate relationship. Jacob Moore had taught him well. Some lessons were learned on their homemade backyard shooting range and some at his father's side as they held up gas stations, diners and liquor stores. Others were taught with fists and belts. His dad's last lesson had been taught through his failure.

Wayne shook his head, remembering. His father had gotten careless, cocky. Had taken on a large city bank without adequate backup, without considering all the ramifications and obstacles. Had seen only his past successes and the promise of a bigger payday. He'd paid for his hubris with his life, shot by the security officer as soon as he fired his own weapon.

Lesson learned. Stick to small jobs. Keep it simple.

Small-town banks had smaller payouts, but also a smaller risk of capture. And the number-one goal, above the take, was not to be captured. Stay out of jail and be free to do another job on another day. Wayne wasn't sure how many days he had left, but if he didn't get some money for all his medical bills, they were sure to end sooner rather than later.

After a last check of his supplies, his weapons, his escape plan, Wayne climbed in his old beater sedan and headed for his target.

Chapter 1

Five excruciating months had passed since Helen had been murdered. Five months of grief, loneliness and, most of all, guilt. He hadn't taken her life, but that didn't exonerate him from his other wrongs. He'd taken her for granted, not given her what she deserved, acted the fool when he'd had a good woman who loved him.

Dave Giblan sat at Helen's graveside, his bad leg stretched in front of him and the moisture from the latest spring rain soaking through his jeans. He made biweekly visits to her grave, often bringing flowers to brighten the still-raw earth from her burial. Flowers he should have given her more often while she was alive. Instead, he'd laughed at his boss's advice to show Helen his feelings, his appreciation of her. Now it was too late.

Grunting as he shoved to his feet, he swiped at the

damp seat of his jeans and whispered, "Bye, Helen." Turning, he headed back to his pickup. He still had a slight limp, minor pain and stiffness following the surgery to repair his broken leg last December. The accident, a fall from a ladder, had been so random, so senseless…and just a few days before Helen was murdered. He lost both his girlfriend and his job within days of each other.

The McCalls swore that he'd have a job again when his leg was fully healed, and he could do the work of a ranch hand again. But since making that promise, they'd hired two new hands. Although he'd heard the Double M was climbing out of the financial quicksand it had been sinking in, he was skeptical they had the means to pay a third hand. Especially one who had a limp that may or may not ever go away.

He moved slowly down the grassy cemetery hill, using the cane he'd borrowed from the McCalls for use on uneven terrain. The handcrafted wooden cane with a simple scalloped design near the hand grip had belonged to the late father of the senior McCall, Michael.

Once back to his truck, he checked the list he'd left on the passenger seat. He'd been by the hardware store, taken his rent check to the post office, refilled his prescription for his anticlotting medicine and visited Helen. Only thing left on his list was a stop at the bank to cash his unemployment check.

He drove back into the business district of Boyd Valley, a small town nestled at the intersection of the Rocky Mountains and the plains of eastern Colorado. The country station on his radio played a sad song about loss and regret, and he reached over to turn it off. He didn't need a song to tell him that story. He lived it.

Five minutes later, he pulled into the parking lot of First Bank of Boyd Valley. The lot was largely empty. Only a couple of cars in the customer section. The convenience of online banking was rapidly shrinking the need for brick-and-mortar banks, human tellers, personal service. Just one more way the town, and the sense of community, was shrinking, dying in this age of technology.

Call him old-fashioned, but Dave preferred to do his banking in person, preferred to see the face of the teller who cashed his checks. His mother had been a teller in this very bank when he was growing up, and although she was gone now, buried in the cemetery just a few rows over from Helen, Dave felt her presence in the bank. Rose Charmand was the only teller there who still remembered working with his mother, and she always had a smile for him. Most days she'd also share a story about her memories of him as a kid, afternoons he'd spent behind the counter doing his homework, eating the lollipops that were supposed to be for the customers and waiting for his mother to drive them both home.

Today as he approached the window where Rose worked, her smile flashed brightly, as usual, before an odd shadow crossed her face. When her gaze darted toward the vault, Dave glanced in the same direction, curious what had distracted Rose. A woman with glossy gold hair and a knockout figure stood just inside the vault at the wall of safe-deposit boxes. A sense of déjà vu skittered down Dave's spine as he watched the woman. Brow furrowed in confusion, he faced Rose.

"Morning, beautiful," he said with a half grin for the older woman. He slid his check across the counter. "How's life treating you?"

"As well as a woman my age can expect," Rose quipped. "The usual? Deposit half, half in cash to you?"

He nodded, then glanced back at the golden-haired woman in the vault. "Who's that?"

Rose glanced up briefly from counting out bills. "You don't recognize her?"

"Her back's to me. Maybe if I saw her face…"

The teller kept shuffling money, her eyes down, as she mumbled, "Honey, that's Lilly Shaw."

Even as the name registered, the woman turned. Helen's sister.

His breath stuck in his throat. Though they didn't resemble each other in more than hair color, the sight of her brought a flood of memories that drowned him with fresh waves of guilt and grief.

Why was she in town? Why had he picked *this* moment to deposit his check? He really couldn't bear a confrontation with Helen's last living relative. The one person who loved Helen as much as he had. Maybe more so. Lilly hadn't taken Helen for granted. Hadn't needed to be badgered for demonstrations of affection. Would never forget an important anniversary. Could never be accused of half-assing their relationship.

His gut rolled. The last time he'd talked to Lilly, at Helen's twenty-fifth birthday celebration, she'd looked him straight in the eye and called him a first-class jerk. She threatened him with bodily injury if he hurt Helen, a vow he'd laughed off. He'd told Lilly she had nothing to worry about, that the complaints Helen had about him were just her sister blowing off steam. Things between him and Helen were fine.

He knew the instant Lilly spotted him. Her gaze, which had passed casually over him at first, darted back to him in surprise, her steps faltering. The very next second, the soft, feminine curves of her face hardened. Her lips pinched, and flinty disdain filled her eyes.

He'd avoided Lilly at Helen's funeral. He'd been too swallowed up in his own shock and heartache to face Lilly's accusations and criticism. But he deserved anything Lilly could dish out. She'd been right about his lackluster attitude toward his relationship with Helen, and now he lived every day with regrets he could never correct.

At the very least, he owed Lilly an apology. Well, he owed Helen an apology, but with Helen gone, Lilly was as close as he'd get to earning forgiveness for his blithe attitude while Helen was alive. He wiped his damp palms on the seat of his jeans and headed toward her. Her brow furrowed, and her gaze dropped briefly to his bad leg as he limped toward her. Had Helen told her about his accident, his surgery, his temporary unemployment?

Lilly's shoulders squared as he approached. Blinking hard, as if battling back tears, she glanced toward the door and took a few quick steps in that direction.

He blocked her path, wrapping his hand around her arm when she tried to brush past him.

"Lilly, wait. Please."

"I have nothing to say to you." Her green eyes glinted at him, and she tugged at her arm. "Let me go."

"Give me just five minutes. Please." He heard the

rusty sound of his voice and paused to clear it. "I want to apologize."

His request stilled her attempt to get free. She narrowed a suspicious glare on him. "An apology. For what?"

"For…lots of things. The way things went down between me and Helen."

She scoffed. "Isn't Helen the one who deserves that apology?" She tipped her head in mock enlightenment and added, "Oh, wait. She's dead. It's *too late* to apologize for the way you treated her."

Guilt pooled like acid in his gut. "I know that, but—"

"But nothing, Dave!" she said, her voice rising.

The other customers in the bank glanced their way. The security guard, a retired sheriff's deputy who'd once busted a sixteen-year-old Dave for trespassing on school grounds after hours, put his hand on his utility belt and strolled over. "Is there a problem here?"

"No, Deputy Hanover," Dave said, flashing a tight smile. "I just need a moment's privacy with Ms. Shaw."

Hanover glanced to Lilly for her response. After a few seconds to consider, she frowned and gave the security officer a nod. Deputy Hanover stepped away, and Dave guided Lilly out of the main lobby toward a corner near the loan offices.

"Look…" he said and sighed. Now that he had her ear, what did he say? He hadn't prepared anything in the last few weeks on the off chance he might run into Lilly. He'd honestly thought he'd never see her again.

"I—I had a ring. Have a ring. An engagement ring," he began awkwardly.

Clearly his opening caught her off guard. She blinked rapidly and gave her head a small shake. "Excuse me?"

"I was going to give it to her on New Year's Eve. I had this whole thing planned with dinner and driving out to this lookout spot and—"

"Why are you telling me this?" she asked in a low growl.

"Because… I want you to know I *did* have feelings for Helen." He scrubbed a hand on his face, deciding what needed to be said next.

She arched a delicate eyebrow, her expression cool. "You *had feelings* for her?"

"Yes! I was serious about her, not just playing at a relationship."

"Evidence would say otherwise."

He opened his mouth to protest, but she held up a hand to cut him off. "You can't even say you *loved* her. You have to use phrases like you *had feelings* for her." She gave a bitter laugh. "Yeah, that's a sentiment that will make a girl want to marry you. 'I *have feelings* for you, Helen. Let's spend our lives together.'"

He took a deep breath and exhaled. Even as irritation with her sarcasm scraped through him, he reminded himself he'd earned Lilly's scorn. He flexed and balled his hands at his sides, trying to recalculate. To find the right words. He might not get another chance to set things right with Helen's only family. Maybe earning her forgiveness shouldn't matter to him, but…it did.

"I screwed up with her. I know. She was a great, kind, terrific person, and I blew it. Okay? I know that!" He took a cleansing breath, his stomach knotting as he added, "And I did love her. I only… It's just hard to say the words now because she's… It makes it harder now that she's…"

"Dead," Lilly said, her stare penetrating and unnerv-

ing. "My God, you can't even say that word? Helen is *dead*. Say it."

"Why?"

"I want to hear you say it."

He swallowed hard. "She's dead."

Lilly's mouth puckered a bit, and she glanced away. But not before he saw the sparkle of tears that filled her eyes.

Dave poked his fingers in his jeans pockets, shifted his weight…then shifted it back when his bad leg protested with a dull throb. "Lilly, I'm sorry."

Her gaze darted briefly to him.

"I'm sorry for your loss."

She drew a slow tremulous breath. "Thank you. And… I'm sorry…for your loss, too."

She caught him off guard with that, and he had to work to suppress the rise of emotion in his throat. "Why, um, why are you in town?"

"I'm in Boyd Valley to close her house and put it on the market, if that's what you mean." She gave him a matter-of-fact look, and her tone had regained its sharp edge. "I'm at the bank to empty her safe-deposit box." She raised both eyebrows now in a way that said, "Satisfied, Mr. Nosy?"

He wasn't sure how to respond. He hadn't even known Helen had a safe-deposit box. And knowing that Lilly was preparing to sell Helen's house, was getting rid of all the things that represented the life of the woman he'd loved, gave him a sick feeling in his gut. After a beat too long, he finally managed a flat "Oh."

She snorted a wry laugh. "You have such a way with words."

He gritted his back teeth, then took a moment to push aside her biting comment. Rather than answer her quip with one of his own, he said, "If you need any help with the house—"

She shook her head. "No. I can do it by myself."

"Are you sure? 'Cause I can—"

She shot him a hard look, so he dropped the matter.

"Was that it? You just wanted to tell me you had a ring? You thought I needed to know you *had feelings* enough to plan a proposal that never happened?"

Okay, now her mocking was starting to tick him off. He had to take a couple breaths to swallow the snide reply that frustration, annoyance and his own grief pushed onto his tongue.

He rubbed the back of his neck. Cornering her was probably a bad idea. He should have waited, gone to Helen's house and taken the time to think about what he wanted to say. Waving his hand in dismissal, he mumbled, "More or less."

Lilly hiked the strap of her purse higher on her shoulder and jerked a nod. "Goodbye then." She took three stiff strides before turning back toward him. "I did find some men's clothes at her house that I assume are yours. If you want them back, and anything else of yours you left there, you can come by later today. Anything still there on Saturday goes to charity."

With that, she marched toward the front door of the bank…just as a man wearing a dark hoodie and wielding a gun stormed through the entrance and shouted, "Everybody on the ground! You try something heroic, you die!"

Chapter 2

Lilly froze when she saw the gun wielded a scant few feet from her. Her brain blanked for a couple of stumbling heartbeats as she tried to process the horror. Was this really happening?

In the next second, the man in the black hoodie grabbed her arm and swung her around. He snaked his arm around her throat and held her against him as a human shield. The truth of the situation slammed into her like a fist to the gut. *Bank robbery. Hostage. Gunfire?*

Gunfire! Her ears rang from the loud shots the robber fired, as well as from the screams of the other women in the bank.

"I said no heroics!" the robber shouted, his arm aiming off to her right.

Fresh terror washed through her. She registered the movement of people dropping to the floor and covering their heads, as though watching through water. Someone to her left sobbed.

The robber pushed her forward, and she stumbled, her feet as heavy as concrete blocks.

"You, behind the counter," he shouted, waving the gun toward the tellers. "Let me see your hands! No alarms or I shoot you. Got it?"

The two tellers gaped at him, their hands shaking as they lifted them over their heads.

"Got it?" he asked again in a roar.

Their heads bobbed, and the younger teller whimpered, "Please, don't shoot. I have babies at home. They need me."

The gunman swung his weapon toward the young mother behind the counter. "Do what I say, and you'll live to see those kids again. Start filling bags from the drawers. Make it quick!" He turned slowly, dragging Lilly in a 360-degree pivot with him as he checked the room. He paused when he spotted a man on the floor with his cell phone out, pointed toward the robber. He fired his weapon two more times, shattering the phone and wounding the man's hand. "Really, asshole? Is a video for your Twitter feed really worth dying over?"

As the robber continued turning, Lilly's gaze darted toward where Dave had been standing. Some part of her brain knew he was her best chance of assistance. But he was no longer standing where she'd left him. Her breath sawed in panicked gulps as she scanned the lobby. She spotted him hovering over the security guard, who was lying on his side, blood staining the front of his uniform shirt. *Blood.* Lilly's gut swooped.

The robber noticed Dave, too. He swung the handgun in his direction and yelled, "Hey, cowboy! I said no heroics. On the ground, hands where I can see 'em. Now!"

Dave lifted both hands, which were smeared with red. "Whoa. Easy, man. The old guy is bleeding out from where you shot him. I'm just trying to help him." Dave put his hands back on the guard's wound, clearly trying to staunch the bleeding. "You could say I'm helping you, too. You don't want a dead security guard added to your rap sheet."

The gunman glared at Dave, then whipped his attention back to the tellers. "Where's that money? Let's go! Let's go!"

The older woman behind the counter shoved a stack of bills toward him along with a bank bag full of cash. The robber, obviously needing to free the arm he had around her neck, released Lilly, shoving her toward the floor. "You get down and don't move."

She obeyed, and when she glanced up at him, he waved his hand toward her large hobo-style purse. "Give me the bag."

Again, fear and disbelief rendered her motionless.

"Do it!" He kicked at her and grabbed the strap of the bag, snatching it off her shoulder with force. Jerking open the snap closure, he jammed handfuls of bundled bills into the purse.

Frowning, he paused in his frenzy and waved a banded stack of cash at the older teller. "Ones?" He leaned across the counter and smacked the woman's face with the money.

The woman gasped and pressed her hand to her cheek as she staggered back from the counter. Lilly tensed, hot anger flaring in her gut.

"Do you think this is a game?" he shouted at the teller. "That I did all this for *ones*?" Then a movement or noise must have caught his attention, because he whirled around, swinging his weapon toward the lobby. "Stay down! Hands out where I can see 'em!"

A ripple of murmurs and gasps rose from the customers and employees hunkered on the floor. Lilly cut a glance toward Dave.

Helen's ex had a glacial stare pinned on the robber. Although he was mostly flat on the floor, one hand was still out of sight, under the injured security guard, presumably tending to the man's wound.

Then Dave's gaze flicked to Lilly's and locked. Softened with concern and questions. Her heart gave a soft bump, and an odd warmth spread inside her. Dave's concern for her made her feel less alone, less frightened.

But a moment later, Dave returned a steely glare to the robber, who'd finished grabbing up the bagged money and stuffing her purse with bills. The thug backed toward the door, making his getaway.

Knowing that some punk was able to come in here, shoot people and take what wasn't his, then waltz out again, offended Lilly on a deep, cellular level. Rage flared in her core like a blacksmith's furnace. She wanted to launch herself at the man and claw his eyes. Wanted to scream in his face the way he'd—

A man from the street entered the bank, walking blindly into the robbery. The thief spun around. Panicked. Fired toward the new customer. Lilly jolted, stunned.

The man from the street grabbed his side, then turned and ran out.

Screams filled the bank lobby as the robber fired again toward a desk where a secretary had crawled to hide. When the robber aimed his weapon at the front counter of the bank, Lilly rolled toward a stuffed chair in the waiting area outside the loan offices.

Two more shots rang out. Different weapon. Different pitch to the blasts.

Shaking, she peered out from behind the chair. The robber was hunched forward, his shooting arm limp. Spitting out a curse, his booty clutched in his left hand, the robber scuttled toward the exit. Another shot boomed from the new weapon, shattering a glass partition at the bank entrance. And then…silence. As if everyone in the bank was holding their breath, uncertain. Was it over?

Lilly sat up slowly, trembling, her mind reeling, her heart slamming against her ribs. A groan, a sudden movement near the fallen guard, drew her attention. Dave had surged to his feet, a gun in his hand, and he jogged, limping, toward the door where the robber had fled. The expression he wore was determined. Murderous.

He'd kill the sonofabitch, Dave swore, gritting his back teeth in pain as he rushed out of the bank. Given a clear shot, he would stop that bank-robbing cretin from maiming innocent bystanders, assaulting old ladies and killing security guards ever again. But his bum leg slowed him down. He didn't make it to the parking lot before the robber had climbed into a rusty sedan and was racing onto the main road through town. Dave knew better than to fire at a moving vehicle on a city street. Too many drivers shared the road, too many people had poked their heads out of nearby businesses, likely having heard the gunfire.

Growling under his breath, he lowered the revolver he'd taken off Deputy Hanover, and raised a hand to rub his face. He stopped when the blood on his palm caught his eye. A sick feeling swelled in his gut. He'd tried to help the fallen guard, but the older man had died even as Dave tended him. He'd had his hand on the man's chest and felt the slow drub of his heart stop.

"Dave!"

He faced Lilly as she stepped out of the bank, warily eyeing the parking lot and the gun still in his hand. He sighed heavily. "He got away."

Even to his own ears, he sounded defeated. Could he have stopped the robbery? He'd known Deputy Hanover had a revolver on his belt, but for better or worse, he'd made aiding the wounded man his priority.

"Did he hurt you?" he asked Lilly.

She shook her head. "Just scared me." She blew out a tremulous breath. "I've never had a gun pointed at my head before. *So* not fun."

He twisted his mouth in wry agreement. "No."

Her gaze dipped to the red staining his hands. "Is any of that blood yours?"

"No. It's Deputy Hanover's." Dave furrowed his brow, felt a knot of emotion tighten his throat. "He didn't make it." The answer scraped from his throat, as rough as sandpaper.

"No, he didn't," she said. "I checked on him before I came out here. I'm sorry."

Regret poured through him. He'd weighed his options, tried to balance the risk of agitating the robber and drawing more fire on innocents against the possibility of putting an end to the crime in progress. When the scumbag had shot at Gill Carver and his cell phone, he'd made his choice to act. But he'd had to work to get the weapon out from under the dead security guard's hip without drawing attention.

Too little, too late.

That had become a theme with him. Forget roads. He was paving entire interstates to hell with all his useless good intentions.

The whine of a siren filtered through the rattling thoughts and recriminations in his brain.

"We should go back inside." Lilly touched his arm. "You don't want to be standing out here with that gun when the cops arrive."

His cheek twitched in a weak grin. "True that."

Dave followed Lilly back into the bank, his leg throbbing from the recent abuse of diving to the floor, crawling around and attempting to run with his full weight on it. Inside, the other customers and personnel of the bank were huddled in clusters. One group tended to Gill Carver, the man whose hand had been shot, and that was the direction Lilly went first. Another group surrounded the branch manager, who held a phone to his ear, and a few women were comforting the younger teller, who seemed to be hyperventilating. Someone had draped their coat over the fallen security guard, covering his wound and face.

Dave laid the revolver on the ground next to Hanover, nudging the weapon out of sight with his toe. He grabbed a bunch of facial tissues from a box on a secretary's desk, along with a squirt of hand sanitizer, and cleaned as much blood from his hands as he could. Drying his palms on the seat of his jeans, he headed over to Rose Charmand, who sat in one of the lobby chairs with another woman crouched beside her.

She gave him a wobbly smile as he approached. "Well, that was a bit more excitement than I'd expected for today."

Dave kneeled, grunting in pain, and took Rose's hand. "Are you all right? I saw him hit you."

"With a stack of money," she added and gave a hooting laugh. "That's one I can cross off my bucket list!" She held up a finger, gnarled with arthritis, and added, "No, wait. Not getting slapped with money. Rolling naked in money. *That's* what's on my bucket list."

Dave flashed her a grin while trying fervently *not* to picture the septuagenarian doing anything naked. He squeezed her hand. "I'm glad you're okay."

From the corner of his eye, he saw Lilly approach and squat beside Rose's chair, next to the other woman. Rose acknowledged Lilly with a smile. "Oh, good. You made it. I called this meeting today to discuss the future of the kingdom. Who will reign when I'm gone?"

Dave arched an eyebrow. "How hard did he hit your head?"

The woman next to her chuckled. "Can't blame a

concussion for that craziness. That's typical Rose. Best evidence yet that she's fine."

"Are you fine? Both of you? Any injuries or short-ness of breath?" Lilly asked, giving both of the women a close look.

Dave regarded Lilly, remembering vaguely that Helen had said her sister was an ER nurse in Denver.

Rose and the other woman both shook their heads.

"How is Gill's hand?" Dave asked, nodding toward the injured man.

"Mostly just cut up as the phone busted in pieces. Someone wrapped it in a shirt. He'll be fine until he gets to the ER for stitches." She drew a deep breath and added, "The bullet is lodged in the floor, mere inches from where his head was."

Dave bit his bottom lip to catch the curse word he refused to say in front of Rose.

"Hmph," Rose said, her expression pinched with dis-taste. "Too bad the bullet didn't get Gill in the ass, so he'd know what we feel whenever he's around shootin' off his mouth."

The teller beside Rose covered a laugh, and Dave bit the inside of his cheek to contain his amusement. Gill might be a pain in the butt, but he didn't want to ap-pear insensitive in front of Lilly, who frowned at Rose's harsh remark.

"I'm going to check on Shelly. Don't give away my claim to the throne," the other woman told Rose. With a wink, she stood and moved to the group comforting the sobbing younger teller.

Dave and Lilly locked gazes for a moment before Rose said, "You two do know each other through Helen, right? I saw you talking before that—that...*jackass* came in waving his gun."

He wasn't sure why, but hearing Rose curse after he'd censored his own reaction brought a brief grin to Dave's face. Lilly's countenance remained grim, however, and he sobered quickly, remembering Deputy Hanover... and the subject of his previous conversation with Lilly.

"Yes," Lilly said, her tone subdued. "We know each other." She held his gaze and said, "You're limping." A statement, not a question.

"Yeah. Broke my leg and had a rod put in back in December. Helen didn't tell you?"

Her expression reflected a moment of realization, then sadness. "Oh, right. She did mention it. In all this confusion, I just..." She waved her hand vaguely and didn't finish the thought.

The memory of Helen hovering at his side after he'd broken his leg made his heart squeeze, and he tore his gaze from Lilly's before she read too much in his eyes.

A sound at the front door and new voices drew his attention as deputies from the sheriff's department entered the building. Within minutes, the tense process of questioning and evidence-gathering began.

Lilly twisted her fingers in the hem of her shirt, trying her best to answer the deputy's questions. The loan office and the branch manager's office had been commandeered for interviews, and after two tedious hours of waiting, she'd been called in to give her statement.

She'd finished recounting the events, up to the point where the robber was making his getaway and Dave had returned fire.

"Where did Mr. Giblan get the gun?" the officer asked.

She shrugged. "I don't know for sure. I assume he used the security guard's gun."

"Did you see a weapon on Mr. Giblan when you spoke to him before the robbery?"

Lilly shook her head. "No. But I wasn't looking for one."

"How many shots did Mr. Giblan fire?" the deputy asked.

"I don't—" Remembering the deputy's previous request to think hard when she'd voiced her uncertainty, she closed her eyes and let the terrifying moments replay in her head, working to recall specifics of something she'd rather blank from her mind. One bang. Two. The robber jerking, then his arm going limp.

"Maybe two? I think at least one shot hit the guy. He hunched forward, and his gun arm seemed to go slack." She reviewed the scene again, and a chill raced down her back. "I think he fired again as the robber ran out. The glass by the main door shattered." What she knew for certain was that Dave had stopped the gunman from firing any more random shots at the bank customers. His actions had probably saved lives.

"Dave made the right call. He's a hero," she said, more voicing her thoughts than answering the deputy's questions. "He stopped the guy from hurting anyone else." She surprised herself, defending Dave's actions even before anyone criticized.

The deputy frowned. "Officially speaking, our office cannot condone or encourage vigilantism."

Vigilantism? The word conjured images in her brain

of old Westerns with cowboys hunting down bad guys and taking revenge on all degree of criminals and cretins. She pictured Dave on his knee beside the older teller, his hand clutching hers as he comforted her and joked about her bucket list. The word *vigilante* didn't mesh with the gentle man she'd witnessed in those moments.

"And then what happened?" the deputy asked.

She retold the robber's escape, Dave's pursuit, how she'd checked on the guard and found him dead, before following Dave outside.

"Did you see the suspect after you left the building?"

She shook her head. "He was gone by then. Dave said he'd driven off in a hurry in a—"

"I can't use hearsay, ma'am. Only what you saw or heard, firsthand."

She flipped up her palm. "Then that's all I have. Dave and I went back inside and checked on Mrs. Charmand and the other patients' conditions until—"

"Patients?" the deputy said, interrupting her again.

She blinked, thinking about what she'd said. "Oh, well, I guess that's how I think of them. I'm a nurse, and my focus was treating injuries. Sort of triage. Checking everyone's physical and mental condition. There was another customer there who also has medical training— as a veterinarian—who was helping out, as well. He was keeping an eye on the man with the injured hand while I surveyed the rest of the group."

The deputy nodded and glanced down at his clipboard. He handed her a business card. "If you remember anything else that could be helpful, please contact us."

Out of habit, she reached behind her for her purse.

Stopped. Her shoulder gave a small twinge as she re-membered the violent tug when the robber had ripped the bag from her. The thief had her wallet, her keys, her phone and a dozen other things she'd miss. Her favor-ite hairbrush. That perfect shade of plum lipstick she'd just bought. The Dior sunglasses, a splurge she'd bought on her last vacation with Helen. The butterfly key chain her mother had bought her when they'd gone to Dollywood when she was nine years old. *Every lily needs a butterfly, and you are the prettiest flower of all.* Her sentimental fondness for and collection of butter-fly-themed items began that day. A hollow ache filled her heart for the lost memento.

Sighing, she stood and exited the small office. Now what? She had no car keys to get home. The thief had… Another realization slammed her like a gut punch. The bank robber had everything she'd just taken from Helen's lockbox. The jewelry pieces that had been their mother's, Helen's passport and birth certificate and God knows what else that had been in those little boxes and envelopes she'd scooped into her purse to examine later. Irreplaceable things that Helen had treasured.

Anger, grief and residual fear flashed through her in an overwhelming flood. Her knees buckled as she walked into the lobby of the bank, and she sank—crumpled, really—into a chair near the front door. Tears filled her eyes, and she pressed a hand over her mouth to muffle the scream she wanted to let loose. Instead, she cried, shoulders shaking and her chest aching as she struggled for a breath between sobs. Other than the day she'd learned about Helen's murder, she'd been strong, she'd held it together. But the loss of the things from Helen's lockbox felt like losing her sister all over again.

"Lilly?"

She jerked her head up. Dave stood beside her, his eyes narrowed with concern. She dashed her hand under her eyes, swiping at the tears. "What do you want?"

He lowered himself awkwardly onto an adjacent chair, favoring his right leg, which he extended stiffly in front of him. He leaned toward her and pitched his voice low. "Are you all right?"

She dismissed him with a snort. "Peachy."

"Can I do anything?" he asked, his voice a soft rumble. Compassionate. Soothing. The way it had been when he'd spoken with the older teller. To continue to rebuff him with sarcasm in light of his kindness would only make her look bitchy, so she modulated her expression and simply shook her head.

"Okay," he said after a brief pause in which he studied her with an unnerving scrutiny. He pushed back to his feet with a soft grunt of pain as he put weight on his bad leg. "Goodbye, Lilly. I'll be by the house later this week to get my things."

The house…

"Dave, wait." She dabbed at her runny nose and drew a cleansing breath. "Could you…drive me home? The robber took my purse…with my keys. You could get your things now, and I could get the spare keys for my car and come back up to retrieve it." She hated asking anything of the man who'd failed her sister in so many ways, but her proposal was the most logical solution to two issues.

Dave scratched the back of his head as he considered her request for all of three seconds. "Um, sure." He spread his hands. "Of course. You ready?"

She stood and smoothed the seat of her slacks. "Yes. More than ready."

Lilly followed him out to his truck, and he held the passenger door for her while she climbed in the cab.

"Sorry about the mess," he said after he slid behind the steering wheel. He tossed a few fast food wrappers and empty drink cans behind the seat. "I'd have cleaned up if I'd known you would be—"

"Don't bother," she said giving him a flat look. "My opinion of you and how you treated my sister is not going to change in the next twenty minutes while you get your things from her house."

Dave firmed his mouth, and his eyebrows dipped in a low line over his dark brown eyes. Bedroom eyes, she could remember Helen calling them when she'd first started dating Dave and she'd gushed to Lilly about her handsome new boyfriend.

Okay, he was handsome. She'd give him that. But the mess in his car underlined the impression she'd formed in subsequent conversations about Dave. A man who was just too casual in his relationships, in his house-keeping, in most aspects of his life. No plan for the future. No commitments and few responsibilities.

She spotted a distinctive cone-shaped plastic sleeve on the floor and bent to pick it up. The grocery store sticker on the plastic wrap verified what the contents had been. *Fresh floral arrangement, $8.99.*

"Wooing a new girlfriend?" she asked, knowing her tone was brittle and not caring.

He started the engine and sent her a cool look. "No. Visiting the grave of the woman I miss every day."

His reply shocked her. Shamed her. She hadn't been to Helen's grave since the funeral. She planned to go before she left town, but…it was too painful, and she hadn't yet mustered the nerve to go.

"Oh." She let the wrapper fall back to the floor. "Sorry. I…shouldn't have assumed—"

"Like I said earlier," he said, facing the road as he drove, "I was going to give her an engagement ring on New Year's Eve."

Lilly's heart contracted. "She'd have said yes. She loved you, despite—"

He cut a sharp gaze toward her, his dark eyes full of pain, but said nothing.

Lilly cursed under her breath. "Dave, I guess it's obvious I'm no fan of yours. You strung her along for five years, forgot important anniversaries—"

"I know."

"—dismissed her unhappiness when she tried to talk about it, flirted with other women in front of her—"

"Now that's not true!"

"—stood her up on her birthday—" Lilly's volume grew as her anger heated.

"That wasn't my fault!" he argued, matching her volume. "There was an emergency at the Double M, and I couldn't get away. I explained that to her, and we went out the next night!"

"And you were always making excuses for your shortcomings. Never taking responsibility for your screwups with her!"

He smacked the steering wheel and shouted, "I know I did! I hate myself for it!"

She fell silent, studying him. He flexed his hand then squeezed the steering wheel. His jaw clenched, and his nostrils flared as he breathed deeply.

After a moment, he cut a dark glare toward her, his tone calmer, quieter. "I regret it every hour of every day. She deserved better. I let her down. I *know* that."

Lilly turned toward the side window, blinking away the tears that stung her eyes. Why had she lit into him like that? Berating him wouldn't change the past, wouldn't bring Helen back. Helen had loved him, despite his shortcomings, and she'd be appalled to know Lilly was calling him to task for the things she'd confided in sisterly phone conversations. Venting, Helen had called it. Maybe all women needed to let off steam now and then about their mates' foibles. If she'd vented to Helen about Alan's faults and transgressions, would she have been in a better position to have saved her own marriage? She'd never know. Alan was gone, remarried, and she was…

Lilly closed her eyes. Never mind what she was. Where she was. What she'd do next. She just had to keep putting one foot in front of the other. One day at a time. She might be alone in the world, but she would not wallow in self-pity. She would be strong, like her mother had been after Dad left.

But in the short term, she simply wanted to complete her business with Dave Giblan and see him on his way so that she never again had to see the man who was a painful reminder of Helen's too-short life. After that, she'd pour a large glass of wine and put this horrible day behind her.

* * *

After their brief shouting match, Lilly grew sullenly silent. Dave wasn't proud of himself for responding to her anger and accusations with the heat he'd used. After all, everything she'd said was true, was something he'd castigated himself for in the last few months. Most everything. But the fact that he had a legitimate excuse for missing her birthday dinner was cold comfort in hindsight. Had he not been so prone to disappointing her, the birthday dinner would have been more easily forgiven. Instead it had been just another letdown on a long list that she'd reported to her sister.

"How long will you be off work?" she asked, breaking into his thoughts.

He rubbed his leg almost without thought and sighed. How long, indeed? "I should be released by the doctor to return to limited work in another month or two."

"Good."

"Yeah, except…"

She turned and met his glance. "What?"

"The McCalls told me when I broke my leg that I'd have a job waiting when I was ready to come back, but…they've hired a couple replacement hands already. One is a woman. A former rodeo champion."

"Really? A woman?" she asked, clearly intrigued.

"You ever meet Zoe Taylor at the diner in town?"

She nodded. "Good food. Nice lady. I remember her."

"It's her daughter they hired. Back right after Christmas. Then earlier this spring they brought on another guy. I can't see them taking me back and letting one of them go, so…"

"Maybe they'll keep them and take you back," she offered.

"Not unless they've recovered more from their financial setbacks than I've heard. Things were real tight last year." He shook his head and squeezed the steering wheel. "I'm guessing I'll have to look elsewhere for work."

She hummed her acknowledgment then aimed a finger out the side window. "This is your turn."

He faced her and lifted a corner of his mouth in a sad smile. "Yeah, I know."

She twisted her mouth in a chagrined frown. "Oh, right. Sorry."

An-n-nd…the awkward silence was back.

When they reached Helen's house, Dave parked in the side drive and cut the engine. Even before he could unfasten his seat belt and hobble around the front end of his truck, Lilly was out and hurrying up the front steps. She walked to the end of the porch, where she lifted a flowerpot with a dead plant—some kind of Christmas plant that still had tinsel and tiny red balls on it—and extracted the spare key hidden there. Dave stared at the brown needles and wilted boughs of the tiny tree while Lilly unlocked the door. Helen would be crushed to know her plants had died. She'd had the golden touch with so many domestic things. Cooking, gardening, sewing. He'd teased her about it, calling her "Mary Homemaker." Now he wished he could tell Helen how much he regretted teasing her. That, in truth, he admired her talents.

The familiar squeak of the screen door hinges snapped him from his deliberations. Lilly pushed open the front door, and he followed her inside.

"The box of stuff I've been collecting for you is in the back. Wait here while I get it." Lilly waved a hand toward the sofa in the living room as she headed down the hall.

Dave didn't want to sit. If Lilly was selling the house, this could be the last time he was here. He had a load of memories, both good and bad, invested in this house, and he wanted a last look around. Closure, he thought people called it.

He wandered into the kitchen, the heart of Helen's home, and he pictured her at her stove cooking up one of her many drool-worthy dishes. She'd loved cooking, baking, creating new foods that were state-fair blue-ribbon quality. He scanned the counters, imagining the cookie jar and cake stand full of her latest indulgent dessert. He'd definitely eaten well while he'd dated Helen.

He spied a glass hummingbird figurine on the windowsill over her sink and went to pick it up. He'd given her the hummingbird for her birthday the first year they'd been dating. She'd fawned over it in a gift shop when they'd gone hiking at Rocky Mountain National Park, and he'd doubled back to the shop without her knowing to buy it. One of the few romantic gestures he'd ever done for her. His lungs tightened with grief when he thought of the bright smile she'd given him when she opened the gift. Why hadn't he tried harder to make her that happy all the time?

He would keep the hummingbird, he decided, as evidence that he hadn't been a complete heel and a reminder of one of their better days. As he reached for the figurine, he noticed odd stains in the sink. The spots looked like…blood. Frowning, he followed the trail of drips from the sink toward the hall. Another line of blood spots went from the sink toward the back door. And there, on the door frame, was a smear of red. What the...?

A prickling uneasiness skittered up his spine. He moved to the back door to get a closer look at the smudge and, through the decorative glass door, he noticed a familiar-looking car parked behind the house. A sedan that seemed to be held together by rust and prayers.

With his next breath, he connected the dots and remembered where he'd seen the battered sedan...

And horror constricted his lungs.

He spun to run to the bedroom, to get Lilly out of the house before—

A chilling scream ricocheted down the hall, and Dave knew.

Once again, he was too late.

Chapter 3

Steeling himself, Dave slid one of Helen's best knives from the butcher's block. He sent up a silent prayer as he moved as quickly and quietly as he could down the hall toward the master bedroom. He pressed his back to the wall. Stopped outside the bedroom and leaned sideways to peer around the door frame.

"I know you're out there, man," a voice said from inside the room, along with Lilly's muted whimpers of fear. "Get in here, before I blast a hole in this one's pretty head."

Dave hesitated. Did he dare? Was following the robber's demands his best move, or was there some better course of action he couldn't see?

He touched his pocket in search of his cell phone, and his heart sank as he remembered he'd left it his truck, charging. He mouthed a vile word. His thoughts were scattered, adrenaline hiking his pulse and blood thundering in his ears. He only had a knife. The cretin had a gun, one he'd been quick to use at the bank.

"Do it, man! I swear to you, I'll shoot her!"

Dave believed him.

Sticking the knife in his jeans at the small of his back and covering it with his shirt, he raised his hands and crept into the bedroom. His eyes went first to Lilly, wanting to assure himself she was unharmed. She stood trembling, at the business end of the robber's gun, and her terrified eyes pleaded with Dave for help. He gave her a small nod, trying to reassure her he'd do whatever he could.

He shifted his attention to the robber, sizing him up with a rapid up-and-down glance, then a closer scrutiny of the punk's face. The robber from the bank had shed the black hoodie, his countenance now fully visible. He was younger than Dave had estimated when he talked to the cops after the robbery. Midtwenties maybe. Large ears. Extremely short brown hair. Rounded nose. Acne scars. A wan complexion. His expression was pinched, his face sweating despite the cool temperature in the house. His breathing was shallow, fast.

"Well, well," the gunman said, curling his lip. "If it ain't Mr. Hero from the bank."

Remembering the blood he'd seen in the kitchen, Dave dropped his gaze briefly to the dark stain on the man's side, just under his arm. Pain, then. That'd explain the guy's pale appearance and rapid breathing. Dave had a brief moment of self-satisfaction, knowing one of his shots at the bank had hit the robber.

When the thief's glare narrowed on him, any smugness vanished. The robber had the upper hand now, and Dave could only pray he wouldn't be vengeful. And what were the odds of that mercy?

"Get in here!" The thug jerked his head toward the bathroom door. "Get the belt from that robe and bring it here. Hurry up!"

Dave glanced at the bathrobe in question, a light blue silky number. Lilly's he'd wager, since he was certain he'd never seen it on Helen. Again he hesitated, hating to comply but seeing no option while the guy had a gun on Lilly.

Maybe before he'd hurt his leg he'd have felt more confident in his ability to overtake the robber, but his bum leg slowed him considerably. When he didn't move for a couple seconds, the robber swung the gun toward him and fired into the wall just inches from his head.

Lilly screamed, and tears spilled onto her cheeks. "Do what he says, Dave. Please."

"Yeah, *Dave*," the guy mocked. "Do what I say. I can't promise no one will get hurt, but it's still the wiser choice."

Expelling a harsh breath and trying to keep his back and any evidence of the knife facing away from the robber, Dave moved slowly to the robe. He removed the belt and carried it to the robber.

In a move Dave had been unprepared for, the robber dropped his grip on Lilly and shoved the gun under Dave's chin instead. "Now hand her the belt."

He did.

Lilly took the silky strip of fabric and swallowed audibly.

Keeping the weapon trained on Dave's head, the robber eased behind him, yanked up Dave's shirt and pulled the knife from Dave's jeans. He scoffed, "Nice try, Hero, but I wasn't born yesterday."

He tossed aside the knife, and it clattered as it fell onto the linoleum floor of the bathroom.

"Now, you,—" he looked to Lilly "—tie his hands behind him."

Lilly met Dave's eyes, as if asking what she should do. The robber noticed her hesitation, her subtle eye consultation, and shouted, "I'm not playing around here, lady! If either of you tries something, I will shoot you both in a heartbeat and lose no sleep over it. Now, move!"

She edged past Dave and gave his hand a squeeze before pulling his wrists together. He kept his arms slightly apart, allowing for some slack in the belt as she wrapped it loosely.

Dave heard the robber huff a frustrated breath. "What did I just say?"

When neither of them answered him, he yelled, "What did I just say?"

Lilly gasped and whispered, "I... I'm not—"

"No tricks! Tie him *tighter*."

"It's okay, Lilly," Dave said, hoping to ease her guilt.

She drew the belt tighter, still allowing for a degree of comfort and a slim chance of freeing his hands later.

"Tighter!" their captor growled.

She cinched the belt marginally tighter, then inhaled sharply when the thug grabbed the belt and jerked it, hard.

"Now tie it off and find something to bind his feet."

* * *

Lilly's stomach churned sourly as she knotted the ends of her belt around Dave's wrists. Without Dave's assistance, how was she supposed to escape the robber? Maybe the bastard had no intention of leaving them alive to bear witness to his crimes. But if that was the case, why hadn't he killed them yet?

He swung the gun toward her again, and her pulse leaped.

"You got some rope somewhere? Or tape?" He shifted his gaze to the boxes she'd been packing. "Where's the tape you've used on these?"

"I, uh, don't remember."

The gunman stepped toward her, making a low growl in his throat. "Find it."

As they started out of the bedroom, the gunman smacked the butt of the gun against Dave's head, and he slumped to the floor, unconscious. Lilly gave a cry of distress. Anger, fear and concern for Dave tangled in the plaintive sound.

"Let's go. I've got plans for you." He jerked his head toward the door to the hall, and steered her toward the front of the house. "First, find that tape, then you're gonna take care of this." Lifting his shirt, he dipped his chin and his gaze to the wound in his side.

"Me?"

"You're a nurse, ain't cha?" he asked, lifting a thick eyebrow.

She blinked, and an itchy feeling crawled down her spine. "How d-did you know?"

His dismissive expression was the equivalent of a shrug. "Went through your purse to find anything that

I thought would help me. Very informative, your purse. Found your name badge from the hospital in Denver. What's the name again? Lorna? Lisa?"

She held her breath, disgust writhing in her gut.

"Lilly?" he asked, and she couldn't stop the cringe. He laughed. "Lilly. We have a winner."

Violated was too mild of a word for what she was feeling. Her skin crawled as if he was pawing her, stripping her naked and—

Bile surged up in her throat. *I've got plans for you...*

He could still do much worse to violate her than going through her purse, learning details of her life against her will. They entered the living room, and she spotted the large roll of packing tape, one of many she'd bought, on the coffee table.

He jabbed the gun in her back. "Get that tape."

She retrieved the roll and carried it back to the bedroom, the muzzle of his weapon poking her between the shoulder blades. Following his orders, she removed Dave's boots and socks, then lashed Dave's feet together.

"Keep going," her captor said when she would have stopped at a few layers. "More around his ankles, then tape his legs to the bed, so he can't go anywhere."

Her heart in her throat, she bound Dave's feet to the leg post of Helen's bed. When she finished securing Dave, she crawled to his head and examined the red knot on his forehead. The goose egg was swelling outward. A good sign. Maybe he'd escaped damage to his skull, his brain. Then she lifted his eyelids to check his pupils. They were responsive to light, which was also good, and he groaned as she probed him, which was even more encouraging.

"What are you doing?" the gunman snarled. "Get away from him."

"You hurt him. He needs medical attention."

The man sneered. "Screw him. It's his fault I'm not headed to Mexico right now. *I* need medical attention."

Her gaze darted to the bloodstain on his shirt. "How bad is it?"

He raised his shirt again to show her the bullet wound. "Hurts like fire, but you're better able to say how bad it is."

Inhaling deeply for composure, Lilly tried to push aside her fear and focus on the robber not as her captor and a murderer, but as her patient. She examined the gash on his side but didn't touch it. Her hands hadn't been sanitized. "It's deep, but it looks like a flesh wound. I need more light and a chance to wash my hands before I can examine it any closer. It needs to be irrigated and disinfected for starters, probably a butterfly bandage or stitches."

Inspiration struck.

"Yes, definitely stitches." She pinned the man with the steadiest look she could, praying for the authority in her voice that would cover her duplicity. "You need to go to the local ER. Stat. Without cleansing and stitches, the wound can fester, lead to sepsis—"

His eyes narrowed. "Sepsis?"

"That's when infection spreads throughout the body. Sepsis can lead to organ failure and death."

The gunman frowned and cocked his head. "Bullshit."

She squared her shoulders. "I'm serious. Sepsis is dangerous. That wound, left untreated, could easily spread infection throughout your body and make you very ill." She squeezed her hands in fists at her sides, trying to stop them from shaking. She was taking great liberties, exaggerating the seriousness of his condition, and he couldn't know she was trying to scare him with medical horror stories. "Why do you think so many people died in the old days from things as simple as a stab wound or strep throat? They didn't have the means to fight infection the way we do now. Simple infections spread and overwhelmed patients' defenses."

He seemed to be considering her warning, but the doubt never left his gaze. The muscle in his jaw worked, and he leaned close enough for her to smell his fetid breath. "I ain't going to the hospital."

His tone was dark and low. Final.

Her heart beat hard enough for him to see the quivering of her shirt if he looked. She pressed a hand to her chest to calm the skittering sensation there. "You should. You need—"

"Shut it! Anything needs doin', you do it. You think I stopped off here at your house instead of hightailing it out of town 'cause I like your decorating?"

His comment sent a jolt through her. Her mouth dried. "What?"

"I said, you're gonna doctor me. Now get to it!" He grabbed her arm and shook it. "Whatcha need? You got a first-aid kit or something?"

She shook herself from the shock of his comment about why he'd retreated to Helen's house and waved vaguely toward the bathroom. "I'm, um, sure we can find s-something in the bathroom."

He waved her that direction with the muzzle of the

gun. "Get on with it then. I don't want none of that sepsis stuff you talked about."

She moved to the master bathroom, which adjoined the bedroom, casting a glance to Dave as she passed his prostrate form on the ground. His eyes were closed and he was still, but she thought she saw the muscle in his jaw tense as they walked past. Bound hand and foot as he was, she knew he would be no help to her if things went south with the bank robber.

She was on her own. As usual. She should have been used to the feeling, but somehow, under the circumstances, "on her own" was emptier. Bleaker. Scarier.

Lilly opened the cabinets in Helen's bathroom and rummaged the shelves for anything she could use. First-aid disinfecting spray. Hydrogen peroxide. Bandages. Tylenol. Sterile pads.

"Take your shirt off," she said as she set the items on the counter around the sink.

Giving her a wary eye, he set the gun on the rim of the bathtub behind him and carefully peeled off his T-shirt.

She washed her hands and dried them on a clean towel, then began ripping open sterile pads to begin cleaning the wound. "Can you raise your arm? I need better light on it."

Grunting, he held his arm up to shoulder level, then winced when he tried to move it higher.

"That's good. Hold it there." She really wanted to irrigate the gash but didn't see anything—a squirt bottle or syringe—for the sterile wash. She began dabbing at the wound with a sterile pad soaked with disinfecting spray. Cutting a quick glance to her captor as she worked, she asked, "What did you mean about coming here instead of getting out of town?"

"What do you think?" he scoffed. "On top of a place to lay low, I needed doctoring and couldn't go to the ER. When I found your hospital name tag in your purse, I knew you could fix me up."

A sick feeling washed through her, and she stilled as the truth sank in. The cretin had come here because of *her*. Her life, *Dave's life*, was in danger because the robber had sought her out. Horror crawled through her and soured in her gut.

"But…" She paused for a breath, forcing her concentration back to his wound. "My name tag is for a Denver hospital. How did you find this house?"

"The envelope full of goodies in your purse. All the documents listed someone named Helen Shaw with this address."

Lilly's heart seemed to slow. *The things from Helen's safe-deposit box.* The nausea swirling through her intensified.

The thug continued, "Figured that had to be where you were staying while in town." He snorted. "I ain't as stupid as I look." He turned his head to eye her. "So should we be expecting Helen to join us soon?"

Tears filled Lilly's eyes, and she whispered hoarsely, "No."

"You sure about that? If I find out you're lying to me—"

"She's dead." Lilly met his gaze directly, angry that he'd forced her to speak the words she'd been trying to avoid since December. "She was murdered right before Christmas."

He held her stare as if searching for deception, then muttered, "Damn. That's gotta make for a sucky holiday."

She scoffed bitterly. "You think?" Dropping her gaze to continue dressing his wound, she grumbled, "Kinda like the sucky days that poor old security guard's family will have thanks to you?"

His lip curled up on one side, and he stuck his face close to hers. "I did what I had to. Better him than me."

She bit the inside of her cheek, knowing that debating the morality and necessity of his actions wouldn't be productive. She swabbed his wound harder, not caring any more if she hurt him.

He hissed in pain. "Hey, take it easy!"

"You want it cleaned or not?"

His only answer was a scowl.

As her initial flood of fear and adrenaline receded, lulled by the familiarity of the task at hand, a new feeling swelled inside her, boosted by her anger and grief over Helen, fueled by her disgust for the man who'd invaded Helen's house and terrorized her. A boldness. A realization that if she was going to die today, she didn't want to go quietly.

Maybe, if she could get the gunman to see *her*, make some kind of connection with her, he'd have a harder time shooting her.

After another moment of working to clean the wound, she asked, "So you got a name?"

"Of course I do. Everyone does." He arched an eyebrow as he turned a smug look on her. "But I ain't telling you mine."

"Is that fair? You know mine, but won't tell me yours?"

He gave a brittle laugh. "*Fair?* What do you think this is—kindergarten? Life ain't fair. Deal with it."

"No. Life is certainly not fair. A fair life wouldn't have seen my sister murdered, my father leaving us when I was nine, or my mother dead from breast cancer when she was barely fifty."

He flinched. If she hadn't had her eyes fixed on the wound she was doctoring, she might have missed the small shudder that rolled through him.

"What?" she asked, eyeing him.

"What *what*?"

"Do you know someone who died of cancer? Your mom?"

He angled a glare at her.

"Was it breast cancer?" Keeping half her attention on his expression, she finished disinfecting the bullet wound and moved on to clean the rest of the blood from his arm and chest.

He snatched his arm away to unbuckle the analog watch from his wrist. He turned to the sink, took a rag from the tiny shelf over the toilet and began washing his arm and chest for himself. "My mother died of a drug overdose in a crack house in California," he said coldly, his resentment obvious. "At least that's what my dad told me."

"Oh. I'm sorry."

He snorted. "Good riddance."

"Then someone else had cancer?"

He pressed his mouth in a grim line and shot her another quelling stare. "Shut it."

She raised her palm in acquiescence. "Fine. Fine."

As she turned toward the supplies she'd piled on the sink to find a butterfly bandage, she moved his watch out of the way. His hand clamped hard on her wrist. "Don't touch that."

"I was just moving—"

He gave her wrist a shake and another firm squeeze. "I said, don't. Touch. My watch."

She gave the watch another look, curious what about it made him so protective of it. She could tell by the well-worn leather strap that it was old. The face was scratched and the gold-toned metal case showed wear. A family heirloom perhaps? The thing didn't look valuable but she knew well enough that you couldn't put a price on sentimental items.

She nodded, and he released her arm. After picking out a bandage for his wound, she faced him in time to see him lift a hand to his chest and rub a neat, red scar there. A surgical scar, if she wasn't mistaken. And it clicked.

"*You* had cancer!" she blurted before she could catch herself.

His head snapped up, and the startled, pained look in his eyes spoke for itself. In the next moment his countenance darkened, and his nostrils flared as he exhaled harshly. "*Have*," he growled. "The damn thing came back."

Chapter 4

Dave's head throbbed, but when he tried to raise a hand to his aching skull, he found his hands bound behind his back. He groaned and blinked against the overhead light that glared in his eyes.

He was on the floor. Why was he on the floor and—?

Angling his head, he discovered his feet were bound as well. A surreal notion of danger flooded him, setting his senses on full alert even before he could muddle through fog that muddied his brain. He turned his head, squinting against the light as he tried to place himself. The decor was familiar, yet…different. Helen's room? Why—?

Reality crashed on him like a boulder, crushing him. Helen was dead. Bank robbery. Gunman at Helen's house.

Lilly! His breathing accelerated, keeping time with

his pulse, as he thought of Lilly alone with the bank robber. If he'd hurt her, if he'd...*touched* her... He couldn't
even think the more accurate word without fury scorching his veins. He tried to sit up, and the pounding in his
head sent him back flat on the floor. Slowly.

So...head injury. The robber had smacked him on
the temple. *Hell*...

A movement to his left snagged his attention, and he
angled his head to peer into the shadows under Helen's
bed. A fluffy black-and-brown cat with a white chest
blinked at him. Meowed softly.

But... Helen didn't have a cat. So where...?

The sound of voices drew his attention away from
the cat and toward the bathroom.

"I'm sorry." Lilly's voice. "I didn't—"

"Shut up!" A male voice. Presumably the robber. "I
don't want to talk about it. I don't want to talk at all!
Just finish up with this and keep your trap shut. Okay?"

The man's hostility set Dave on edge. The guy was
armed, unpredictable and currently alone with Lilly.
Dave rolled on his side and curled his body so that he
could see his feet. He had a thick band of clear tape
around his ankles. Then tape had also been looped
around the leg of the bed. He was useless to defend Lilly
if the dirt wad tried to hurt her.

"Do you want something for the pain?" Lilly asked,
her voice drifting in from the bathroom. "I have Tylenol
here, and I think I have ibuprofen in my purse. Assuming you didn't lose the bottle when you snatched my
purse from me."

"Screw that. I have some of the good stuff. Serious

painkillers." There was a beat of silence, then the robber bit out a curse. "Left my pills in the car," he grumbled.

"I can get them for you," Lilly offered.

The cretin chortled. "Like hell you will. You're going in there with your buddy. Are we done here?"

"I—"

"Never mind that." He heard a clatter. "We're done."

Dave tensed as he realized they were returning to the bedroom. He had no plan, and he scrambled mentally. Should he pretend to still be unconscious? Was there anything nearby he could use as a weapon? His hands might be bound behind him but if the opportunity arose…

"Well, look who's awake. Won't be trying any more of your stupid tricks now, will you, *Hero*?" The robber shoved Lilly's shoulder. "You. Get over there with him. On the floor."

Lilly gave the gunman a disappointed look. "Is that really necessary? I'm not—"

"Yes," the man replied, his expression sour. "It *is* necessary. Until I figure out what I'm gonna do with you two, how I'm gonna get out of town with this delay… Hell, *if* I'm going to leave town. Maybe hiding out here for a couple days is my best bet. Huh?"

Lilly stood motionless, staring at him. Her shoulders were back, and her eyes glowed bright with challenge.

Dave's stomach swooped. What was she doing? Challenging a desperate man with a gun was asking for trouble. The thug had already proven his willingness to kill innocent bystanders. Dave tested the bindings on his wrists for the hundredth time. Nope. If the gunman attacked Lilly, he'd be useless to her. His incapacity clawed at his soul. He had to find a way to protect Lilly, to rescue her from this lunatic before she was hurt.

"Go!" The man gave Lilly's shoulder a nudge and took a roll of packing tape from the top of the dresser.

Lilly trudged over to Dave and squatted beside him on the floor, taking a moment to check the bump on his head. "How do you feel? Any nausea? Double vision?"

She touched his face, just below the spot on his head that ached from the robber's assault. Even the slight pressure of her fingers sent lightning bolts streaking under his skull. He sucked in a breath, startled by how much his head hurt—and by how good her cool touch felt on his skin. Despite the pain from the knot on his brow, Lilly's soft caress, the concern in her green eyes and the subtle floral scent that surrounded her were a heady combination.

Dave shook his head slowly. "No. None of that. Just a sore skull."

The screech of tape ripping from the roll redirected his attention to the robber. "Yeah, boo-hoo. You shot me. This—" he pointed to the bandage on his side just below his armpit "—ain't no picnic, either. So stop your griping."

Dave's attention went to the revolver tucked in easy reach in the waist of the man's threadbare jeans.

"He wasn't griping," Lilly said, glancing over her shoulder. "I asked him about his symptoms."

Dave lifted an eyebrow as he glanced at Lilly, surprised to hear her defend him. She might hate him for his history with Helen, but they were united by their captivity at the hands of the bank robber. A frail and unfortunate connection, for sure, but not one he would dismiss. They needed to trust and depend on each other if they were going to survive this ordeal.

"Hands behind your back," the cretin barked, kneeling beside Lilly.

Sighing, she complied. "What are you going to do with us?"

Dave was wondering the same thing. If the robber meant to kill them, wouldn't he have done that already? Why bother binding them and holding them hostage if he meant to be rid of them?

"I don't know." The thug began wrapping the packing tape around her wrists, and she grimaced. "This wasn't supposed to happen. Mr. Hero there screwed things up when he shot me. I should be a hundred miles from here by now."

"Going where?"

The robber jerked a startled gaze toward Dave when he spoke. "Away from this Podunk town. That's all you need to know."

"In that rattletrap?" Dave said and scoffed. "You'd be lucky to make it fifty miles before something essential fell off or gave up the ghost."

The thug narrowed his eyes on Dave. "Did I ask you?"

"Just sayin'." Dave wasn't exactly sure where he was going with his comments, but an idea niggled at the back of his head. He followed where the forming idea led him. "If you plan to make your getaway in that thing, you're gonna need some work on the engine at least."

"And you know this how?" the robber grumbled, pausing from his work binding Lilly's wrists.

"I followed you outside the bank when you drove away. I heard the motor." He lifted one shoulder. "I work on farm machinery primarily, but the ranch trucks need tweaks every now and then. I know engines."

The robber held his stare for a tense moment before tearing off the tape and dropping Lilly's hands. "Well, I can't hardly take the thing into a shop around here and wait around while they give me a tune-up, now can I? Cops all over the state are looking for me by now."

His gut felt as though snakes were writhing inside him, biting his flesh and filling his blood with poison. He swallowed hard and said, "I'll do it."

Beside him, Lilly stiffened. The robber blinked in surprise, then twisted his face with skepticism. "What?"

"I'll fix your engine." Confidence in his impromptu idea flowed through him, emboldening him. "If you'll let us go, unharmed, then I'll do whatever repairs are needed to get you on the road and out of state."

Lilly gaped at him. The robber sat back on his heels and rubbed his cheek.

A bubble of hope swelled in his chest. This could work. He cocked his head in question as he eyed the robber. "So…do we have a deal?"

Chapter 5

Dave held his breath, while in his mind, the details of his plan began spinning out and taking shape. This could work, if—

The thug snorted. "Nice try, Hero. But I wasn't born yesterday. If I let you two go, your first stop will be the police, and I'll have cops on my tail inside of twenty minutes."

Dave's hope deflated a little, but he wouldn't give up. "We won't go to the cops."

"Sure, you won't," his captor said, sneering. "And the Easter Bunny and Santa Claus are real." He faced Lilly. "Feet together, Lilly."

"How about this," Lilly said, complying with his demand. "We give you twenty-four hours to drive as far out of Colorado as you can before we go to the cops."

The robber gave Lilly an ugly grin. "But that arrangement still has you going to the cops. And that is the deal breaker." He tore another long strip of tape from the roll with a jarring *rrriipp* and began binding Lilly's feet.

Dave gritted his back teeth. At least they were talking, negotiating. He knew that, deep down, the guy was intrigued, tempted. The thug had to know his car was crap and was on the verge of breakdown. The promise of repairs that would facilitate his escape had to be enticing the thug on some level. "Then don't let us go."

Lilly's head swiveled toward him, her eyes wide, her mouth slack.

But he had the robber's attention, and he continued, "I fix the crap-mobile, and you leave us safe and uninjured, still bound, right here in the bedroom. You drive away, scot-free. But you have to swear not to hurt us. We are not injured in any way. That is *my* deal breaker."

He cut a brief look to Lilly, praying she'd trust him, and met her baffled expression.

The robber stood and tossed the rest of the tape roll on the dresser. He twisted his mouth as he glared at Dave. "We'll see. I ain't making any deals now. I'm hurtin' and need time to rest, regroup. I'm better off hiding here while the cops spin their wheels lookin' for me." He rubbed his side, carefully touching his bandage before walking into the bathroom. When he returned, he wore his shirt and had the gun in his hand again. Scowling, he divided a hard look between them. "I gotta get my pain pills outta my car. Don't try anything while I'm gone, or I swear I'll start shooting off toes."

The hardwood floor vibrated as the robber stomped out of the room.

Dave muttered under his breath, calling the cretin every foul name he could think of.

"You forgot 'bastard' and 'son of a bitch,'" Lilly said quietly.

"Hmm. Didn't forget 'em. I was saving them for you."

She chuckled wryly, as he'd hoped she would, then fell silent. He searched for something, anything he could do to encourage her and buoy her spirits. As bad as things looked for them, he needed her not to give up, not to accept defeat. He'd rather she be fighting mad than fearful or hopeless.

She scooted across the floor, pushing with her bound feet and wiggling her bottom a little at a time, until, back to back, they could lean against each other. He heard—and felt—Lilly heave a sad sigh. "I'm so sorry I got you into this, Dave."

He furrowed his brow, certain he hadn't heard her correctly. "What? How…?" He gave a short dry laugh. "How is any of this your fault?"

"He's here at the house because of me. He told me that when I was cleaning out his gunshot wound."

"Are you saying you know him? I noticed he used your name."

"No. Nothing like that. It's… He took my purse. Remember?"

He grunted an acknowledgment.

"Well, he saw my hospital ID in my purse and decided I was going to fix him up. He found Helen's address on the stuff I took from her lockbox. I'm the reason he's here. And I'm the reason *you're* here, because I asked you to drive me and get your things."

Her forlorn tone gouged at his heart. He wished he could comfort her in some way. A hug, a smile, a pat on the back, but none of those options were available to him. "Stop it."

"Huh?"

"Stop blaming yourself. I could just as easily say it was my fault. If I hadn't shot him, he wouldn't have needed medical attention, and he wouldn't have come here."

He felt the movement, the stir of her hair as she shook her head. "No. I'm glad you shot him. You saved lives. He was panicking and firing at anyone who moved. Things were spiraling out of control, and you helped put an end to his reign of terror."

Dave expelled a weary breath. "Until he ended up here, holding us hostage."

She snorted. "Yeah. Right."

"Look, Lilly, if anyone is to blame for our situation, it is him. *He* robbed the bank. *He* broke into the house. *He* tied us up. Don't take this on yourself." He turned his head, wishing he could look into her eyes as he pleaded with her, but could only manage a glimpse of her slumped shoulder. "Okay?"

"Okay." She didn't sound convinced.

"Now say it like you mean it."

"Okay!" Her answer was edged with irritation, but he preferred that to her self-pity.

Dave inched his hands to hers and hooked a couple fingers with hers, the closest he could come to holding her hand while his wrists were bound as tightly as they were.

"I'm going to find a way to get you out of this mess, Lilly. I promise."

"Don't you mean get *us* out of this mess?" She gave a low, wry chuckle. "Seems to me you're right in the middle of it yourself."

"True enough, but…you're my priority. If something happens to me, so be it. But I will do everything in my power to see you through this ordeal safely. I swear."

She was silent, and he could imagine her skepticism.

"I know I don't have a good track record, based on the promises I made Helen, but… I want to make up for all that." He felt Lilly stiffen, her back straightening behind his. "For disappointing her. For falling short too many times. Her death was a wake-up call. Too late to do anything for her, I know. But… I will try to do better. For you."

They sat in the silent room for several minutes. Then her hand moved. Her fingers curled to grip his more tightly. And a lightness spiraled through him. He'd been given a second chance. Although he'd failed Lilly's sister, he had an opportunity to make a difference for Lilly.

Somehow he would. Or he'd die trying.

Lilly flinched when she heard the back door slam and the heavy footsteps of the robber returning.

"Listen, Lilly. If, at any time, he shoots at us," Dave said, in a hushed and hurried voice, "get low. Try to get under the bed. I'll do my best to cover you."

Lilly's heartbeat accelerated. While she'd been dwelling on the horridness of their situation, Dave had been working through strategies, possibilities. Plans that involved him sacrificing himself to protect her. "Dave, you can't—"

"Just do it! Roll under the bed if at all possible. I'll—"

"Hey!" The robber appeared again at the door of the bedroom, an orange prescription bottle in his hand, and he sent them a warning look. "What are you two talking about?"

Dave sat taller, and against her back, she felt the tension enter his body. "Nothing."

The robber stepped into the room, his expression darkening. "Don't lie. I heard you talking."

"He was asking me if I was all right. If you'd hurt me," Lilly said, hoping her apparent cooperation would win points, maybe a degree of trust. "I told him you hadn't. That I'd helped you with your wound and that was it."

The robber lifted an eyebrow and nodded slowly. As if remembering the pills in his hand, he twisted off the childproof lid, shook out a capsule and swallowed it without water. When he pressed the cap back on, he fumbled the bottle. It fell to the floor and rolled toward Lilly. The robber grumbled and trudged over to pick it up.

Lilly cut a quick glance to the prescription bottle, reading the label to see what he was taking, an address, anything she could glean about the man before he recovered the pills.

The chain-drugstore logo jumped out at her and below that *tramadol* and *Wayne Mo—*

Their captor snatched up the bottle and shoved it in his pocket.

"Wayne," she said quietly, and he jerked is head around to glare at her.

"What?"

"That's your name. Isn't it? Wayne."

He frowned as he blinked at her. "How'd you guess?"

"It was on the pills."

He twisted his mouth in frustration and defeat but didn't confirm her assertion.

"Tramadol," she continued. "That's heavy-duty stuff."

His pale-eyed stare met hers. "Cancer causes heavy-duty pain."

Dave raised his chin, his attention clearly snagged by this information.

The robber—*Wayne*—angled his head as he growled, "That's right, Hero. I got cancer. So what? It doesn't change a thing about this situation." He motioned with the gun, indicating all three of them. "Now, you two behave yourselves while I go find something to eat and get some rest. I need to be sharp to figure out what's gotta happen next, and right now, I feel like crap."

He stopped at the door and pulled something from his back pocket. "Oh, and in case you were hoping to get your hands on this—"

He held up her cell phone, and Lilly's gut swooped. Obviously he'd ransacked her stolen purse.

"—thinking you'd call the cops or someone would track you by it…think again."

He stashed the gun in his waistband to free that hand and pried the protective, butterfly-decorated case off her phone. Wayne flipped over her phone, and thumb-scrolled one-handed through her screens of personal information.

"By the way," he said with a smirk, "Gloria sends her best. Says she knows how hard this is for you and proposes you two go out for drinks when you get back." He thumb-scrolled again, still reading her texts.

Lilly clenched her back teeth, fighting tears of outrage for his violation of her privacy. She hated being at this man's mercy, feeling so helpless.

"Jillian is canceling for the thirtieth." Wayne flicked a casual glance at her. "Forgot her kid had an orthodontist appointment. Wants to reschedule when you get back." With a gloating grin twisting his mouth, he gazed at her from under hooded eyes. "Maybe she should say *if* you get back. Alan says the alimony check will be late next month. Still waiting for a client to pay their bill before he can pay you." Wayne cast her a curious look. "Alimony, huh? Good news, Alan. You may soon be off the hook for that."

"You ass," Dave grumbled, his tone venomous.

Wayne ignored him and continued, "Gail P. sent a picture of a kid with ice cream on his face with an *L-O-L*. And someone named Isaac wants to trade work days on the weekend of the fourth. And, finally, your phone bill is ready for viewing and will auto-draft on the fifteenth." He met her eyes and cocked his head. "There. All caught up. Now…"

Digging his fingernails into the side of the phone, he pried off the back, tapped out her battery, pinched the SD card from the slot and dropped the rest of the phone on the floor.

"Don't!" she cried desperately, knowing what he had in mind a fraction of a second before he stomped the screen and shattered the device to sad pieces. Carrying the SD card in his fingers, he disappeared into the bathroom, and she heard him flush the commode.

She drew a deep breath, searching for the stoicism she wished she could present Wayne. Despite her best efforts, her sigh still shuddered with emotion. As Wayne emerged from the bathroom, she firmed her jaw and forced steel in her spine. She met his gloating grin with disdain in her glare.

"Problem solved. Now, keep it quiet in here." Wayne strode to the door and shot them a minatory look. "Nothing has gone right today, and I've got to make a new plan."

Chapter 6

Pressing his hand over the throbbing wound just under his arm, Wayne sank onto the sofa and rocked his head back to stare at the ceiling. The cottage-cheese texturing overhead was the same kind he'd had on his bedroom ceiling as a kid. Unlike this one, the ceiling in his bedroom had had spider webs dangling in the corners and a water stain by the light. He'd stared at the popcorn bumps many a night listening to his parents argue… or screw. Or hearing his mother rant about nonsense when she'd get high.

His bedroom had grown silent at night the day his mother OD'd. She'd gone out to meet up with her dealer and had never come back. No great loss there, he'd told himself stoically. With her death, he and his dad were free to do their own thing. Move around the country. Never look back.

Only time he missed her was when his dad vented the drunken rage he used to take out on his mom on him. The beatings forced Wayne to grow up fast. He'd learned to hide on the nights his dad drank, and as he gained his own muscle, he'd learned to fight back. His dad said facing the belt had toughened him up, taught him respect. Maybe it had. Mostly the beatings added bitterness to the love-hate relationship he'd had with his old man.

Moving slowly, Wayne raised his feet to the couch and stretched out, his gut full of sour reproach. If his dad could see how things had gotten screwed up today, he'd be laughing his ass off. Or smacking him around to teach him a lesson. He'd scorned his dad for checking out at the St. Louis hit. Today, Wayne had blown a much smaller job. Who was the real screwup?

His head swam muzzily as his pain pill started kicking in, and Wayne closed his eyes, his dad's voice echoing in his head. *Rule number one is don't get caught.*

He could still remember the night his dad had first suggested holding up a bank. They'd already robbed a couple of convenience stores and mugged an old lady as she left an ATM. His dad got the notion to do a bigger job after watching some old Western on TV. Wayne couldn't remember now how old he'd been at that time. He'd learned to mark days according to the different places they'd lived, staying one step ahead of the law.

"We could do that," his dad had said as the movie's bank robbers rode out of town on horseback, whooping over their success. They'd been in West Virginia. Early November. He knew that because he'd been nursing a stomachache after eating a whole bag of fun-size Snickers they'd bought on clearance the day after Halloween. A storm had blown up outside, and the bare branches of the hickory tree in their yard had been clawing the window in an eerie way, like a goblin trying to break into their house. He hadn't been scared. Not of the storm or the scratching sounds at the window. But his father's plan to escalate their thievery disturbed him. His dad was getting greedy. Even then Wayne had known his father's greed would lead to carelessness. To mistakes that could get them caught. Jailed.

He dreaded the idea of prison more than death. Penned up for the rest of his life. Trapped in a steel-and-concrete cage. No sir. That was not for him.

Wayne's stomach growled, and he slid his hand from his aching side to his belly. Lilly had to have something around this place he could eat. Wincing as the bandage pulled at his wound, he climbed off the couch and investigated the shelves of her pantry. He found potato chips. *Baked.* He rolled his eyes. What a waste of a potato.

Her bread was whole grain, and the closest thing to lunch meat in her refrigerator was some funky, swanky cheese spread that smelled like feet. He returned to her pantry and located a jar of peanut butter. No sugar added. He frowned. What was wrong with the woman? Was she afraid of flavor? Didn't matter how much "health food" you ate or how much you exercised, everyone died eventually. And even the fittest people got cancer.

Fuming silently over the injustice of the disease that had changed the course of his life, he slapped together a couple of sandwiches and searched the refrigerator for something to wash down his dinner.

Spying a yuppie IPA from some microbrewery he'd never heard of, he scoffed at Lilly's choice of beer and pulled out one of the squatty bottles. Tucking the bag of chips under his arm, he carried his sandwiches and drink into the living room and settled on the sofa to eat. He used the remote on the coffee table to turn on the small flat-screen television and scrolled through the channels. He paused briefly on a movie channel playing *Shawshank Redemption* and shuddered. No way in hell he'd ever go to prison. He'd eat a bullet before he'd let himself be caged like an animal.

He scrolled on through the channels until the image on the screen stopped him. His face. Blurry and in black and white. Shaded by his hoodie. But definitely him. A screen shot from a surveillance camera at the bank.

He'd known security cameras were everywhere these days. He'd worn the hoodie for that reason. Somehow during the robbery, the hood had slid back far enough to capture a shot of his face. Hell and damnation!

He gripped his sandwich so hard the peanut butter oozed out onto his hand. He licked the mess from his fingers and hiked up the sound. The local news was detailing the bank hit and warning the community to be on the lookout for him. Not to approach him, as he was believed to be armed and dangerous.

Wayne sat back and chuckled to himself. *Armed and dangerous*. He liked that. He should get it tattooed on his back or something.

As he took another large bite of his sandwich, he realized that the news broadcast—his image being sent out to viewers in the area—complicated his escape. With all eyes watching for him, hoping to cash in on the reward offered for him, his chances of getting out of town unnoticed had just grown slimmer. His best bet now might be to hunker down here at Lilly's for the long haul and let the hunt for him cool down.

The image on the screen blurred, and when he blinked, his eyelids were heavy. His pills were kicking in, making his head feel thick, slow. Sleepy. But before he'd nap, he had one more thing to do with his hostages. Grunting in pain, he hauled himself off the couch and picked up the revolver.

After Wayne had left, closing the bedroom door behind him, Lilly had wilted against Dave. The stress of the past few hours had sapped her energy, and one of the tears she'd tried to hold at bay leaked through the fringe of her eyelashes.

"So…add one phone to the list of items he owes you," Dave said, clearly trying to keep his tone light, but the underlying anger was palpable.

Scoffing, she rolled her eyes. "I'm as likely to get a new phone outta Wayne as I am to get next month's alimony outta Alan."

"Alan, huh? I guess I never knew you were married."

"Was married. Definitely past tense. For the last five years." She tried to dry the teardrop from her cheek with her shoulder but couldn't reach the right spot, so she let it slide down and drip from her chin. With a sniff, she tried to compose herself. Knowing that Wayne was going to sleep for a while, she allowed herself to lower her guard, just a bit, needing the break to recoup a bit of her own mental focus and strength.

"That would explain why Helen didn't mention a husband in connection to you."

"Yeah. She was pretty offended on my behalf when we found out about Alan's other women. She was content to wash her hands of him when it ended and encouraged me to do the same."

"Women...plural?" Dave asked.

"Mmm-hmm. You caught that, huh? He was a serial cheater." She really didn't want to rehash the whole Alan debacle right now. Her nerves were raw enough as it was.

Dave made a soft, nondescript sound, then muttered, "Sorry."

"Not your fault."

"No, but between Alan and Wayne, I'm not feeling too good about being among the male representatives in your life. Especially knowing you're not too keen on me, either."

"Yeah, well." Lilly shoved down the sour taste at the back of her throat. Now was not the time for an Alan pity party. She *had* moved on. She told herself this surge of heartache and bruised emotions was just a symptom of her current vulnerability and fatigue. She purposely shifted her thoughts. Groaned aloud. "Geez, I hope I backed my photos up to the cloud. I can reconstruct my contact list, but I had pictures on that phone of—" *Helen*. She swallowed, unable to push the name out past the sharp constriction of grief that strangled her.

"Yeah," Dave murmured, and his fingers groped to find hers again and squeeze.

As much as she appreciated his attempt to sympathize with her, his comforting gesture only wrenched the knot choking her tighter.

"Do you know what kind of cancer he has?" Dave asked after a moment of silence.

"No. He wouldn't talk about it. But based on where his scar is, I'm guessing breast or lung."

"Huh."

"What? Men can get breast cancer, too."

"Yeah, I know."

"Why does the kind of cancer he has matter?"

She felt Dave lift a shoulder. "Don't know." He kept his voice quiet, barely more than a whisper. "I guess I'm just trying to gather any information I can. Putting together a picture of who and what we're dealing with."

She wasn't sure how Wayne's cancer could provide them an escape, but she knew Dave was on the right track. Gathering information of all kinds could yield something unexpected. "If I can get alone with him, I'll see what I can learn about him, his family, his plans for us."

A low rumbling sound vibrated from Dave's chest and into her own. "I don't like the idea of you being alone with him."

Lilly sighed. "I don't, either, but I feel like he'll be more open with me if you're not around. I don't think he likes or trusts you."

"Well, it's mutual."

"Dave, hostility will only work against us. I want him to see us as more than just hostages, but as people with lives, with feelings, with potential that will be lost if he kills us. I think I can form a personal bond with him if I'm given the chance to talk with him."

Dave sighed. "That's all well and good, but that kind

of plan takes time. I don't get the impression we have time to chitchat and reason with him. I think our best plan is to try to get out of this tape and make our escape while he's asleep."

"Get out of the tape? How?" Lilly tested the tape around her wrists and winced as the adhesive ripped the fine hair on her arm.

"Well, he used your packing tape, right? Packing tape generally has lower tensile strength than something like duct tape. I think we can tear or saw through it."

She chuffed a short laugh in disbelief. "With what?"

"My keys are in my pocket. I can't reach them, but you might be able to."

Lilly's pulse tripped. "Okay. But…"

When she didn't finish her comment, trying to think through the ramifications, Dave said gently, "But what?"

She swallowed hard and glanced at the door. "I just think…we need to have the whole plan worked out. If we get our hands and legs free, but wake Wayne in the process or can't get out of this room, he'll just tie us up again with something sturdier. And we'll lose any advantage we might have. He could even get ticked off enough, panicked enough, that he shoots us rather than risk our getting away and reporting him."

"I suppose. But I'd hate to waste what may be our best chance to free ourselves. If we get out of these restraints, maybe the two of us could surprise him, overpower him."

She imagined that scenario in her head, and fear rippled through her. "He has a gun."

"I know. That has to be our main consideration going forward. Disarming him eliminates our main threat and levels the playing field, so that is priority one. Despite my bum leg, I think I can be faster than him. It's something we practice when it comes to calf roping."

She chuckled mildly, trying to lighten the mood despite their circumstances. "Calves carry guns these days?"

"No." His tone acknowledged her attempt at humor, then he explained, "But you want to subdue them as quickly as possible. And with as little struggling. The more they struggle, the more likely they'll hurt themselves. Or you. A calf hoof to the face could break your jaw or concuss you or…" He sighed. "Never mind all that. Point is, I think I can get the gun from him…if my hands are free."

"And how do we do that?"

"If you lie on your side and scoot close to me, I'm betting you can get your hand in my pocket and get my keys."

Lilly visualized what he was describing, and heat flashed through her. She didn't miss the fact that she'd be groping blindly around his crotch, her fanny snuggled close to him. "O-kay." When her voice cracked, she cleared her throat. "I—I can do that."

At least Dave had a plan, was making an attempt to free them. That was more than she had.

"Good. C'mon." He straightened his leg and lay back on the floor to give her access to his pocket.

She wiggled away from him a few inches, scooting her bottom across the floor, and stretched out beside him. Lying on her side, facing away from him, she reached with her bound hand to find him. She heard him shift, groaning as he scooted closer.

"Are you okay?"

"The change in position made my head throb and the room spin, but I'll live."

And he was dealing with a leg that hadn't finished healing from serious surgery a few months ago. Despite his assertions to the contrary, Dave would be at a disadvantage should their attempt to get away lead to a physical confrontation. But Wayne was contending with cancer pain and his gunshot wound...

Lilly closed her eyes as Dave snuggled up behind her, and she sent up a prayer that they wouldn't have to find out whose injuries were the greater liability.

As he positioned himself, Dave's body heat, his soap-and-leather scent enveloped her, and the occasional brush of his thigh against hers or his chest at her back sent a tingling sensation to her belly. With her wrists taped together, her range of motion was seriously restricted as she felt blindly for his pocket. Her fingers found the soft cotton of his T-shirt over the taut plain of his belly, and he hissed.

She jerked her hand back. "What? Did I hurt you?"

"No. I'm...ticklish." Was that embarrassment she detected in his tone?

He grunted. "Ignore me. Just...try again. Lower." His body skimmed along hers as he moved to better align her hands with their target.

An awkward awareness shot through her, along with a ripple of something she refused to call pleasure. She was not, *not, not* attracted to her late sister's boyfriend.

Chapter 7

Lilly's hands trembled as she tentatively searched behind her. She found the stiffer denim of his jeans, felt a belt loop, the cold metal of the button at his fly. With a gulp, her fingers skittered away from the button like a spider retreating from a broom.

"Come on, Lilly. You can do it. This is no time to be shy," he said, and his breath fanned the back of her neck. A not-unpleasant shiver swept down her spine. She clenched her teeth and scolded herself. *Get it together, Lil. This is no more sexual than when you treat injured men in the ER. Now suck it up, and do your job.*

"Right," she muttered aloud, steeling herself. She groped again, found the edge of his pocket and wiggled lower so she could push her fingers inside. Tight as his jeans were, her movement was restricted all the more.

But she twisted her hand, slid her fingers around the lining of the pocket. Searching. But found nothing. "Is this the right pocket?"

"Yeah. Keep trying." He angled his body closer to her, but it was no use. With her wrists bound, she couldn't dig deep enough in his pocket to reach the bottom, where the keys rested.

"All right, never mind," he said, his voice sounding husky. Thick.

A fresh jolt shot through her. Had her groping turned Dave on? The idea both shocked and mollified her. She felt a tad less guilty about her reaction, knowing that Dave, too, had noticed and responded to the intimate nature of the task. But as she scrunched away, she also frowned her displeasure that he hadn't had the self-control, the common decency, to rein in his body's reaction. Helen had only been gone for a few months. How could he—?

She expelled a harsh, shamed sigh. *Black pot, meet black kettle.*

"New plan," he said, his voice stronger, steadier.

Lilly rolled to look at him. "I'm all ears."

He hitched his head, indicating she should roll on her side again. "Hold your hands out. I'm going to see if I can bite through the tape, a little at a time."

"Good idea." She held his gaze—for a moment too long, she realized, when an uncomfortable look filled his face. His nostrils flared as he sucked in a slow breath and slammed his eyes shut. She drew her own shuddering breath and moved to her side, holding her arms out to him.

Dave's unshaven chin scratched her hands, and his

hair tickled her arms as he tried to find the right angle to begin his task.

"Where's a gerbil when you need one, huh?" she quipped, trying to distract herself from the tug as he gnawed at the edge of the tape.

"A gerbil? What's that supposed to mean?"

"You know, because they chew *everything*. Cardboard, wood, electric cords, your school assignment. You didn't have a hamster or gerbil growing up?"

He nibbled a bit of tape and paused to spit it out. "Nothing that small. A dog. Horses." He started chewing the tape again, then hesitated. "Which reminds me. I'm guessing that's your cat under the bed? The fluffy black, brown and white one with big eyes."

She gasped. "Maddie is under the bed?"

"Someone is under the bed."

She rolled until she could look past a storage box under the bed and found her cat huddled near the wall. "Hey, sweetie! Oh, poor scared girl!"

From under the bed, a loud rumbling purr answered her. Maddie crawled until her head barely poked out from under the bed frame and gave a squeak-like meow.

"Think if we tied a message around her neck, she'd carry it to the nearest neighbor?" Dave asked. "'Help, we've been taken hostage by a lunatic. Send the police.'"

"Yeah…no. I can barely get this girl to find the cat treats I drop on the floor for her, even if I point them out. I seriously doubt she could find the neighbor's house. Isn't that right, Maddie-pie?"

The cat *merped* and edged closer, purring and requesting a pat with a bump of her head on Lilly's shoulder.

"So no *Timmy's-in-the-well* Lassie rescues?"

She turned her head to glance up at Dave with a weak smile. "Not from Maddie. Best we'll get is if Wayne tries to pick her up, and Maddie scratches his eyes out trying to get away."

Dave lifted an eyebrow, and the corner of his mouth twitched. "So there *is* hope?"

She rolled her eyes.

"Come on," he said with a jerk of his head. "Time's wasting. Give me your wrists again."

She sobered, glanced toward the door, then inched back into a position where he could gnaw at the tape binding her wrists.

His lips brushed the inside of her wrists from time to time, and she had to bite the inside of her cheeks to keep from moaning.

This is the man whom Helen called you about so many times, crying and hurt by his apathy or lack of commitment, she reminded herself, trying to squelch the fluttery sensations that tickled her belly. Then a different vibration caught her attention as the floor quivered, and the thud of footsteps signaled Wayne's return. As if sensing danger, Maddie scurried back under the bed.

"He's coming back!" she warned Dave in a whisper a fraction of a second before the door opened.

Wayne, who had a plate in his hand, glared at the two of them, huddled so close together. His lips pressed into a grim line of displeasure, and he set down the plate with a thump on the bedside table. "What are you doing?"

"Nothing." Sitting up, Lilly twisted and inched her body until she was leaning against the side of the bed. "We were just…trying to get more comfortable. You have the tape on our wrists too tight, and I know my shoulders are hurting from having my arms crooked behind me."

Wayne stared at her for several seconds, his narrowed eyes skeptical. With a grunt, he grabbed her under the elbow and half lifted her to her feet. "Get on the bed."

"Why?"

Wayne lifted an eyebrow. "Don't you think you'd be more comfortable there? Stay on the floor if you like, but not by him. You can get on the bed or be tied over there to that desk." He waved a finger toward the heavy rolltop antique that had once been her grandmother's.

"Bed." As she flopped on the mattress, feeling a bit like a fish floundering on a dock, she cut a quick look to Dave, whose expression and posture reminded her of a snake. Dangerous. Tightly coiled. Ready to strike. She tried to signal him with a subtle shake of her head. Wayne, too, was edgy and could prove lethal if provoked. Until they were in a better position to act, they needed to appease Wayne, not rile him.

As she scooted into place on the mattress, she glanced at the plate Wayne had brought in and spied a sloppily constructed peanut butter sandwich. "What's that?"

"I thought you might be getting hungry," Wayne replied gruffly.

The smile she offered him was genuine. "Thank you. That was…nice."

He shrugged the shoulder on his uninjured side and grunted. "Yeah, well…you were nice enough to patch me up so…" Another dismissive shrug. "Turn around."

When he pulled out a pocketknife, she hesitated, and he took her arm forcefully. "You want your arms tied in front so you can eat or don't you?"

"Yes." She gave him access to her wrists and held Dave's vigilant gaze. She could tell by the way the muscle in his jaw twitched and how his breathing whispered, shallow and quick, that he was mulling a move. She could practically hear the gears in his head turning as he sized up the situation.

Wayne sawed through the loop of tape at her wrists, and Lilly rolled her aching shoulders as she brought them forward and rubbed the offended flesh. Within seconds, he had the roll of tape in his hands and was securing her hands again. When he was finished taping her wrists, he squinted one eye as he sized her up. "You be nice to me, Lilly. I'll be nice to you."

He took the sandwich from the plate and shoved it into her hands.

"Thank you." She nodded and took a bite, even though she had no appetite at the moment. To spurn his gift didn't seem diplomatic at a time when she was making headway in gaining his trust.

"What about me? Move my hands to the front?" Dave asked, his head cocked slightly.

Wayne scoffed. "You shot me." Flashing a cynical smile, he said, "I don't like you, so you get nothing."

Lilly chewed the inside of her cheek lightly as she thought. She had an opportunity here. Wayne didn't have the gun in his hand at the moment, though she figured the lump under his shirt at the small of his back had to be the weapon. Still...even though her feet were bound, her hands were now in front of her, giving her more ability to move, to act. Was there something, *any-thing* she could—

Her thought stopped half-formed when she realized Wayne was removing his belt. A chill slithered through her with the implication.

"What are you doing?" she blurted, recognizing the panic in her voice.

Dave yanked his shoulders back and bared his teeth. "Damn it, man. Don't you touch her!"

Wayne paused, his hand still on the metal buckle. He divided a wry look between them, then snorted at Dave. "You have a dirty mind, Hero." He slid the belt free of the loops on his jeans and jerked the leather taut between his hands. Leaning toward Lilly, he grasped her wrists and poked the end of the belt between her bound arms, pausing only long enough to send Dave a gloating grin. "Although if I did decide to *touch her*, there ain't nothing you can do to stop me, now is there?"

Her heart thrashed in her chest, and she tried to catch Wayne's attention, meet his eyes. "Don't do this, Wayne. This whole thing has gotten out of hand, but it's not too late to do the right thing. Please! Just let us go."

His mouth pinched closed, and he shook his head, avoiding her eyes. "Can't do that."

Wayne tugged her hands, still clutching the peanut butter sandwich, up to the bed's lattice-style headboard, where he wove the belt ends in and out of the thick oak. He buckled the belt, leaving her arms over her head, bound to the bed. "Don't worry, Lilly. If you keep on cooperating with me, being nice to me, you'll be okay." Tugging up his now-loose jeans, he cut a look toward Dave. "You I'm only keeping around as long as I think you might be useful, say, in fixing up my car. Plus, if the cops track me down, I may need a human shield."

The two bites of sandwich Lilly had managed to choke down curdled in her gut.

Dave glared at Wayne. "Do you think you're scaring me with threats like that? That I really care whether you starve me out of some small-minded revenge?" Dave scoffed. "You're wrong."

Dave's challenge wrenched a knot in Lilly's chest. When Wayne left, she really needed to get a handle on Dave's state of mind.

Wayne chortled. "I guess we'll see about that."

Their captor left, closing the door again. The room fell silent, but Lilly's mind roared. The truth of the situation was things between Dave and Wayne could escalate quickly, and she'd be helpless to do anything about it.

Lilly stared at the ceiling for a moment, catching her breath before she asked quietly, "Do you really not care if you die?"

"What?"

"You told him you didn't care about his threats—"

"No! That was just… I don't *want* to die. No."

"Good." Her body relaxed slightly, though the position of her arms over her head was only marginally better than having them behind her. "Could you maybe stop antagonizing him then?"

"Maybe. Thing is, if he does see the need to be rid of one of us or use someone as a shield, I want his choice to be easy. If anything's going to happen to one of us, I'd rather it be me than you."

"Dave…"

"I already have Helen's death on my conscience. I won't have your death there, too."

Her heartbeat scampered. "But…you weren't responsible for Helen's death."

"Maybe not." His breath sawed out heavily "I carry it with me just the same."

Grief was thick in his tone, and sympathy plucked deep inside her. Just a few hours ago she'd reamed him out for his treatment of Helen while her sister had dated him. But his feelings for Helen seemed to be deeper and truer than she'd imagined. She drew a slow breath and closed her eyes, fighting the rise of tears that thoughts of her sister brought on.

Instead she tore the sandwich she still held in half and awkwardly tossed one half onto the pillow beside her on the queen-size bed. Then, pulling her knees up and twisting her body, she got her feet high enough to nudge the pillow toward the edge of the bed. "Hey, heads up. Pillow and dinner incoming."

"Wha—" he began, just as the pillow dropped to the floor with a *poof*. He chuckled. "Thanks." Then he said, "Hey, back off, cat. That's my dinner."

She smiled. "Don't worry. Maddie's never shown an interest in human food. She's probably just wondering what that was that landed on the floor." Angling her head sharply and scooting herself higher on the bed, she took another bite of the sandwich. She didn't know when Wayne might bring food again, and she wouldn't waste the chance to eat. Around the sticky peanut butter she mumbled, "Can you reach the sandwich?" Remembering his hands were behind him, she huffed her frustration. "Will you be able to eat it somehow?"

"Mmph," he grunted in what sounded like an affirmative. She heard spitting noises next, and he said, "Got it…and a bit of cat hair. Can't say I've ever eaten off the floor before, but desperate times and all that… whatever."

"Sorry."

"No. Thanks for sharing. And for the pillow. I dragged it closer with my teeth. My head thanks you."

Remembering the blow he took to his head, she furrowed her brow. "And how is your head? Any new symptoms? Double vision? Nausea?" Not that she could do anything for him if he was showing new signs of a concussion, trussed up the way she was.

"Just a splitting headache."

She took another bite of her half sandwich, and her mind returned to her confrontation with Dave at the bank. "Dave?"

"Hmm?"

"Were you really going to propose to her?"

He didn't answer right away, and she angled her head on the pillow toward that side of the bed, even though she couldn't see him from her position. "Dave?"

The sough of an expelled sigh drifted up from the floor. "I was. And I hate—" he cleared his throat "—hate that she never knew. It would have showed her that I really did care about her."

She noticed he didn't say he *loved* Helen this time but chose to let it slide. She was in no mood for recriminations, painful regrets or arguing. "I'm sorry I laid into you the way I did at the bank. I was out of line."

"Maybe, maybe not. Maybe I deserved everything you said."

"And maybe you're being too hard on yourself. There are two people in every relationship, and both parties share in its success or failure. I know Helen could be pretty…demanding. Insecure." She hadn't meant to say it, but once the words slipped out she realized they were true. She'd shied away from thinking any ill of Helen since her death, but if she was fair, Lilly had to admit her sister had always been…well, needy.

Dave was silent, and Lilly wasn't sure how to interpret his nonresponse.

During the lull in their conversation, she allowed herself to reconsider everything Helen had told her about Dave in this new, more honest light. Staring blankly at the ceiling, she replayed some of Helen's complaints. He didn't call often enough. He didn't remember "anniversaries" for such things as their first date, their first kiss, their first intimacy. Or if he did, he didn't commemorate the events the way she felt he should have, with gifts or romantic gestures. She'd complained that he flirted with waitresses and store clerks, but was it possible Helen was too sensitive? That he was just being friendly with the people in service jobs?

Lilly could definitely remember telling Helen that her jealousy wasn't good for the relationship, that perhaps she was overreacting. And, yeah, *that* comment had gone over with her sister like a lead balloon. And so rather than try to reason with Helen in later conversations, Lilly had just let Helen vent.

Her chest ached as she continued reconstructing memories of her sister that highlighted her sister's weaknesses. It felt like a betrayal to resurrect Helen's faults. But her sister had been human and imperfect like everyone else. For all Helen's good qualities—and she'd had a laundry list of those, as well—Lilly's little sister could definitely have made a relationship with her challenging. Even as a child Helen had demanded more of their mother's attention, had needed constant stroking, praise and encouragement to battle her pessimism and uncertainty. Especially after their father left.

Lilly's gut whirled as it did whenever she thought too much about her father's disappearance from their lives when she and Helen were young—yet old enough to feel the sting of rejection and hurt left by their father's desertion and subsequent disinterest in them.

"Do you really think so?" Dave asked, breaking his silence, his question pulling Lilly from the bleak direction of her thoughts.

She cleared the emotion from her throat. "Think what?"

"That Helen was insecure. Demanding."

Lilly blinked, bit her bottom lip. "I mean… Well, you didn't?"

He hesitated. "Lilly, I don't want to speak ill of her. If she—"

"It's okay, Dave. I know she was difficult to be with sometimes. To be fair to you, I want a full picture. Be honest. No hard feelings."

He grunted, and she heard a rustling as if he was shifting, trying to get more comfortable. "I tried to make her happy. She was a great gal. But I had long hours at the Double M. Most days after work I just wanted to grab a bite to eat and tumble straight into bed." He paused, then added, "To sleep, I mean. I'd be exhausted."

Lilly twitched her cheek, amused that he felt the need to be clearer on that point. "Understood."

"See, the McCalls…they were shorthanded, and I sometimes had to cancel on her when—"

"Dave. I'm not judging you."

He snorted. "You did. At the bank."

She chuckled hollowly. "Yeah, let's put that aside for the moment. Tell me what it was like. How did you try to make her happy?"

"Just…giving her what she asked for. Trying to go to the places she liked or spending as much time with her as I could. But it never seemed enough. Every time I thought I had it figured out, what she wanted of me, it seemed I'd screwed up again. I didn't mean to be such an oaf. But I always seemed to be in trouble with her for something. Not calling when I got too busy, not noticing she'd done her hair different, not bringing a present on our anniversary, falling asleep too soon after sex—"

An uneasy jitter rolled through Lilly when he mentioned his intimacy with her sister. Dave was unquestionably good-looking, in peak physical condition from his work on the ranch, injured leg notwithstanding. Thinking of Dave in sexual terms was dangerous. And far too easy to do. She shook her head as if that alone would clear the images taunting her and tamp down the tingle in her womb.

"—didn't understand why she would get so upset over some things that seemed so unimportant to me, but I tried," he continued, his voice a bit hoarse. "I really did try to remember the little things that she'd complain about and do better. Complimenting her cooking or her clothes. Texting her if I was going to be late, even if it was just five minutes. Flowers or some gift for *every* occasion, no matter how trivial the event seemed to me."

He fell silent, but Lilly said nothing. She sensed that Dave needed to have his say, unload months of frustration and guilt. She truly wanted to hear his side, put things in perspective.

"Problem was," he said and heaved a sigh, "I never knew what days she thought were noteworthy. I'd never kept track of things she thought were cause for celebration."

He paused again, and Lilly recalled a phone conversation just a couple months before Helen's death when Helen had complained bitterly about the fact Dave refused to dress up for Halloween as Raggedy Andy to her Raggedy Ann. Lilly had taken Dave's side on that one, telling her sister that she shouldn't force Dave to wear a costume he was uncomfortable with. Helen's response had been something along the lines of "Fine! We won't dress up *at all* then. We'll be the losers at the costume party with no costume!"

Lilly was tempted to ask Dave how that particular debate had finally come out.

"I mean, really," he said, "Half anniversaries and half birthdays? Aren't the whole ones enough?"

Lilly snorted an indelicate laugh. "That's probably my fault."

"Your fault? How?"

Her heart squeezed as she reached deep into her sepia memories to pull the dusty reminiscences from their shelf. "My birthday is in December, near Christmas, and so as a kid, I always felt like it got lost in the Christmas rush. When I was seven, I asked if we could celebrate my half birthday in June when the weather was nice and I could have an outdoor party with my friends. My mom loved the idea. So it became a tradition, one that Helen decided meant she should have a half-birthday party, too, even though her birthday was in October and was never overlooked. She won, of course, and got two parties. The one in April was small. Just family, her favorite dinner and a cake, but…a precedent was set."

"A precedent. Right," He scoffed quietly. "I think I set a few of those myself that had to be repeated, or topped, every year."

He grew silent, and she thought she heard him chewing, the slight smack of a tongue dealing with sticky peanut butter and no drink to wash it down. She took another bite of her own sandwich, her speculation turning in a new direction. Around the dry peanut butter and bread in her mouth she muttered, "Dave?"

"Hmm?"

"If she was so hard on you, so difficult to please…" Lilly felt the sandwich form a hard knot in her gut as the question she really wanted to ask slipped from her lips. "Why did you stay with her?"

He coughed as if he'd choked on his sandwich. "I—"

"I know. That sounded terrible. What I mean is—"

"Helen wasn't always that way. You know that. She could be so great most of the time. Cheerful and generous and concerned for others. She was so passionate about her cooking and crafts. And, well, we had fun together. Usually. Interspersed with arguments." He hesitated. "Sometimes I wondered why *she* stayed with *me*."

The sadness in his tone shot a pang straight to her heart. Lilly shook her head even though she knew he couldn't see it. "Dave, don't say that."

"It's true."

"It sounds to me like you were, if not the best boyfriend ever, at least—" she hesitated, choosing her words carefully "—doing the best you could with a… demanding girlfriend. I believe you when you say you tried to make her happy, and in the end, that's what matters."

Of course, Helen wouldn't have been with Dave, wouldn't have stayed with Dave, if he weren't a good guy at his core. And everyone had faults. Maybe Helen had overblown Dave's shortcomings. Hearing Dave's side of things made her reevaluate everything Helen had told her. His tardiness meant he was dedicated to a hard job that had unpredictable hours sometimes. His forgetfulness of special occasions was often a disagreement over what constituted a special occasion. His apparent lack of commitment…

Her pulse stumbled. Considering Dave had a hard time saying he *loved* Helen, was his planned marriage proposal a concession to pressure from her sister or had he truly loved her enough to want family and a lifetime commitment with her?

And why was she even debating the issue now? Wasn't it a moot point since Helen was gone?

He grunted. "Was it enough that I tried, though? If she wasn't happy—"

"She was." Lilly needed him to believe that. Letting him go on torturing himself would be cruel. "I know she complained to me, but she gushed sometimes, too.

When I got my divorce, I remember her saying she hoped that one day I'd find a guy as great as you. But being the protective older sister, I guess I focused on her complaints. I wanted her life to be perfect. Especially since our childhood—" a knot of emotion clogged her throat, and she croaked "—wasn't."

Inhaling deeply, she silently prayed he didn't press her to explain her comment.

After a moment, he said quietly, "Yeah, I get that."

So he knew? How much had Helen told him? She pushed aside the unsettling memories and searched for a new topic. Things had grown far too maudlin, and they still had to figure out a plan of escape.

Chapter 8

Dave followed Lilly's lead, and when she said no more about the ugliness of her and Helen's childhood, he let the topic go, as well. For long minutes, he stared blankly at the ceiling. He had quite enough to think about, thank you, in light of all Lilly had already said regarding Helen's temper and neediness. Josh and Zane McCall had said much the same about Helen a time or two when he mentioned their arguments. Dave had felt the need to defend Helen, which made him question whether he thought, on some level, Helen was right for wanting more from the relationship.

But Lilly had known Helen better than anyone. Had loved Helen better than anyone. And still Lilly was giving him credit for trying to make things works with her sister. The accusations and anger in Lilly's tone at the bank replayed in his mind. How much of that bitterness was just her grief talking?

A warm furry head butted his cheek, distracting him. If his hands had been free, he'd have patted Lilly's cat. "Hey, fuzz. What's up?"

Her cat chirped a meow.

"Say, Maddie, you have a blade on you? Or maybe a really sharp claw I could borrow?"

The cat sniffed his mouth, and Dave chuckled when the feline's long whiskers tickled his chin. "That's right. I ate peanut butter. You smell it?"

"What?" Lilly's groggy voice drifted from the top of the bed.

"Talking to Maddie. She seems more interested in sniffing my peanut butter breath than helping slice through the tape on my feet with her claws."

Lilly snorted a short laugh. "Imagine that."

But imaginary help from the cat or not, he did have to find a way to get his hands and feet free. He had to protect Lilly and get the revolver from Wayne. After a good bit of thought, the seeds of a strategy were taking root. And Lilly needed to be prepared for any opportunity that arose.

Lilly shifted on the bed, attempting to get more comfortable. At least her hands weren't behind her anymore. Dave was the one who had to be aching. Besides the way he was bound, he had his bum leg to deal with and the smack to his head. Though he hadn't yet shown any signs of concussion, she needed to stay alert to the possibility. *As if she could do anything for him—*

"Lilly," Dave said, his tone more serious. So serious,

in fact, it caused an uneasy scrape of worry to travel up her spine.

"Yeah?"

"Since it is clear you have a better standing with our captor than I do, you need to know what I've been thinking."

"Okay." Dread coiled inside her. Plans for escape boded ill, promised guns and violence, and the threat of injuries or death. At that moment she longed for the easy rapport and lighthearted teasing she'd shared with Dave earlier in the afternoon. Her nerves had appreciated the brief escape and chance to release some tension with a chuckle or two. She swallowed hard. "What have you been thinking?"

"First, if he lets you out of your restraints for any reason, you need to try to get the gun from him."

Panic pinged in her gut, and she shook her head. "No, Dave, I... I'm a nurse. A healer. I don't think I could ever kill someone."

"I didn't say shoot him."

She exhaled her relief.

"But we don't want him shooting us, either. Here's the thing—if you get the gun from him, aim at the floor, well away from you or me, and fire it as many times as you can. I don't know if he has backup ammunition or not, but he can't shoot us if he's out of rounds."

She had to admit, his plan made sense. But that didn't do anything for the dryness that filled her mouth at the thought of handling the lethal weapon.

"I've been replaying the scene at the bank in my head, counting shots. I think the gun he has is a Glock 17. That means seventeen rounds, assuming he's using the factory magazine. Best I can remember, he fired seven rounds at the bank, one here, so he has nine left."

She frowned. "How do you know this stuff about what gun it is and how many bullets it holds?"

"My uncle had a Glock 17 when I was younger. He and my dad let me shoot it and some rifles at the range as part of my gun-safety training before we'd go hunting together."

"Oh." Again, his explanation made sense, but it didn't alleviate her anxiety about having to handle the weapon herself.

"Of course, he'll try to get the gun back from you, so you have to be quick about it. Get it, aim away from yourself at the floor and fire. No hesitation. Got it? You don't want to find yourself in a struggle with him over a loaded gun."

The quiver in her gut grew, and she whispered an unladylike word.

"You can do it, Lilly."

She was touched by his encouragement, but nothing he said would make her feel better about trying to snatch a loaded weapon from Wayne. She would, though, because Dave was right about the need to eliminate the threat. She swallowed hard. "Is that all?"

"No. That's your first priority, if you get the chance. But if there is any way for you to get out of the house, into my truck, my phone is there. I left it on the seat. I'd been charging it. Get it."

"Right."

"I doubt it has much battery power left at this point, but if it does, call for help."

"Okay." That one was easier to promise. In fact, her

pulse accelerated as she pictured Dave's cell phone in his truck, just steps away…if she could sweet-talk her way out of the restraints Wayne had her in.

Now her mind began sorting through options, tricks, ploys to earn Wayne's trust and win her release. The most obvious answer was to tell him she needed to check his wound, reclean it. But it was too soon for that excuse to be plausible. If they were still here in a few—

"Oof. Uh…oka-a-ay," Dave said, cutting into her thoughts.

The loud rumble of a purr tipped her to the source of his distraction. She smiled. "Maddie?"

"Yeah. I'm now her bed. Center of my chest." Then in a slightly higher-pitched voice, the sort everyone apparently used to talk to animals and babies, Dave added, "Don't mind me. I'm just lying here tied up by a bank robber. Please, use me as your mattress."

She heard a soft *meep* from her cat and grinned. Too bad the cat couldn't be their spy or gopher. Lassie really would come in handy right about—

Or *could* she use the cat to her advantage? She wrinkled her nose as she mulled the idea. The last thing she wanted to do was expose Maddie to danger from Wayne. If he didn't like cats or took a notion to be cruel to her via her beloved pet…

Pain jabbed her chest at the mere suggestion of anything happening to Maddie.

But if Wayne liked animals, could Maddie be a conduit to build a bridge with Wayne? Could she invent an excuse why Wayne would need to release her to care for Maddie? Feeding her or letting her get to her litter box or…

She heard Dave sputter and puff air.

"Hey, move your tail. I...*ack*. Cat, really? There. That's better."

"Everything okay down there?" she asked.

"Yeah, we're fine now. Maddie was just getting a little too up close and personal."

Her cat meowed loudly, as if telling a different story from Dave's, then hopped up on the bed and crossed to her.

"Hey, sweetie." She closed her eyes and savored the contact when Maddie rubbed her head on her chin. Her cat, a small bit of normality in her current surreal circumstances, settled her a little. "You're a good girl, Miss Maddie."

"Mrrp."

"Yes, you are," she cooed, then remembering Dave was listening to her baby talk, she winced and switched to clicking her tongue softly. Some might call her routine with her pet silly, but the interaction, goofy as it might seem to an outsider, was a balm to her after even the worst days. Say when she dealt with child abuse in her position at the ER. Or lost a patient she'd expected to survive. Or had to deal with inane hospital bureaucracy, petty coworkers and paperwork.

Or stumbled into a bank robbery and was taken hostage.

Maddie nosed Lilly's bound hands, asking to be patted, Maddie's favorite thing. Lilly complied as best she could, wiggling her fingers as Maddie rubbed her face on her taped hands.

The bed shook, drawing her out of her musings. "Dave? Whatcha doing?"

"I thought maybe if I wiggled my legs, I could loosen the tape, maybe stretch it."

"Any luck?" She glanced toward her own feet. *Worth a shot.* She turned her feet and tried to create some slack in the layers of tape. Drawn by her wiggling, Maddie moved to rub against Lilly's feet.

"Nothing yet, but it's not like I have anything else to do at the moment. This is gonna be a game of inches, not miles. Baby steps count."

"Right." So it would take time. They had that, didn't they? Time was all they had at this point. She angled her gaze to the belt Wayne had looped through the head rail and the strips of tape that joined her wrists. It was a basic belt with a standard buckle. Could she work the end back through the loop and unfasten the belt?

Scrunching as far up as she could to the head of the bed, she wrenched her wrists and twisted her arms to awkward angles, desperately trying to grasp the loose end of the belt. Her fingers finally brushed the dangling leather and, one millimeter at a time, she nudged the belt closer to her reach.

The wiggling bed told her Dave had not deserted his campaign of inches, either. Maddie, who'd snuggled against her legs for a nap, put her ears back, clearly annoyed by the jiggling bed.

"So you work in an ER?"

His question caught her off guard. "Yeah? Why?"

"Just making conversation. We could be here a while. Tell me about the ER. I bet you see some interesting stuff."

The way he said *interesting* clearly indicated he meant *bizarre*.

She snorted, recalling some of the more unusual cases she'd worked in the past. "You have no idea. Everything they say about full moons and paydays is the truth."

"Paydays?"

"Yeah." Her fingertips batted at the belt, wiggling it the tiniest bit closer. "A little cash in the pocket means an opportunity to go blow off steam, get drunk or high. Drunk or high with some people translates to stupid and risky... and a trip to the emergency room." She sighed when the tenuous hold she'd managed to get on the belt slipped, and she dropped it. Firming her mouth along with her resolve, she flexed and curled her fingers, preparing to try again. "It's amazing to me the things people will try on a dare."

Dave chortled. "Yeah. I've heard stories."

"Fireworks and alcohol are a particularly bad mix, but—" She flicked the loose part of the belt and caught it between her index and ring fingers when it flopped back. "—some folks don't need small explosives to get themselves in a world of hurt."

Easy—easy, she coached herself mentally as she worked to gently shift the belt from her current tenuous grip toward her thumb and forefinger.

"Like eating laundry detergent pods?" Dave asked, his tone wry.

"Good example." Pinching the leather with her weak fingers, she tried to roll the belt toward her stronger, more agile digits. And dropped the belt again. She muttered a curse.

"You okay?" Dave asked.

"Yeah. Just trying something up here, and it's testing my patience and my fine motor skills." Doggedly, she set to work again, deciding if she couldn't fumble the belt over to her dominant fingers, perhaps she could reach the end with her mouth. Could she maneuver the strap of leather with her teeth and tongue?

"Weird stuff has got to be easier for you than—" He didn't finish his sentence, as if realizing something that cut him off. "Well…never mind."

"The tragedies?" She furrowed her brow. She tried not to dwell on the sad cases that were an inevitable part of her line of work. She wasn't inhuman. Far from it. But she needed a certain detachment in order to do her job. "Mmm-hmm. Those are hard. Really hard. And they don't get easier with time, but—" She'd managed to catch the belt again and nudged it toward her mouth. Dropped it again. Her heart sank. Closing her eyes, she drew a cleansing breath and started again.

"But?"

"But…for all the weird and heartbreaking stuff that comes in, you also see the best of humanity, too."

"Oh?"

"Yeah. The folks who risk their lives to help a stranger at an accident. People who show unbelievable courage to help pull someone from a fire or dive in freezing water to save a drowning child."

"First responders," he said.

"Yeah, them. But regular citizens, too." Her fingers stilled in the middle of her ministrations when an image of Dave helping the fallen security guard popped into her head. Pulling the guard's gun to return fire when Wayne seemed to panic…

Her heart thumped harder, and a tingle walked up her spine. Dave's actions today had been heroic. She wouldn't soon forget the way he'd rallied in the crisis and likely saved lives. Maybe not the security guard's, but other people in the bank, had Wayne not been winged by Dave's shot.

"Tell me." Dave's voice diverted her thoughts.

"What?" His comment seemed a non sequitur following her thoughts about him.

"About the best of humanity. I could use a dose of positivity about now."

"Oh, right." She refocused both on the good she'd encountered at the hospital and the belt. She had to get the damn thing off. Her life and Dave's depended on it. She couldn't count on Wayne's favor toward her lasting forever. And when he saw her and Dave as an inconvenience or hindrance...

Huffing, she pushed aside that thought. Positivity...

"Well, there's the people willing to donate blood to save a life. And not just for family members. For whoever needs it."

Dave gave a quiet grunt of acknowledgment. She'd bet her month's salary, based on what she was learning about Dave, that he was one of those people.

"Then there are the husbands and wives whose love is so deep, you can see it, feel it. And you'd know that it was their love that gave the patient the strength to fight against all odds and survive horrible injuries." Those cases gave her hope. True love was out there, and maybe one day she'd find it.

When her throat thickened with tender emotion, she bit her bottom lip and steeled herself. *Stay on task.* To find her happily-ever-after, she first had to live long enough to meet Mr. Right.

She stretched her fingers, grasped the leather strap and flicked it close enough to her mouth to catch it between her teeth. Progress. Angling her head to drag the belt closer to her fingers, she gained a better grasp of the dangling end between her pointer and middle finger. Still not the combination of her most dexterous fingers, but better than before. And maybe...

"So you believe that love is strong enough to fight off death?"

His question surprised her. "I do. They've done studies that show that the mind, especially a person's state of mind and attitude, has a big effect on how well a person recovers from illness and injury. Love can be the motivation to overcome big obstacles."

"Hmm." His hum sounded intrigued.

"You'b neber hearb dat?" she mumbled around the leather strap in her teeth.

"I've heard things like 'mind over matter' and 'attitude is everything.' And while they are chipper sayings that are good for morale, I always believed they were just mantras made up by some spiritual guru to sell DVDs and coffee mugs."

"Naw. I'b seen it in action," she said around the belt, adjusting her head to give her fingers more slack to scrunch up. Mind over matter, Lilly thought as she inched her fingers up the belt, held taut by her mouth. A few millimeters, then a few more. Baby steps...

The bed wiggled some more—Dave was obviously still working to free his feet—and Maddie gave up on sleeping beside her. Fluffy tail swishing, her cat hopped onto the floor, presumably to hide under the bed again.

Lilly was finally making progress with the belt.

Slowly. But she was getting somewhere, and her heart pattered harder with excitement. She resisted the urge to rush, despite the fact that because the sun was setting, the room was getting darker.

"You okay up there? You sound funny."

"I'm fine. Working on somfin."

"Good. Because I'm not getting very far with the tape around my feet." She heard his disappointed sigh.

When she'd inched the belt far enough through the loop that the buckle wiggled, she released the grip she had with her teeth. "Come on…please…"

"Lilly?"

"Hang on…"

The angle that she'd turned her hands meant the tape had twisted tighter and was beginning to cut of the blood flow to her fingers. Her grip was getting clumsier as her hand grew numb. But the buckle frame had moved, the metal prong sliding in the hole. She held her breath, repositioned her fingers another millimeter or two up the strap…

"So if the mind can *will* something to happen, why don't more people survive disease and accidents?" he asked.

A fair question, but one she didn't want to take the time to debate or explain at the moment. Not when the prong was sliding further…out…of…the…

Hole! She exhaled happily as the tiny bar fell free of the belt hole. Now if she could continue to wiggle and push up the strap…

Bit by bit, one tiny step at a time, the leather slid farther through the frame. The closer she got to freeing her hands from the belt, the more her adrenaline surged.

Combined with the numbness from decreased blood flow, the excitement and anticipation made her hands shake. *Steady*, she told herself, taking a short break to draw a cleansing breath and try to calm the trembling.

"Me-ow!" Maddie's yowl jarred her nerves.

She shifted her gaze to the door, where her cat stood on her hind legs and bopped at the doorknob, her signal that she wanted out of the room. Lilly had to blink to refocus her eyes after having her attention narrowed up close for so long.

"Sorry, girl. No can do," she said, turning her attention back to the belt. So close! With the new slack in the strap, she'd gotten a better grip and repositioned her fingers. A little more, a little farther—

She gasped and gave a tiny cry of celebration when the belt slid free.

"What's wrong?" The concern in Dave's voice touched her.

"That was a happy sound. I got the belt off. I'm not strapped to the bed anymore." She struggled to a seated position and leaned over to peer down at Dave on the floor, showing him her freed, if still tape-bound, hands.

"Excellent. Well done!" He flashed her a handsome grin, and pleasure puddled in her core like the joy of indulging in a gooey chocolate dessert. Her pulse raced as if on a sugar high, but she brushed aside the sweet sensation.

Now was not the time to examine her surprising reaction to Dave. Instead she wiggled her way to the edge of the bed and rolled onto the floor beside him. With her hands now in front of her, she'd be better able to attack the tape restraining them.

Dave stretched his hip toward her. "Wanna have another go at getting the keys from my pocket?"

Heat rose up her throat to tingle in her cheeks. "Um, sure."

She scooted closer and slid one hand in his pocket. But like the previous attempt, the tape and awkward angle meant she couldn't dive deep enough in the pocket to snag the keys.

"All right. Plan B," Dave said. "Or are we to plan C or D at this point?"

"Doesn't matter what letter we assign it, if it will work." She was already wiggling and twisting her arms, hoping to make the tape looser, thus giving her more mobility for whatever task was next.

Dave cocked his head. "I think we're back to playing gerbil. Nibble away."

She nodded. "Right."

She brought her wrists to her mouth and bit at the tape, managing to chew off little pieces of the plastic packing tape. One tiny bit at a time. Spit it out. Nibble and rip again.

From the door, Maddie meowed impatiently and stood on her hind legs again to rattle the doorknob.

"Do you know a way to quiet the cat?" Dave pulled a face, reflecting his frustration. "If she keeps rattling that doorknob, Wayne will hear it and think we're trying to bust outta here."

"Maddie, stop!" she called to the cat in a stage whisper, trying to infuse her tone with authority minus the volume. Which, of course, didn't work. Maddie sat down for a moment to blink at her but resumed her meowing and doorknob bapping seconds later.

"She wants out," she told Dave, stating the obvious, "to eat or use her litter box. She won't quit until she gets her way. She's not very cooperative or well trained, I'm afraid."

"Then we have to hurry." Dave met her gaze. "It's just a matter of time before the cat's ruckus brings our friend back down the hall to see about the noise."

She frowned and divided a look between Dave and Maddie. "I'm sorry. I—"

"Forget it." He shook his head in dismissal. "Just… keep gnawing."

She did. Biting, ripping, spitting out the torn bits. After a couple of minutes, she'd chewed through the layers enough to tear free of the looped bindings.

Her eyes darted over to Dave's, and he sent her another approving smile. "Great!"

As she plucked the remaining scraps of tape off her skin, she rubbed her sore wrists.

"*Now* get the keys," Dave said, rocking back and straightening his legs so that she had access to his pocket.

She swallowed hard and steeled herself to go foraging at his groin again. "Okay."

Scooting closer to him, she snorted ironically. "Helen must be laughing her tail off."

"Laughing? The Helen I knew would be terrified for us."

Lilly dipped her chin in agreement. "Well, sure. Because of the unpredictable and dangerous man with the gun. But if she knew I was going spelunking in your jeans just a few hours after having told you off…"

Dave met her raised-eyebrow look with one of his

own. "Spelunking, huh? Don't worry. There are no bats."

She chuffed a short laugh. "It's not the bats I'm worried about, pal."

His eyebrows inched higher, and when she slid her fingers in his pocket, he hissed through his teeth.

She snatched her hand back. "What?"

His mouth tightened. "Nothing. Just…don't take anything that happens down there the wrong way. There are some things I can't control."

Her heart stutter-stepped. Then, drawing her shoulders back, she blew out a cleansing breath. "Whatever."

She jammed her hand deep into his pocket, found the keys with minimal groping and dragged them out with a sigh of relief. "Got 'em."

He nodded, his own expression relaxing. "The house key is probably sharpest."

Four keys dangled from the simple ring. The largest was obviously for his truck and bore the auto company logo. Two were the shape and size she associated with door locks and the fourth was smaller, as if for a padlock or mailbox.

"Two house keys?" She bent her head to begin sawing through the tape lashing him to the bed.

"My place and here."

She glanced up, blinking her surprise at his profile. "You still have a key to this house?"

"Yeah. Who was I supposed to give it to?"

She clenched her back teeth, choking down the spike of grief and frustration that accompanied his reminder of their mutual loss. Once his feet were loose from the bed, she set to work cutting the straps of tape around his ankles. He'd managed to draw the strips tighter, bunched into thick ropes with his tugging and writhing attempts to get loose.

Her fingers were still stiff and tingly after having her own wrists tightly bound, but she hacked at the strips feverishly.

Her cat yowled again and padded the door.

"Stop it, Maddie. No!"

"Wait!" he whispered harshly, turning his head toward her. "Shh!"

She quieted and stilled her hands as Dave angled his head to listen. When she wrinkled her brow in question, he whispered at a barely audible volume, "The squeaky floorboard in the hall—"

Chapter 9

The bedroom door flung open.

Maddie bolted out of the room.

Bleary-eyed, Wayne wobbled and leaned against the door frame for support, apparently without having noticed the cat. "Wha're y'two doin'? I'm tryin'a sleep!"

Lilly curled her palm around the keys and slowly tried to move her hands behind her back before Wayne noticed that her hands were unbound. Of course, she was no longer on the bed, where he'd left her. She held her breath.

"Just talking, man," Dave said, angling his body in a way that clearly meant to hide her.

"Well…don't!" Wayne squeezed his eyes closed, then widened them and blinked as if trying to clear his vision.

How much of the tramadol had Wayne taken? Did he even remember moving her to the bed? His unsteadiness, slurred speech and apparent blurry vision indicated he was pretty doped up. He'd be slower to react, just like a drunk, but also like a drunk, he could be more volatile too.

Glaring at them, but apparently unarmed, Wayne moved into the room, his gait uneven. "Get up."

Dave and Lilly exchanged a look, but neither of them moved.

Wayne grabbed the bedpost nearest him for balance, then kicked at Dave's bound feet. "Get up!"

Dave drew his feet back, got them under him and rose awkwardly to his knees but went no farther. "Give me a second. My feet are numb."

"That ain't my problem," Wayne growled.

While Wayne's attention was focused on Dave, Lilly shifted slowly until her arms were behind her, hoping Wayne wouldn't realize they were unbound. She clenched the keys in her fist, then spotted the discarded wad of tape from her wrists by Dave's hip.

Her stomach swooped. She rose on her knees and scooted awkwardly toward the tape. With her feet still tied together, her balance was off, and she basically flopped on top of the discarded wad of tape. And, naturally, drew Wayne's attention.

"Where d'you think you're goin'?" Wayne grabbed her arm and tugged. "I'm movin' you, too. Can't trust ya not t'chatter 'n' plot 'gainst me, so I'm sep'rating you."

Lilly shot a panicked look to Dave. His even stare and slow nod silently bid her to stay calm. She inhaled slowly and worked to school her expression.

"C'mon." Wayne jerked at her arm. "On y'r feet,

Lilly." He spoke her name as if it were an insult. "You're comin' w'th me."

Muscles tensing, she pushed clumsily to her bound feet, trying to brace herself for what might come next.

Wayne swayed a little and grabbed the bedpost again to steady himself, and when he said nothing for a moment, she hazarded a glance at the floor. The tape was gone. Where—?

At that moment, the wad, which had stuck loosely to the seat of her pants, fell to the carpet with a quiet *plop*. She stiffened, while inside her heart thrashed against her ribs.

Wayne's confused gaze drifted to the flattened ball of tape, and he blinked as if forcing his drug-clouded brain to make sense of what he was seeing.

Dave didn't wait for their captor to catch on. From his position on his knees, he lowered a shoulder to ram Wayne in his wounded side. With his feet still taped together, Dave could only lunge at him. But he aimed well, and the two men toppled together to the floor. While Wayne struggled under the surprise of the attack, Dave used those precious moments of advantage. He smashed his forehead into Wayne's nose, then while Wayne grabbed his offended face, Dave rolled aside and brought his bound feet up to kick out at Wayne, striking in the region of his kidney.

Watching in horror, Lilly held her breath. This could end so badly. And yet she couldn't blame Dave for taking what could be their only opportunity to fight back.

Pivoting, she dropped on the bed and raised her feet to the mattress beside her. She fumbled one key into position in her hand and began sawing frantically at the multiple layers of tape.

She heard a growl and cut a glance toward the men. Wayne had rolled out of Dave's reach and was clambering to his feet. He swiped at his bloody nose with the back of his hand and snarled at Dave, "Son of a bitch!"

Dave struggled to right himself and get his feet under him again, but Wayne now assumed the upper hand and kicked Dave in the chest. Once Dave had toppled onto his back, Wayne lobbed several more strikes with his booted foot into Dave's ribs, his legs, his hip.

Lilly's gut churned, seeing Dave battered so viciously. "No! Stop!"

Having made a slit in her bindings, she ripped hard at the tape around her ankles. She managed to free one leg and stumbled to her feet. She grabbed at Wayne's arm, trying to pull him away from Dave. "Wayne, please! Stop it! Don't do this!"

Pausing, Wayne turned an ugly scowl toward her. "Get off me!"

"Wayne, please. This isn't who you are." Of course, she didn't know that about him. But if she could convince their captor the brutality was unnecessary, if she could continue to form some tenuous bond with him, using his name as often as possible, forcing him to see them as people and not liabilities, then maybe…

She knew the moment he realized she was free of her constraints. His expression morphed from startled to livid in a heartbeat. "What the hell? How'd you—?"

He swept his gaze around the room as if searching for the answer to his confusion. His attention lingered on the discarded leather belt. His face contorted in a snarl, then he grabbed her wrist. "How'd you get free?"

The biting grip on her wrist made her drop the keys, and with them, her heart fell to her toes. She tried to scoop them back up with her free hand, but Wayne got them first. He stared at the keys, scowling, his drug-muddled mind obviously needing time to sort through the implications of his discovery. "Where'd these come fr'm?"

Dave rubbed his bad shin and gave a snort. "Where do you think, genius?"

Lilly shot him a warning glance and said under her breath, "Don't antagonize him."

The look Dave sent her said he didn't agree with her approach, but he acquiesced.

After staring at the keys for another moment and wobbling on his feet, Wayne dropped on the bed and jerked Lilly's arm to force her to sit beside him. He dangled the keys in front of her. "Where's this car?"

The answer should have been obvious. But Wayne *was* drugged up, and, if she wasn't mistaken, she smelled beer on his breath. The idiot! He was obviously struggling to think clearly. "You're in no condition to drive, Wayne."

His face darkened. "Where's it?"

"Stay the hell away from my truck, you bastard," Dave growled.

Wayne turned an evil grin toward Dave. "*My* truck now. My ride outta here…"

When Dave tried to roll onto his knees again, Wayne placed a foot on Dave's chest and shoved him back down.

Lilly intervened before the situation escalated to blows again. "Wayne, listen to me. You've lost blood, and you just took a potent painkiller. You can't—"

"Two."

"What?" she asked.

He blinked at her as if trying to clear his vision. "Pain was bad, so I took two pills."

She had to work to swallow the groan that swelled in her throat. A double dose of a narcotic, possibly with alcohol. Well, that certainly explained his fogginess, slurring and unsteady gait. Didn't she see enough of patients abusing prescription drugs to be inured to the reckless behavior yet? Apparently not.

Keeping her voice calm, she touched his arm with her free hand. "All the more reason for you to go sleep it off. You've overdosed, and until the drug leaves your sys—"

He lurched to his feet, his face reddening. "Don't tell me wha' ta do!" Wayne started toward the hall with staggering steps, then stopped, swayed and clutched the door frame. Turning back to his hostages, he seemed to remember something, and stumbled back to grab Lilly's arm. "Can't leave you…l'se."

Wayne dragged her to the closet and shoved her inside, stopping long enough to use one of Helen's silk scarves to tie her hands together around the clothes bar.

"Wayne, don't!" she pleaded. "You can't drive in your condition and—"

He slammed the door in her face, and she heard him tell Dave in a sneering tone, "Later, H'ro."

Chapter 10

The closet was dark. Except for a tiny line of weak light at the bottom of the door, she was in complete blackness. Lilly gritted her teeth and concentrated on calming her racing heart and gathering her thoughts.

"Lilly?" Dave called to her. "Are you okay?"

"Yeah. But…he tied me up again. My hands, anyway. I—" She stopped when she heard the faint sound of the front door opening and closing, causing the house to shudder slightly. "Damn. He's going to try to take your truck."

Dave muttered an expletive that echoed how she felt. She kept quiet, straining her ears to listen, and before long she heard an engine rev, tires squeal…

And the terrifying thud of a crash, the shriek of crunching metal.

She gasped in horror at the same time Dave bit out another scorching curse.

The truck's horn sounded, a constant blare that told her something was holding it down. Or someone. She could easily picture Wayne crumpled against the steering wheel, injured, unconscious. Maybe even dead.

She held her breath. Waited. But the horn continued blasting, and Wayne didn't return to the house.

Finally Dave asked, "Do you think you can get free? How tightly did he tie you up? To what?"

"It feels pretty tight. My fingers are tingling. It's too dark in here to see anything. Do you remember where the light switch is for the closet?"

"Umm…" Dave said. "It's a pull string to a bulb on the ceiling."

"Okay. Hang on." She turned her face up slightly and shifted her body to the right, left, back, forward, until she felt the tickle of a cord against her cheek. Angling her head, she caught the string in her mouth. With a jerk of her head to pull the cord, she turned on the light. "That's better."

She focused on the knotted scarf and knew immediately she couldn't untie the restraint by herself. So now what? She shifted her focus to the steel clothes bar. No way could she break it, but could she pull it down? Sliding the scarf down the bar to the end and head-butting Helen's winter coat out of the way, Lilly examined how the bar was affixed to the wall. She grinned, finding the heavy rod wasn't anchored at all but rather rested on a small, curved shelflike support bracket.

Moving closer to the apparatus, she twisted her hands beneath the steel bar and pushed up, grunting with exertion. The bar, still laden with so many of Helen's clothes, was far heavier than she expected. But she only needed to budge it an inch or so up and over…

Freed from the support, the bar toppled to the floor, dragging her and all of Helen's clothes with it. Lilly yelped as she tumbled onto the pile of clothes, wire hangers poking her.

"Lilly?" Dave called again, his tone worried.

"I'm okay. The clothes bar fell and…" She grunted as she tried to right herself, struggling to free her bound wrists from the bar and the tangle of hangers and blouses. After a moment of kicking clothes out of the way, she managed to slide the scarf off the end of the steel bar. With a weary huff, she flopped back in the pile of clothes to catch her breath. *You really needed to get back to the gym. You're in terrible shape!*

"Lilly?"

"I'm free of the bar. Just…catching my breath." She closed her eyes, thinking about her next step. Outside the truck horn was still blaring. As a nurse, she knew Wayne would likely need medical attention. But first things first. Her wrists, and Dave's, were still tied.

She climbed over the fallen clothes and opened the closet door. Using her teeth, she pulled at the knot in the scarf, freeing her hands with surprising ease.

"All right then. Let's give this another go." As she rounded the bed to reach Dave, she dropped the scarf on the floor and crouched to pick at the knots in her bathrobe belt, which bound his hands.

"If we get out of this alive, I'll never—"

"Ah!" she said, cutting him off. "First, it's *when* we

get out of this alive. We have to believe we will survive this. We have to *make* it happen."

He slid his mouth into a crooked grin. "Fine. *When*."

She squinted at the belt, trying to figure out the best way to unknot the tight tangle. "Second, never say never. That has proven a surefire way make something happen for me."

"Oh? As in?"

She dug at the knot with her short fingernails but made little progress. "As in… I would *never* get a tattoo. Um, I would *never* use a public men's room. My husband would *never* cheat on me."

She bit her lip as she worked. She hadn't meant that last one to slip out.

He grunted, a sympathetic hum from his throat, but said nothing until he asked, "What's the tattoo of and where?"

"A butterfly and somewhere you'll never see."

He chuckled, and she realized belatedly what she'd said. She was about to make a snarky comment on her goof when he said, "The horn stopped."

Her breath snagged as she let that fact filter through the natural progression of assumptions. Wayne had revived. Moved off the horn. Would he return to the house? She had precious few seconds to get Dave free before—

"Forget my hands. Get my feet free!" His tone was urgent.

She suited his words to action, but he stopped her almost immediately. "No. Never mind. Get the gun!"

She jerked a startled look to him, remembering his earlier instructions. *Fire the gun. Use up the rounds.*

"Go!" His eyes echoed the imperative in his voice. "Hurry! Find the gun!"

Acid crept up her throat. "But what if he has it with him?"

Dave shook his head. "You'll have to wing it. Sweet-talk him. Trick him. But get it from him. This may be our only chance."

"Oh, good. No pressure." She shoved to her feet, her knees shaking. Pressing a hand to her swirling stomach, she edged toward the door.

"You can do it, Lil. I have faith in you."

His encouragement surprised her. She cast a backward glance to him, and the look in his eyes matched his words. Warmth flowed through her, and she smiled her thanks. Taking a deep breath, she crept into the hall, careful to avoid the squeaky loose board that had given Wayne away earlier. Before she reached the living room, she plastered herself against the wall and peeked around the corner to look for Wayne. She heard him on the front porch, grumbling to himself, his gait still unsteady, but it was getting too dark outside for her to see what he was doing.

Lilly swept her gaze around the living room, taking a mental inventory of where things were that she might need, searching for the revolver. Wayne had left the lamp by the sofa on, and its yellow glow illuminated the room. The scissors she'd been using to cut tape and plastic wrapping while she packed boxes were on the end table. Wayne had left plenty of dirty dishes scattered on the coffee table and floor. Two empty bottles of the craft beer she'd bought earlier that week were lying on their sides by the couch. She gritted her teeth, muffling a groan. *Geez!* Two pain pills *and* alcohol? Was the guy trying to kill himself? No wonder he'd crashed the truck.

Before Wayne could get inside, she darted into the kitchen. The lights were off in that room, and the house was getting darker as night fell outside, but she did a quick inventory of what she could see. More dirty dishes, the peanut butter with the lid off…but no gun.

Damn! Did that mean he had the weapon with him? Made sense. Even dangerously drugged and sedated, he'd obviously had the wherewithal to keep the weapon at hand.

She heard the squeak of hinges as the front door opened, and she peered around the kitchen wall just as Wayne stumbled inside. His nose was red, swollen and dripping blood. He had a large red mark on his forehead that Lilly figured would be a nasty black-and-blue bruise in the morning.

He sniffed, then used the back of his hand to wipe the blood leaking from his bashed nose. The red smears on his arm and shirt indicated he'd been doing a good bit of blotting in the last couple of minutes. With lurching steps, he moved toward the couch, swaying into a small occasional table and knocking it over in the process. He blinked at the tumbled table as if confused why it had toppled, then continued to the couch. He dropped onto the cushions, grimaced, then reached behind him and…pulled the gun from somewhere near the small of his back.

Bingo! She held her breath, as he set the weapon on the coffee table next to his dirty dishes and settled back on the couch, closing his eyes.

Lilly said a quick prayer that he didn't have a reason to come into the kitchen before he fell asleep. If she was quiet, maybe she could wait him out. When he fell asleep—which should only be a matter of moments considering how much sedation he had in his blood—she could sneak out to the coffee table and get the gun. She'd take it outside and fire it until the magazine was empty then throw the cursed thing as far into the woods as she could.

She was watching Wayne, her heart thumping a wild rhythm as she mentally made her plan, when something bumped her leg.

A small gasp of surprise escaped before she could stifle it. Clapping a hand to her mouth, she glanced at the floor to find Maddie winding around her legs and rubbing on her shin.

"Me-ow!"

She cringed at the volume of the cat's request for dinner because she had no doubt that was what Maddie wanted. Maddie was a creature of habit and it was past dinnertime for her cat. Maddie would continue to complain in full voice until she had something to eat.

Lilly cast a glance back in the living room. If Wayne had heard the cat, he'd ignored the sound. But she couldn't count on that lasting. She had to risk a little noise in order to satisfy Maddie and quiet her meowing. As quickly as she could, she tiptoed across the kitchen, took a bowl from the cabinet, popped open a can of cat food and dumped it unceremoniously in the bowl. Maddie got a whiff of salmon pâté and voiced her approval. As soon as Lilly set the bowl on the floor, Maddie tucked in, and Lilly exhaled her relief.

Now…the gun.

Leaning to peer around the wall again, she studied Wayne for a moment. He didn't move. At all. Alarm bells rang for the medical professional in her. She narrowed her eyes and tried to watch his chest. Was he breathing? Could she let him drift to sleep knowing he'd overmedicated? Two pills weren't enough to kill him, but…

She had a duty to check on him.

But first, get the gun! she could hear Dave saying in her mind.

She tiptoed out, stepping over the detritus of Wayne's past few hours and her half-completed sorting, and reached for the gun on the coffee table. Before her hand closed around the grip, Wayne gave a loud snort and shifted on the couch.

And his eyelids fluttered open.

Chapter 11

Lilly froze, her heart thundering.

He narrowed his eyes, glancing from her to the gun. "What the—?"

She snatched up the weapon and aimed it at him. "Don't mo—"

But before she could finish the warning, Wayne lunged. Faster than she had any idea a sedated man could move. He grabbed the gun's muzzle as they crashed backward onto the floor.

"Give me that, bitch!" he growled as he yanked the weapon from her hands.

She scrabbled to retrieve it, but he held it out of her reach.

New plan. Get away from *him*. With a firm shove to push him off her, she rolled away and clambered to her feet. She didn't want to get in a wrestling match for the gun. He outweighed her and, even drugged, he was stronger.

Her gut tightened, knowing she'd failed the most basic of tasks in the mission to free them. She eased away from Wayne as he rose to his feet, still swaying drunkenly and glaring at her.

Maybe she could salvage the moment…

"You're hurt." She held both hands out in a placating manner. "I want to help."

"Help? How?" Wayne sat down heavily on the couch, the gun still clutched in his hand. He leaned his head back with a groan and dabbed at his nose, watching her from hooded eyes.

"You n-need an ice p-pack for your nose. I think it's broken." She balled her trembling hands at her sides as she assessed her options. She was untethered, after all.

Did she make a run for it? No. She couldn't outrun a bullet. And she wouldn't leave Dave behind to contend with an irate, armed and unpredictable killer.

So…what then? *Wing it*, Dave had said. *Sweet-talk him. Trick him.*

"I'll, uh—" she sidled away "—just get a rag and ice, um, from the kitchen." She kicked a beer bottle accidentally as she backed away and it clattered as it struck the leg of the coffee table.

As if waking from a stupor, Wayne sat straighter and aimed a finger at her. "Hold it!"

Her breath stuttered from her. "Wayne, you need ice and—"

"How'd you g't…out h're?" He blinked, swiped his hand under his dripping nose again, then winced. Furrowing his brow, he stared at the back of his hand as if startled to see the blood there.

"You're bleeding and need ice on your nose." Stating the obvious was better than answering his question. She might convince him to let her help him, but could she distract him enough to get the gun from him?

She moved again, slowly, and pointed to the kitchen. "I'm just gonna get that ice pack now."

When he said nothing, she eased into the next room and blew out a long breath. Maddie sat in the middle of the kitchen floor, licking her lips and grooming herself.

She gave the cat a disgusted look and muttered, "Lassie would have gone for help and disarmed the bad guy."

Grabbing a towel from a drawer, she began filling it with ice. When she closed the freezer door, Wayne stood in the kitchen, just a few feet from her, gun aimed at her chest. Lilly gasped and dropped a few of the ice cubes.

"Where'd th'cat co' from?" he asked, jerking his head toward Maddie.

"She's been here the whole time, mostly hiding under the bed." She swallowed hard, a new worry growing in her. How would Wayne treat Maddie? Someone with a complete disregard for human life, as he'd demonstrated when he shot the bank guard, could easily be as cruel to an animal.

But he simply grunted a "huh" and returned his glare to her.

She held out the towel bundle. "For your nose."

Instead of taking the ice pack, he seized her wrist. "Y're not s'posed to be out 'ere."

His grip was surprisingly strong, and she winced as his fingers dug into her flesh. "I was just—"

"Move it." He nudged her with the muzzle of the gun, then started toward the door to the hall, dragging her with him.

"Wayne, wait." She tried to slow him down, digging in her heels and tugging against his shackling fingers. "You don't have to do this. If you'd let us go, we promise to—"

"Shut it!" He gave her arm a hard yank. "You're giv'n me a headache."

Headache—right. She changed her tactic as she stumbled behind him down the hall. "You need a doctor. You hit your head when the truck crashed, and your nose is probably broken." She still clenched the ice pack in the hand he'd seized. "Let me help you—"

The bedroom door stood ajar, and he kicked it open wider, hauling her inside.

Her gaze flew to Dave, whose eyes were bright with alarm. His posture was rigid and alert, and he was vibrating with tension.

Wayne shoved her down on the bed and walked over to the dresser, where he'd left the roll of tape.

Leaving the ice pack on the mattress, she stood and stepped forward, her hands spread. "Wayne, please, think about what you're doing. This can only end badly. But if—"

He swung around, raised the gun and fired at the wall behind her.

Lilly yelped, and Dave bit out a curse.

"Get on the bed. Hands behind you," Wayne growled.

Her heart sank. One step forward only to take three

steps back. Body trembling with adrenaline and fear, she sat back down on the edge of the mattress and squeezed the bedspread with her fingers.

Leaving the revolver on the dresser, Wayne staggered over and dropped onto the bed beside her, his expression angry. "Thought I c'd trust you."

"You can," she pleaded. "If you'd—"

"No." He jerked her arms behind her back and began wrapping her wrists in tape. "You betrayed me."

"How? I've tried to *help* you, take care of your injuries. I should check your wound again. Change the bandage…"

He was still taping…and taping. Layer after layer beyond what was needed to bind her securely. When the roll was empty, her threw the cardboard center across the room with a grunt. "There. Let's see you get outta that!"

"Wayne, your injuries need attention. I can help you, if you'd let me. I want to help," she insisted, unwilling to accept defeat. She could still get through to him, reach some bit of humanity in him. Surely…

He took her upper arm and dragged her to the head of the bed, where he found the discarded belt. He looped it around her throat like a noose before weaving the ends through the headboard again and buckling it.

"Wayne," she pleaded, letting the tears she'd held at bay fill her eyes. "Please."

He hesitated, his gaze narrowing on her when the first of her tears spilled on her cheek. But almost as quickly, his expression hardened, and he turned his back on her. Stumbling back to the dresser, he collected the gun, scooped the ice pack off the bed and wobbled to the door.

"Wayne!" she called, knowing what he likely had in

mind when he returned to the front room. "You can't drink beer with your pills."

He paused in the doorway but didn't turn.

"If you drink any more or take any more pills now, you could put yourself in a coma. You've already over-dosed."

Shifting the ice pack to his gun hand, he grabbed the doorknob and slammed the door shut.

"That bastard," Dave grumbled. In a softer tone, he asked, "Are you hurt?"

"No. Just...*so* frustrated." Lilly exhaled in disappointment. Her body sagged in defeat, only to have the belt around her throat tug tighter. Her heart scampered at the implications of her predicament. Any twisting or shifting to try to get free of her new restraints could draw the belt tighter. She could breathe for now, but if the leather strap cinched much tighter, she could strangle. "Can you see what he did with his belt this time?"

"Hell, now what'd he do?" She heard a grunt, and the bed wiggled some as his feet kicked the side. He sat up and peered at her over the edge of the mattress. His face hardened, but his eyes were full of sympathy for her. "Damn it, Lilly. I'm sorry. Can you breathe?"

"As long as I don't move." She sighed, knowing that it would be a long night, that any time she nodded off and let her head droop, she'd pull the belt noose tighter.

Dave's lips firmed, and he gave a nod as if he'd made a decision. "Hang on."

She gave a short wry laugh. "Not much else I can do but hang out here."

The bed jiggled some more, and Dave growled under his breath. "C'mon, c'mon! Ahh!"

"Dave? What—?"

"Almost…there…" The words sounded as if they'd been pushed through clenched teeth.

Lilly used her feet to scoot an inch or two higher on the bed, carefully repositioning. Only then did it dawn on her that Wayne hadn't bound her feet. Not that it mattered. She wasn't going anywhere with her hands taped to hell and back and the belt ready to hang her if she slumped. She closed her eyes and tried not to let defeatist thoughts fill her mind. As bleak as their situation was, she had to keep believing that she and Dave could find a way out, a way to survive.

Doubt demons nipped at her, trying to drag her down. She'd let negativity win after her divorce, and she'd sunk into an abyss that had taken months to drag herself free from. In hindsight, she could see that a lot of her doubts were rooted in her father's departure when she was young. If Daddy couldn't love her enough to stay, why should she expect her husband to love her any better?

A knot of emotion gripped her throat, and she forced herself to relax, to redirect her thoughts, to dig deep for an optimism that would help her through this mess.

"Yes!" Dave said, and the relief in his tone pulled her from her morose musing.

"What happened?"

Rather than an answer, she heard more grunting and shuffling. And then Dave's head rose above the mattress, and he struggled awkwardly to his feet.

"You got your feet loose!"

He flashed a cocky grin that made her pulse scamper. "I did."

"But…how?"

"Persistence. And the metal edge of the mattress frame." Dave rolled his shoulders and gave each of his legs a shake. "And pain. Damn, it hurts to pull leg hair." He eyed his discarded socks and boots and blew out a puff of air. "I guess you don't want the boots on the bedspread?"

"Um…" She was still processing his freedom and the possible ramifications. "Huh?"

He turned and sat on the bed next to her and scooted close to her. "No dirty boots on the bed. Helen hated that."

She blinked at him as he settled on the mattress, anxiety knotting her gut. "You're not going to try to confront Wayne again, are you?"

Even as she asked, she wasn't sure if she was hoping his answer was *yes* or *no*. The idea of Dave challenging Wayne in any capacity sent cold frissons of fear trickling through her.

He propped himself against the headboard and sighed. "I'd like nothing more than to go mano a mano with him, but as long as my hands are tied, so are my options. I took a shot earlier when he was unarmed, and you saw how badly that went. So…" He huffed. "You know the expression 'Discretion is the better part of valor,' right?"

She angled her gaze toward him. "I do." She paused, flashing him a teasing smile. "A little surprised that you do, though."

He scoffed his affront. "Oh, brutal, Lil! You think because I herd cattle for a living that I'm uneducated?"

She blinked. Despite the humor in his tone, she heard defensiveness, as well. "I didn't say that. And I was teasing. Touchy touchy." Then, because she needed to distract herself from the echoing memory of Wayne firing his gun and the pain of the tape biting her wrists, she added under her breath, "Betcha don't know where the saying came from."

Dave angled a narrow-eyed, speculative glance at her. After a moment he said, "Shakespeare?"

"You don't sound too sure."

"Because I'm not. Totally guessing here."

She nudged him with her shoulder, grateful that he'd picked up her attempt at distraction. Her nerves were raw, and anything she could do to keep herself from dwelling on her failed attempt to disarm Wayne was welcome. "Then it was a good guess. It *is* from Shakespeare."

He chuckled, the sound a sexy low rumble from his chest. "Damn, I'm good. My mother would've been so proud, me getting a Shakespeare question right."

She snorted. "Why is that?"

"She used to teach AP English lit and creative writing at my high school."

"Used to? She's retired?" Lilly asked, gladly latching on to the new topic of conversation and intrigued by the peek into Dave's family history.

"Yes, years ago. She passed away last year. Alzheimer's." Then, as if reading her mind he explained, "I was a surprise, late-in-life baby. She was seventy when she died."

"Oh." She bit her bottom lip and sighed. She knew a thing or two about the struggle of taking care of an ill parent. "Did Helen tell you about our mom? That she was bipolar?"

Why had she said that? She usually kept that aspect of her childhood to herself.

"She told me your mom had bouts of depression,"

he said, his tone gentle. "I figured it was because your dad left, because of your financial struggles."

"That played into it, too. But she was ill. I didn't know that was the reason for her mood and behavior swings until I was older and learning about such things in college. We didn't talk about it. It just…was our life."

Without thinking, she slumped a bit and the belt tightened. When she coughed and turned her head, trying to loosen the strap around her neck, Dave sent her a worried look.

"Here." He adjusted his position, snuggling close to her and pushing his shoulder up right next to her cheek. "There. Lean on me to sleep. I'll help you stay upright and that should keep the belt from choking you."

"That's so… Thank you, Dave." She felt a tender ache tug below her ribs. Something more than gratitude. Affection? Could she really have done a complete about-face in her feelings for Dave in less than twenty-four hours? Helen had been right about his charm. And she'd seen his courage, his caring.

She closed her eyes and felt the weight of the day, the stress and fear, sitting heavily on her. She needed sleep but her mind wouldn't quiet. Feeling Dave beside her, his body propping hers, gave her a measure of peace and security, though. At least she wasn't going through this horror alone. As selfish as it was of her to be glad he was there with her…there it was. Misery loved company.

She thought about Helen, how her sister had been alone when she was killed. She hated to imagine her sister's final moments, her pain, her terror. A familiar acid bite gnawed her gut. She'd probably never have true peace in regard to her sister's murder. And Dave had known the man who'd killed her. How much harder must it be for him to grapple with?

"Tell me about the man who killed Helen," she said quietly. "The police said he claimed it was an accident."

"Yeah. That's what he said." Dave sighed, making the shoulder she rested her cheek against lift and fall. "Roy isn't a bad person. Not really. Just someone who made a lot of terrible, tragic mistakes."

"Then you believe him? That it was an accident?"

"I do. That doesn't make losing her hurt any less. And I can't say I'll ever find the grace to forgive him. I know that sounds horrible, but it's all still too recent, too raw, to go there yet. Maybe one day…"

Bitterness grew in her. "I'm not sure how I can ever let him off the hook. He took my sister."

"I get that. But I believe forgiveness isn't about letting the other person off the hook. Roy will pay the consequences of his actions, serve his time. Forgiveness isn't about forgetting, either. It's about letting go of the anger that is living in you. You only hurt yourself by holding on to anger."

Lilly blinked, stunned by Dave's insight, then chastened herself. Why couldn't she have that kind of practical wisdom?

"I…guess so."

"Forgiving is about giving yourself a chance to heal," he said, his tone as much a balm as his words. "It's not for them. It's something you have to do, for yourself."

Tears filled her eyes again, and she gritted her teeth and worked to suppress the urge to cry. With her hands bound, she didn't need to get weepy and make her nose run.

Helen had told her she'd had deep, meaningful conversations with Dave through the years. He was a thinker, always analyzing and trying to make sense of the world. And he was spiritual, her sister had said, raised going to church. What he said made sense to her, and she let the sentiment settle inside her.

"For myself," she muttered softly, then added, "I have a lot of people I need to forgive."

"Am I one of them?"

"I—" She angled her gaze, trying to see his face, but she couldn't. "Not anymore. I know I came at you with both barrels earlier. And I'm not saying I think you were totally innocent of all the stuff Helen complained about, but now that I know you better…"

"Hmm. There's always another side, huh?" He sounded thoughtful, and her curiosity was piqued.

"Do you have someone or something in mind?"

"Lots. Besides what Roy did to Helen, I'm mainly thinking about Wayne. Your idea to get to know him makes sense. To make this situation more personal for him. Why's he doing all this? Who does he care about? Does he have family, a girlfriend or wife, kids? If we knew him better, we might have better luck negotiating with—" Dave yawned, then continued, "Excuse me. I still keep rancher hours, which means I've been up since before the sun."

"We should both sleep. I don't see any way we're getting free tonight, and we need to be sharp tomorrow. Who knows what could happen once Wayne's had time to think about the situation."

"Right." He rested his cheek on the top of her head, his breath stirring her hair and warming her scalp. The position of her body snuggled against his, and vice versa, made the shared conversation in the dark bedroom feel even more intimate.

Dave had both provided her comfort and stirred up restless notions that churned in her mind. Forgiveness, personal healing…getting to know Wayne and how he ticked.

What motivated their captor? How could they use what they knew to save themselves?

Even when she and Dave had fought back, Wayne hadn't killed them. Yet. She ruminated on that fact. Why had he not killed them?

Dave had been smart, offering his services to fix up Wayne's rattletrap getaway vehicle. And she'd been needed for her medical services. Was it as simple as that? Was Wayne keeping them alive as long as they were potentially useful to him? Or was there still a seed of humanity, an inkling of conscience, that shied from the idea of cold-blooded murder?

He'd killed the bank guard, yes. But it was possible, in his twisted logic, that he saw that kill as necessary to execute the bank heist. So what would happen if and when he felt stronger and was ready to make his run for the Mexican border? Would they be unneeded at that point?

They couldn't become expendable. When Wayne viewed them as a liability, she feared he'd find it too easy to be rid of them. For good.

Chapter 12

A muscle cramp woke Lilly the next morning, and when she automatically tried to reach for the seizing muscle, the belt noose jerked against her neck. She muttered a curse word and gritted her teeth against the pain.

Either her movement or her cussing, maybe both, woke Dave. "Lilly? What happened?"

His voice was craggy with sleep, but just his presence beside her, knowing he'd propped her up through the night, filled her with a gratitude and reassurance that took the edge off her physical discomfort. She'd faced so many difficulties in her life without anyone to support her, but she wasn't going through this ordeal alone. "Muscle cramp, but then the belt tightened on my throat, and— Not a good way to wake up."

His drowsy gaze softened with sympathy, and the

soft stir of butterfly wings joined the gnawing ache of hunger in her belly. As much as she hated the fact that Dave was in this position, had even been injured, she couldn't deny the selfish consolation she took in having him with her.

"Think I can do anything to help?" He shifted on the bed to face her more directly. "I'll be fumbling blindly, but I can probably loosen the belt some."

"If you could—"

The bedroom door opened, and Dave stiffened and sat straighter, clearly on full alert.

From the hall, Wayne glared at them with bloodshot eyes. He held the gun in one hand and leaned heavily against the door frame. His nose was swollen, slightly crooked and horribly discolored. His rumpled clothes, creased brow and dark scowl all said he felt miserable, and his churlish mood echoed that assessment. "Get up." He motioned the gun in a small circle. "You're gonna help me."

He glanced at Dave, frowned, but didn't say anything about the fact that Dave was not on the floor where Wayne had left him. Still, Wayne's dour expression didn't bode well for how the day might go.

Lilly raised her chin and asked, "Help with what?"

Their captor moved into the bedroom, his gait slow and dragging, but he was no longer swaying. "My side is throbbing, my head feels like crap and I'm hungry." He gingerly touched the bridge of his nose with his free hand, then added, "And your cat has been yowling at me from under the dining table for the last couple hours."

Lilly raised her eyebrows, her pulse quickening when

she thought of Maddie, vulnerable to Wayne's ill temper. "You didn't hurt her, did you?"

Wayne met her eyes with a look that said he was offended by the suggestion. "No. But you need to do something to shut her up. She's driving me crazy."

"She wants breakfast."

"Yeah, well, so do I," he groused. "So you can fix *both* of us something to eat while you're at it." He moved closer, raising his shirt and pointing to his bullet wound. "But first you're going to do something for this. It feels worse today than yesterday."

"Serves you right," Dave grumbled under his breath.

Lilly sent her co-captive a quelling look and quietly shushed him.

Even without a close examination, she could tell Wayne's wound was inflamed. The skin around the bandage was bright pink and looked swollen. "I'll do what I can. What you really need is an antibiotic and the kind of thorough cleaning and disinfecting you can only get at a doctor's office."

"Where, by law, he'd have to report the gunshot wound and bring in the cops? Nah, that ain't happening," he said, stepping up beside the bed and staring down at her. "You'll have to do what you can."

After stuffing the gun in the waistline of his jeans, he reached for the belt that cinched her throat. Wayne stared at the leather strap, his brow beetled in confusion. "How'd this get around your neck like that?"

"You don't remember?" Dave asked.

"Would I have asked if I could remember?" Wayne snapped, curling his lip.

"You put it on me like this. But you were pretty

doped up last night on beer and pain pills. It's no wonder you don't remember." Her tone scolded him. "You're
lucky to have woken up this morning."

Wayne glowered at her. "I don't feel lucky. I feel like
hell." Dividing a look between them, he asked, "Which
one of you jerks broke my nose?"

Dave chuckled darkly. "You did that to yourself,
man." He gritted his teeth and added, "When you
crashed my truck."

Wayne arched an eyebrow, staring back at Dave with
an expression that said their captor was playing catch-up,
mentally trying to recall the past evening. And coming
up blank. "Whatever."

"Wayne," Lilly said, "*please* cut my hands loose. I
have to pee in the worst way. Have a heart, and let me
use the bathroom before we do anything else."

With a growl rumbling from his chest, Wayne unfastened the belt and used his pocketknife to saw through
the tape at her wrists. "Don't be long," he said, tipping
his head toward the bathroom.

"Thank you," she gushed, earnest in her enthusiasm.
Rubbing her sore wrists and rolling her stiff shoulders,
Lilly scrambled off the bed and hurried to use the fa-
cilities.

"And no tricks!" Wayne added. "Remember I still
have your boyfriend out here."

Through the closed door, she heard Dave counter,
"She's not my girlfriend."

"What. Ever."

Hearing Dave deny any relationship between them
caused a strange jab to her gut. He spoke the truth,
but for him to purposely distance himself from her...

Well, it hurt. Which was ludicrous. But there it was. She flashed mentally to Alan's parting words when he'd walked out of their apartment, their marriage for the last time. The empty maw of wondering and unanswered questions surrounding her father's disappearance when she was nine years old. Helen's death. So many people she'd loved...gone.

Huffing her frustration with herself—wrong time for a pity party—Lilly finished her business, washed her hands and face and finger-combed her hair. Feeling markedly better even with the few rudimentary ablutions, she returned to find Dave and Wayne in a glaring match.

"How'd you get your feet loose?" Wayne asked.

"Tooth fairy." Dave slid his feet to the floor and rose from the bed with a grunt.

Wayne raised the revolver and aimed it at Dave. "Where do you think you're going?"

Dave rolled his head from side to side, stretching his neck muscles. "Bathroom."

The testosterone-fueled staring match intensified for a few tense seconds before Wayne hitched his head. "Hurry up."

Dave arched one eyebrow. "Free my hands so I can go?"

"Not a chance."

"Then how am I supposed to—?" Dave clamped his mouth shut without finishing the sentence and glowered at Wayne.

Wayne smirked. "Get the *tooth fairy* to help you."

As he moved toward the bathroom door, his shoulders back and squared, Dave sent Lilly an embarrassed look. She moved toward him, prompting Wayne to wag the gun as he barked, "Hey! Get away from him."

"No funny business. I promise," she said, edging in front of Dave and raising her shaking hands to the button on his fly. Lilly held Dave's gaze as she unfastened his jeans for him.

A complex brew of emotions swirled in his dark brown eyes. Everything from gratitude and humility to the unmistakable spark of sexual awareness. Under other circumstances, her gesture could have been the prelude to any number of erotic acts, and the heat that zinged between them as she lowered his zipper left no question that they were both mindful of the implied sensuality. He continued staring in her eyes, the muscle in his jaw twitching for several seconds after she'd dropped her hands to her sides.

"Not your girlfriend, huh?" Wayne said with a snide scoff. "Right."

Dave shot a lethal glare at Wayne and disappeared into the bathroom for several minutes.

As she and Wayne were waiting for Dave to finish his business, Maddie appeared at the bedroom door and peeked in with a squeaking meow.

"Coming, Maddie girl." Lilly started toward the door, but Wayne raised the gun and stepped into her path.

"Nope."

His movement sent Maddie scuttling quickly back down the hall.

She frowned at him. "Really? I can't even feed my cat without you pointing that thing at me?"

"That's right. I'd be stupid to let either one of you

out of my sight while you're untied. Are you saying you think I'm stupid?"

Lilly fought for patience and composure. *Slow breath in...and exhale.* "No."

She had practiced showing a calm countenance when her nerves were shredded while dealing with panicked or unreasonable patients in the ER. Drug addicts faking symptoms to score a hit. New mothers who were sure their crying babies must be dying. Grown men who become combative when faced with the necessity of a needle stick.

"We wait for Hero." He used that excuse to bang on the bathroom door. "Hurry up in there."

"His name is Dave."

The doorknob rattled, and Lilly stepped over to help Dave open the door. She glanced down, and he gave her the same awkward grimace as she rezipped and buttoned his fly.

"Thanks," he said quietly.

"All right, all right. Break it up." Wayne wedged himself between them and stuck the gun under Dave's chin. "You, sit on the bed where I can see you. You move, you lose a toe." He waggled the gun to let Dave know how the toe extraction would be performed. Facing Lilly, Wayne nodded to the bathroom. "You, start doctoring."

When she glanced back at Dave, his hard stare unnerved her. He shifted his eyes to the gun, then back to her face with a lift of his brow. *Get the gun.*

Lilly's stomach somersaulted. She'd never fired a gun. Even holding the weapon yesterday had made her sweat. And what if, like yesterday, Wayne snatched the revolver back and, furious with her for her bold move, shot her, or Dave or Maddie or…

Wayne closed the lid on the commode and raised his shirt. "Let's go, Lilly."

She nodded to the gun. "Can you put that down while I work?"

He rolled his eyes at her. "No."

Shoulders drooping, she carefully peeled back the bandage from his gunshot wound and set to work. The gash was definitely showing early signs of infection, so she recleaned the wound, coated it with antibacterial cream and replaced the bandage. As she finished, she heard Dave's low murmur, and glanced into the bedroom to find that Maddie had returned and was on the bed, begging attention from Dave.

"Sorry, cat. No hands." He tried to give Maddie's fuzzy cheek a rub with his elbow, and she responded with her trademark purr.

"What about this?" Wayne asked, drawing her attention back to him as he pointed to his broken nose.

"The two *i*'s. Ice and ibuprofen to fight the swelling."

"What about resetting it?" he asked.

She pulled a face. "I don't dare try. I'm not trained for that, and anything that close to your brain is risky. But if you see a doctor in the next couple weeks, he or she can set it."

Wayne's expression clearly said he didn't like her answer but he didn't argue. "So…you got any ibuprofen?"

"Your tramadol will help, too." She cringed internally at recommending he add another of the narcotic painkiller when he'd just gotten the overdose out of his system. But if he was sleepy and slower to react…

Wayne seemed to be considering. "Naw. Not yet. I need you loose to fix breakfast. I'll take a pill once the both of you are secured again."

So...he planned to let her remain unrestrained while she cooked for him. Her heart raced as she considered the ramifications. With a poise that belied her fluttering pulse, she opened the medicine cabinet on the wall over his head and took down the bottle there. Lilly shook one out for Wayne, swallowed one herself for her sore muscles and offered one to Dave.

When he nodded, she took the pill out to Dave with Wayne shadowing her. She dropped the pill on Dave's tongue, and he swallowed it dry, holding her gaze the whole time. His impatient, raised-eyebrow look silently asked why she wasn't trying to get the weapon from Wayne. Unable to verbally explain her concerns about the plan, she flashed an apologetic frown, hating the disappointment and frustration in Dave's eyes.

"Now," Wayne said, "feed us."

She faced her captor, tilting her head. "What do you want?"

"Anything. But I'm sick of peanut butter. I saw eggs in there, and other good options in the cabinets. Surprise me." He waved the gun toward the door. "You, too, cowboy. Let's go."

She considered a symbolic protest of his sexist demand. But since she and Dave needed a good meal, as well, and everyone's temperament would be better with a full stomach, Lilly headed to the kitchen. She dug through the refrigerator and found eggs, the fresh vegetables she'd intended for a salad and bread. Helen likely had other potential delicacies stashed in her pantry, but Lilly had never been the gourmand her sister had.

One large garden omelet, which she divided three ways, a pot of coffee and whole grain toast later—plus kitty kibble and canned salmon mush for Maddie—they settled in the living room and tucked in. Wayne claimed the recliner facing the sofa, and Lilly sat on the couch next to Dave. She forked bites to her fellow hostage, an indignity Dave obviously endured only because he was famished. But she could tell he held the humiliation against Wayne, who still refused to untie Dave's hands.

When he finished his breakfast, Wayne took the bottle of tramadol from the table beside the recliner and shook out a tablet.

"When did you last take one of those?" Lilly asked, narrowing a concerned look on him.

"Why do you care?" Wayne popped the pill in his mouth, washed it down with coffee, then swiped his upper lip with his sleeve.

"Because you took too much last night and weren't in your right mind."

"Case in point, my wrecked truck," Dave grumbled.

"Bite me," Wayne snarled back.

Lilly divided a peevish look between the sniping men. "Everybody chill."

Dave slumped to a more comfortable angle on the couch, leaning his head back on the cushions with a sigh.

Setting aside the pill bottle, Wayne kicked back in the recliner and put the revolver on his lap. He said nothing for a long time, only stared at her and Dave for a few minutes before he flicked on the television, scrolled through the channels and turned it off again. "Will the chemo make me sick?" he said without preamble. "Will I lose my hair?"

Lilly perked up, seeing an opportunity to make the vital personal connection with Wayne she'd been seeking. "It depends. Some chemo meds cause nausea, but treatments are getting better. And there are things the doctors can do to minimize side effects. Did the treatments make you sick last time?"

He pursed his lips and shook his head. "Didn't do chemo before. Just surgery to take out the tumor. Couldn't afford chemo then." He flashed a sly grin. "But now I can."

Dave grunted. "You really think you can cover the cost of cancer treatments with the amount you stole from a small-town bank?"

Wayne tapped his thumb on the arm of the recliner as he regarded Dave with disgust. "Not *one* small-town bank haul. But I'll add my take from the other day to the haul from my last three bank heists and should be in pretty good shape."

Lilly jerked her chin up. "You robbed three other banks?"

"In Indiana, New Mexico and Missouri. Not in that order, but…" Wayne chuckled at her startled look. "You didn't think this was my first rodeo, did you? Hell, I've been robbing banks for years with my dad. Convenience stores before that. Since I was a kid. He taught me real good. Both what to do and, by his mistakes, what not to do."

"Your father? Wow. Model parent," Dave said flatly.

Lilly moved her hand to Dave's knee, silently imploring him not to antagonize Wayne.

"Where's your dad now? Why isn't he with you?" she asked.

"One of those mistakes he made got him killed. Shot by a cop." Wayne fingered his watch, and Lilly wonder if he even realized he was doing so.

"I'm sorry," she said, meaning it.

"Are you?" Wayne tipped his head and narrowed his eyes on her.

"Sorry you lost your father? Yeah. I'm not heartless. The manner of his death…" She twisted her mouth.

"He asked for it," Wayne finished for her.

"I didn't say that."

He shrugged, then winced and put his hand over the freshly bandaged bullet wound under his arm. "I am saying it. He got greedy. I told him we should stick to small banks, and he wouldn't listen."

"Tell us about the watch," Dave said, surprising both her and, judging from his expression, Wayne, too. Especially since Dave's tone sounded genuine and encouraging, not hostile.

Wayne didn't respond for a moment. His gaze dropped to the timepiece, and his gaze lost focus, as if he were deep in thought. Finally he said, "It belonged to my grandfather first. He picked it up in France while on leave during the Second World War. He called it his 'lucky watch,' because when he was wearing it in the trenches one day, the strap broke. He bent over to pick it up, and a sniper's bullet whizzed right over his head. If he hadn't bent over for the watch, he'd have caught it center mass."

"Wow," Lilly said. "That is lucky."

"My dad got it when Gramps died, and he gave it to me on my birthday when I turned twenty-one. It's the only thing I have from my gramps." The way he looked at the watch and rubbed the face with his finger showed the sentimental value the watch held for him.

"Has it been lucky for you?" Lilly asked.

"Well, let's put it this way," Wayne said, still stroking the face of the watch with his thumb. "The first job we did after Dad gave me the watch was the one that got him killed. I was wearing it, not him."

Lilly and Dave exchanged a look, and she winced as she faced Wayne again. "Oh."

"And since I've had it, I've gotten cancer, twice, and this last job scored me this—" he pointed to the bullet wound on his side and sent Dave a scurrilous look "—and this." He aimed a finger at his busted nose. "Lucky?" He made a face to reflect his skepticism. "But I don't really believe in superstition much. I only keep it with me because it was my gramps', and he was the one person ever really cared anything about me."

Lilly let the comment about who had or hadn't cared about Wayne slide. That was a can of worms that could go sideways quickly.

"You could say it was lucky for protecting you the day your dad was killed," Lilly offered, trying to lighten the mood.

"And the bullet I put in you could have been six inches to the right and hit your heart. It was lucky I was just trying to stop you, not kill you." Dave gave Wayne a smug grin. "'Cause I usually hit what I'm aiming for."

Wayne returned a narrowed glare.

"It's always a matter of perspective." Lilly infused her tone with as much cheer as she could. "Happiness in life is more about a good attitude than what happens to you."

"Really?" Wayne lowered his brow and scoffed. "Is that what you told yourself when your sister was murdered?"

His gibe hit its mark, stealing the air from her lungs and tightening her throat with a fist of grief.

Dave tensed and sat up, growling, "You prick."

Wayne snatched the gun from his lap and fired a shot into the sofa, inches from Dave's shoulder.

Lilly screamed. Maddie raced down the hall to hide. Dave's jaw tightened.

"I'm getting tired of your mouth, Hero. Consider that your last warning." Wayne angled the gun and flashed a gloating grin. "'Cause I generally hit where I'm aiming, too." He cast a quick glance around the room, his attention stopping on a framed picture of Helen and Dave hanging on the wall over the TV. He aimed the gun again and fired, hitting the photograph where Dave's face smiled. "See?"

Lilly lifted a shaking hand to her mouth. She swallowed hard, struggling to keep her breakfast down.

Beside her, Dave sat motionless, his jaw set and rigid with a dark glare pinned on Wayne.

"So I'm guessing that's your sister?"

Lilly glanced to Wayne when he spoke and found him studying the picture he'd just shot. "Yes." The word was no more than a rasp.

"And she was Hero's girlfriend?"

When neither of them answered, Wayne glanced at

Lilly, and she gave a small bob of her head. He continued staring at Lilly, then back at the picture for a moment. "Yeah, she was pretty enough. I'd have done her. But you're hotter."

Lilly blinked, stunned by the crass comment. "What?"

"You heard me. You're hotter than your sister was. Hero shoulda been doing you instead."

Dave shifted forward, and she saw Wayne's remarks for the provocation he'd likely intended. She put her hand on Dave's thigh and squeezed. "Don't."

Wayne chuckled and leaned back in the recliner. "Then again, now that sister's out of the way, maybe that's his plan."

She felt the tremor of rage that shuddered through Dave. She tightened her grip on his leg, her fingers digging deeply into his muscles. "Please, don't," she whispered under her breath to him.

The mantel clock ticked loudly, counting off the tense seconds and keeping time with the anxious drumming of Lilly's heart. The mutual hatred between Dave and Wayne was a powder keg, and she had to find a way to keep it from igniting. The best way to do that, until she thought of a better idea to end this nightmare, was to keep them apart.

She cleared her throat to loosen the muscles, which were knotted with fear and stress. "I think we should go back to the bedroom. I'm sure you'd probably like to rest."

"Aw, c'mon, Lilly. We were just starting to have fun." Wayne folded his arms carefully over his chest, the revolver still in his grip.

"This isn't fun, Wayne. It's cruel. Why are you being cruel to us?" The hoarse quality of her voice surprised her. She'd thought she was doing a better job than that of keeping her emotions in check.

Their tormenter pulled his head back, angling his head, as if confused. "Cruel?" He waved the gun, motioning to where they sat on the couch. "You think this is cruel? Breakfast? A chance to stretch your legs and pee?"

"Taunting us about Helen's death is. You understand my sister was *murdered*—" her voice cracked on the word "—just a few months ago, don't you?"

Dave looked away, staring at nothing apparent in the adjoining dining room.

"Yeah. So you said." Wayne narrowed a speculative gaze on her, and he was quiet for a few moments, then asked, "Did they catch the guy that done it?"

"Yes," Dave said without looking at anyone. "He confessed."

Wayne snorted. "Idiot." He paused, his jaw moving as if he was deep in thought. "Innocent until proven guilty, ya know. With the right lawyer, he mighta gotten off."

Dave turned his face toward Wayne, so clearly wanting to tear into their captor that Lilly feared for Dave's life. One more heated comment could push Wayne over the edge. Especially now that he'd taken his painkiller, a class of drug known for muting a person's inhibitions and practical reasoning, much like alcohol.

"You want to know what real cruelty is?" Wayne asked.

She didn't. She saw enough proof of some people's meanness in the emergency room.

"My daddy. Now *he* was cruel." Wayne's face contorted with anger and agony, obviously reflecting on a tragic past.

"I'm sorry, Wayne," she said, because she truly was. No one deserved abuse.

He seemed not to hear. "He was an especially mean drunk. Whippin' me with his belt wasn't good enough when he was drunk. He set out to really hurt me then." His throat convulsed as he swallowed. "Really can't say I blame Mama for taking off like she did. A person can only get beat on and burned so many times before they've had enough. Bitch shoulda taken me with her, though. Dad took everything out on me once she left."

Lilly's chest tightened, and her gut roiled. She saw in Wayne's face the pain of rejection he'd likely never admit—that of a small boy abandoned by his mother. Or maybe she was projecting her own devastation over her father's departure. And Alan's. She firmly pushed those memories from her head. She had quite enough to deal with today without letting those dark emotions out from where she kept them locked away.

Lilly refocused her attention on Wayne and what she was learning about him. Considering all he'd endured as a kid, the criminal lifestyle foisted on him by his father, he must have felt he had no other choices in life. She could imagine with the cancer he was battling and the wrong turns his last bank heist had taken, he was probably feeling rather hopeless, desperate, trapped.

She swallowed hard, then murmured, "I hope you know you are better than this. Life can be more for you."

Wayne angled his gaze without turning his head. "Better than what?"

"Robbing banks. Shooting guards. Holding us hostage. Your dad may have led you into that way of life, but you can change. You can rise above it."

He shifted on the recliner and lifted his face more fully to her. "What are you saying, Lilly? You think I'm some kind of lowlife you can look down on?"

His sneer and the darker tone of his voice warned her to tread lightly. "No. I'm saying it's not too late to change your path. Your past, your father's abuse, your track record do not have to dictate where you go from here."

Dave gave her a side glance that said he was skeptical of her contention but understood what she was trying to accomplish.

"See," Wayne said, pointing at Dave, "even he knows that's a load of crap. I can't undo the past. It is what it is, and I done what I've done. Can't unshoot someone or unhold up a liquor store."

"No. But you don't have to let it determine how you move forward from here. The things you've done are just actions, they don't dictate your heart. You can turn your life around. If you send good out to the world, good will come back to you."

"So it's my fault I have cancer and that my dad was an ass?" His eyes glittered with anger. "That what you're saying? Because I put bad stuff out there, robbin' banks, karma gave me cancer?"

"No! Not at all. I mean, we all have to face the consequences of our actions. Your dad chose to rob a larger bank and got shot. You chose to drive Dave's truck while impaired and crashed, breaking your nose." Beside her Dave growled under his breath.

"But plenty of things happen for no reason we can understand," she continued, knowing she had Wayne's attention. "You didn't ask to be born into a family where your mother would leave and your father would beat you. You didn't do anything to deserve cancer. But you can change the things you can control. Change what's inside you. Forgive your father for his cruelty."

Wayne's scoff was loud and defiant. "Like hell. Why should I?"

"Because," she said and drew a slow breath, "as someone wise recently told me, forgiveness isn't about letting the other person off the hook. Forgiveness means not letting the other person control you or your emotions anymore. Forgiving means letting go of old hurts so that you can heal and move on."

Dave angled a look at her, lifting an eyebrow at her, as if to say the sentiments were wasted on Wayne.

Wayne's expression was dubious, too.

Still, she had the opening and she wouldn't waste it. "You can *stop* robbing banks. You could even do something to help other kids from abusive homes. And…you can do right by us. Let us go. Holding us, hurting us, gains you nothing but more trouble down the road."

Wayne rolled his eyes so hard she was surprised she didn't hear his brain rattle.

With a sour look and a curled lip, he said, "You know, same as me, there's only two ways this'll end. Either I get away and go down to Mexico or South America somewhere to get treated for my cancer, or the cops will get me, and I'll get locked up for the rest of my days."

"That's not true. The future is not written yet. You could negotiate a plea that—"

"Shut up," he barked, turning his head away. "I'm tired, and you're giving me a headache." He glared at her. "A worse headache than what I already had."

Lilly sighed and sank back in the sofa cushions. So much for her plan to win Wayne over with her encouragement. She could only hope that somehow she'd planted a seed in him that would take root. But would Wayne see the light in time to save her life and Dave's?

About thirty minutes later, Wayne's eyelids started drooping as his latest dose of tramadol kicked in. He hadn't yet moved her and Dave back to the bedroom prison, and Lilly began hoping their captor would nod off while she was still untied. Her plan A had failed, but was there hope for a plan B?

After his third yawn in as many minutes, however, he seemed to realize he was fading fast and scooted out of the recliner. "Get up, both of you."

He used the gun to wave them to their feet. Moving to one of the partly packed boxes Lilly had been filling with Helen's books, Wayne found another roll of packing tape and hitched his head toward the back of the house. "Time to go to your room."

Her heart sank, both for the failed attempt to convince Wayne to release them and the thought of being bound hand and foot again.

Dave's expression reflected the same frustration and dejection as they were marched down the hall. Before

Wayne could dictate otherwise, Dave climbed on the bed and leveled a challenging glare on their captor, as if daring him to force Dave back down on the floor.

"Turn around. Hands behind your back, Lilly," Wayne said. He set the gun on the dresser, out of her reach.

"Wayne, can't we come up with another way to—" she started, only to be interrupted by the jarring *rrrriip* of the tape unwinding from the roll. She'd have nightmares about that sound when this was over... God willing, she survived the ordeal. Dave was eyeing the weapon on the dresser, speculation plain in his eyes.

"Wayne," she began again, hoping to capture their captor's attention, in case Dave was planning a move. "Tying us up is not the answer. Please, just let us—" She grunted when he grabbed her arm and spun her around.

"Let you go?" he finished for her as he pulled her arms behind her. "Just give it a rest, Lilly! That *ain't* happening."

He wrapped the tape around her already sore and adhesive-chafed wrists, and she winced. "I'm just trying to find an out for you, Wayne. For all of us. I don't want anyone else to die."

He leaned close, his breath smelling of coffee and the old blood in his sinuses, and whispered, "Then do as you're told, and keep your pal in line." He flicked a finger toward the bed. "Up."

While she climbed on the bed, he jerked Dave's feet together and taped them, then secured his hands to the headboard. Her feet and hands were given similar treatment next.

After retrieving the revolver, Wayne paused at the

door and grumbled, "Keep it down back here. I need to sleep."

As soon as the door closed, Dave directed a hard look at her and whispered, "I thought I was clear about our plan, our priorities, if opportunity presented itself."

She furrowed her brow. "What?"

"You had plenty of chances to get the gun from him. Why didn't you?" The accusatory edge in his tone stung.

She glanced away from his dark, razor-sharp gaze and took a moment to compose herself. "I didn't think I could."

"Your hands and feet were both loose. It was the perfect chance. I would have distracted him, dived in to help with the slightest cue from you."

"I…was scared to. I'm not sure I could have fired it, emptied it before he got it away from me."

"I'd have run interference for you."

"And likely gotten yourself killed for it! Last time I tried to take control of the gun, he got it back in an instant and aimed it at me." She shuddered at the memory. "I chose not to take that risk." Squaring her shoulders, Lilly lowered her voice, which had grown louder as her passion rose. "I saw a chance to get in his good graces, a chance to build a useful bond with him, and went that route instead."

Dave closed his eyes and leaned his head back on the headboard. "Oh, Lilly…"

"And I was making progress until…"

He cracked one eye open and turned his face toward her. "Until? Go on. You're going to blame me for ruining things. For letting him get under my skin."

"Well…no. He was the main provocateur."

The muscle in his jaw jumped as he ground his back teeth together. "What he *is* is a first-class bastard. A psychopath."

"Agreed."

"So why are you still trying to negotiate with him? Begging him and—" He made a sound of disgust and shook his head.

"I still think I can reach him, convince him to let us go unharmed."

"You're dreaming."

"Maybe. But it's a dream worth pursuing. I'm not willing to quit fighting for any chance to save our lives. Are you?"

He huffed his frustration. "Of course not."

"'And what do we say to the God of Death?'" she said, quoting one of her favorite TV shows.

He jerked a startled gaze to her and answered, "Not today."

She smiled knowingly at him, and he expelled a harsh laugh. "It just…sticks in my craw knowing so much of our fate is in his slimy hands. I've had to mind my words and yield to his will simply because of that damn gun so many times that I'm choking on it. But—" he angled his head to meet her gaze, his voice dropping to an intimate murmur "—if swallowing my pride is the sacrifice I have to make to see you safe, I'll do it a thousand times."

The sentiment brought a lump to her throat.

Based on what she was seeing for herself about Dave, she knew he would indeed sacrifice for her, up to and including his own life. That thought sent a chill through her, because Wayne was showing signs of growing more hostile, more volatile. Especially when under the influence of his pain meds.

"So…you know *Game of Thrones*?"

"I do."

"Helen called me a dragon geek for watching it. For loving it as much as I do."

Lilly snorted. "She told me."

His gaze narrowed. "And…you like *Thrones*?"

"Hadn't expected to, but…what can I say? Great storyline, creative world building, spot-on character development. I mean, Tyrion…"

"I know! Right?" He chuckled and, after a beat, quoted, "'That's what I do—'"

"'I drink and I know things.'"

They shared a smile, then she offered another famous line from the popular fantasy drama. They continued this way for a while, passing the time reciting the dialogue from television shows and movie scenes they both loved. They moved on to word associations, random favorites and trivia, anything to keep their mind off the passing hours and the aching in their muscles.

"Dark chocolate?" he said, quizzing her.

"It's okay with the right red wine," she replied. "Cilantro?"

"Love it, but my brother thinks it tastes like soap." He shook his head, grinning, "In fact, once when we were eating out at this primo, five-star restaurant for my mother's birthday…" And he launched into a humorous story about his childhood that led to her telling a memory of her own. And back and forth they continued, learning tidbits about each other and trying not to dwell on the nightmare sleeping down the hall.

She'd just finished recounting the comical calamity that was her seventh birthday party, complete with the neighbor's dog eating the cake, a sudden rain shower that soaked the piñata and her father popping the inflatable bouncy house when he jumped on it, when Dave grew strangely pensive.

"What?" she asked, sensing his mood swing.

"Oh, just…" He sighed. "I guess Helen told you she found him?"

Shock rendered her frozen, breathless. When she recovered enough to speak, she rasped, "Found…who?" But she knew. Who else could Dave mean? Who else from her and Helen's past needed finding? Certainly not the fireman who responded to…

"I take it from your reaction that you didn't know."

Lilly fought for a shallow, quavering breath. "No. Tell me."

"Um, all she said was that she used some legal documents—your parents' divorce papers, I think—as a starting place to track him down. She said she wanted closure."

"Oh, Helen."

"Um…when she found your father's new address, she sat in the car and watched the house for a while. A lady with a small boy pulled up to the house first and unloaded groceries. Then a girl who looked to be about ten got off the school bus. The kids were in the yard when your dad got home. His hair was grayer, but she was sure it was him. She heard the girl call him 'Daddy,' and the boy ran to get a hug as your dad got out of the car."

Her heart thrashed against her ribs like a trapped animal fighting to get free. "He has a new family."

"Apparently. She said she didn't speak to him. Just started the engine and drove away."

"Damn him," she muttered under her breath. Lilly blinked back the tears that pricked her eyes. She would not shed any more tears for that man. He'd made his choice, and she'd dealt with the repercussions of his decision in ways no nine-year-old should have to. But someone had to cook and clean and buy the groceries when their mother slipped into one of her depressions.

He angled his head toward her. "I'm sorry, Lil. I shouldn't have said anything. I figured Helen had told—"

"No. I always begged her to let it go. What was done was done. But she couldn't believe he left without good reason." She scoffed. "Poor Helen. I guess she got her closure."

"She did. She said knowing he was happy, even if it wasn't with her, gave her a little peace. She wouldn't begrudge him the love he'd found with his new family. She loved him enough to let him go."

Helen had found peace over their father's abandonment? The idea rocked Lilly to her core, because his memory still hurt her so deeply. She sniffed hard when her nose started to run. "When was this?"

"About three years ago."

She exhaled and shook her head, trying to clear the melancholy. "So now I know. Good for her. I'm afraid I can't be as magnanimous."

Having apparently recovered from her gunfire-wrought fright, Maddie grew bold enough to climb on the bed with them and crawl onto Lilly's lap. Her cat nuzzled her arm and nipped at her elbow, asking to be patted, and Lilly sighed. "Sorry, Maddie-cakes. I'd like nothing more than to hug you right now, but my hands are tied. Literally." She chuckled without humor. "Don't often get to say that, huh? My hands are literally tied."

Dave hummed an acknowledgment, then said, "The man was an idiot."

"Huh?"

Dave turned his head to pin her with a probing stare full of compassion and conviction. "I'll tell you what I told Helen that day. Your father was an idiot to leave. He gave up the right to know what a beautiful, vibrant woman you became."

Her breath caught, and she felt as if she were falling into Dave's mahogany gaze.

"He forfeited the chance to know you, to love you, to watch you make a difference in the world, and he is so much poorer for it."

"Dave…"

"Only an idiot would give up a chance to be with you," he whispered.

And she lost a piece of her heart to him.

Chapter 13

"Hey, wake up!" a gruff male voice said the next morning, waking Dave from the best sleep he'd had all night.

Most of the evening he'd stared into the darkness, listening to Lilly breathe and sweating over how he could get them out of this mess alive. He knew he needed to rest while their captor slept, so his mind would be as fresh and clear-thinking as possible. But when he tried to quiet his brain in search of Z's, his stiff muscles and throbbing skull conspired to keep him in only the lightest stages of sleep. Apparently, though, somewhere in the wee hours he'd drifted off, because the room was lighter now. And he hadn't heard Wayne come in the room—a failing all on its own.

Dave wanted to rub his bleary eyes, needed to stretch

the dull ache from muscles bound in the same awkward position too long. While he mentally grumbled over his hand constraints and discomfort, Wayne raised a booted foot to Dave's bad leg. "I said, wake up!"

Dave gritted his teeth and muffled his grunt of pain. "What do you want?"

"Get up and you'll find out."

He'd promised Lilly not to let Wayne bait him. Continuing the hostilities between them would only prove more dangerous as Wayne lost patience and grew more agitated.

The bedsprings squeaked as Lilly roused and raised her head from his shoulder. "What's happening? Dave?"

Her voice was craggy with slumber and held an edge of fear. He wished he could hug her, hold her, soothe the worry that vibrated in her tone. But, of course, he was trussed like a Thanksgiving turkey and unable to do more than stare at Wayne. "I don't know what he wants. Are you okay?"

"I— Yeah. Wayne, what—?"

"I've decided to take Hero up on his offer." Wayne crouched beside the bed, and Dave saw the revolver in his hand. Inches from his nose. He focused on the barrel, where the tiny manufacturer's inscription confirmed his suspicions. A Glock 17, fourth generation.

He'd been keeping count of the rounds fired. Seven at the bank. Four warning shots at the house. Six rounds left.

"What offer?" Lilly asked, echoing the question that nudged Dave's brain.

Wayne grabbed Dave's arm and tugged. "Sit up."

Dave struggled to a seated position, a task made more

difficult because of his pounding headache and lack of good leverage. He turned a wary eye toward Wayne, startled to see his captor set the gun on the bedside table and reach in his pocket. The weapon was almost in reach... if he'd had free use of his arms, which he didn't, but—

His attention shifted abruptly when Wayne drew a small folding knife from his pocket and flicked it open. Dave tensed, drew back. "What the hell, man?"

Lilly gasped. "Wayne, don't be rash. Please!"

Their captor held up the blade and glowered at Dave. "You said earlier that you knew engines. Said you could fix up my car. I think you called it the crap-mobile?"

Dave held his breath. Clenched his teeth. Jerked a small nod.

"Good. Here's what's going to happen." Glaring at Dave, he waggled the knife as he spoke. "You're gonna get my car up and running, ready to drive me at least outta state before I swap vehicles somewhere."

Dave figured Wayne would be better off trading vehicles sooner rather than later, but he wasn't going to give the robber tips on how best to escape.

"You're going to work fast, and you're not going to try anything funny, because the whole time you're working, I'm gonna have this bad boy—" he paused long enough to pat his hand on the grip of the Glock "—pointed at Lilly's head."

Dave's stomach lurched. His first priority, until this whole mess was over, was to keep Lilly safe. Having that thug pointing his gun at Lilly only made his plan to get the weapon away from him more difficult. He took a slow breath and took a page from Lilly's playbook, tried to stay calm and be friendly, reasonable. "Why don't we leave Lilly out of this? You said yourself you like her. You may even need her nursing skills again for your injuries before this is all over."

From the corner of his eye, he noticed Lilly's startled glance, but he kept his focus trained on Wayne. "If I do anything you don't like, shoot me instead."

"Dave, no," Lilly said under her breath.

He cut a quick side glance to her. "It's okay, Lil. I don't plan on getting shot."

That much was true. If anyone took a bullet, he intended for it to be Wayne.

Their captor narrowed his eyes and divided a look between him and Lilly, as if considering the proposition. "You're right—I do like her better. But I also don't like being told what to do. She goes outside with us, if for no other reason than to keep you in line. 'Cause it's obvious you like her, too, and I think you'll do exactly what I say just to make sure I don't hurt her." He used the knife to slice through the tape around Dave's ankles. "Now get up, and I'll let your hands loose."

Easier said than done. With his arms still bound behind him and his bum leg stiff from disuse, finding the right balance was awkward. But Dave would be damned if he'd let Wayne see him struggle. Dave swallowed the groan that rose in his throat as he struggled to push slowly to his feet without toppling sideways.

Grabbing Dave's arm, Wayne turned Dave around.

Lilly gasped and cried, "No, wait! Don't cut it. Please. I really like that bathrobe and without the matching belt, it won't be, well— Can't you just untie the knots?"

Wayne made an impatient sucking noise with his

mouth. "He's pulled the knots too tight. I can't untie them."

"Then let me try," she said. "Not only are my fingers smaller, but I knit as a hobby. I'm used to untying tiny tangles and knots that get in my yarn."

Clearly Wayne wasn't happy with the delay. Finally, he huffed his resignation, and wiggled his fingers, indicating she should raise her arms. Shifting to kneel on the bed, she leaned forward to give him access to her wrists. He slit the tape binding her arms, and she half moaned, half sighed when her hands were released.

In any other circumstance, Dave would have found the sound pure seduction, but… Hell, who was he fooling? The sensual noise that purled from her throat sent a wave of heat flashing through him. Judging from Wayne's raised eyebrow and the sleazy grin tugging the corner of his mouth, their captor had noticed the sexy quality of the moan, as well. Dave set his jaw, itching to smack the slimy smirk from Wayne's face.

Lilly plucked gingerly at the sticky mess clinging to her wrists, gritting her teeth as the tape pulled at her skin.

"Come on already! We don't have all day." Wayne gave the tape a rough yank, and Lilly yelped as the remaining adhesive ripped from her chafed skin.

"Hey!" Dave protested.

"What?" Wayne snapped back.

"You didn't have to do that." Dave gritted his back teeth, reining in his anger. "I warned you not to hurt her."

"You need to shut the hell up!" Wayne shouted back,

snatching the gun off the bedside table and taking a threatening step toward him.

Dave bristled and widened his stance, ready to fight if needed, even with his hands still tied.

"Whoa, whoa, whoa!" Lilly said over them both, then loosed a shrill whistle.

Both men shot startled looks toward her. She motioned with her hands for both of them to quiet down. "Wayne, Dave, come on. Everyone take a breath. I'm fine." She directed the last statement toward Dave, then to Wayne she said, "It's all good. Let's calm down, and try this again?"

She waved a hand toward her feet. "If you would?"

Nostrils flaring, Wayne sent a dark glare toward Dave, then sliced through the tape at Lilly's ankles. Thanks to her slacks, she was able to peel it off hastily and wad it in a ball. Rubbing at her wrists, she slid off the bed and eased past Wayne. "Can you two be civil for two minutes? I gotta—" She hitched her head to the bathroom.

Wayne stiffened as she took her leave and closed the door.

Dave shoved his feet into his boots while they waited for her. "We need food and something to drink, too. I'll cooperate if you will. It's a two-way street."

"You'll get food when I say so." Wayne glanced toward the closed bathroom door and shouted. "Hurry up, Lilly!"

She returned a moment later and sidled toward Dave, giving Wayne a stiff smile. "Now, I'll just work this belt loose, and we can all go outside and take a look at your car. Dave will get it fixed right up, and you can be on your way. Win-win for everyone. Right?"

Wayne pressed a hand to his side and took a shallow breath. "Well, you got it partly right. I'm not so sure Hero there will come out of this a winner if he don't start being a little smarter and stop pissing me off."

Lilly put a hand on Dave's forearm and squeezed, giving him a quelling look and mouthing his name. She circled behind him and began plucking at the belt knots.

"Hmm. You really did pull these suckers tight. Geez." She gave his fingers a friendly squeeze, and Dave's heart thumped.

"I need...something." She moved away and scanned the room.

Wayne tensed and aimed the gun at her. "What are you doing?"

She raised both hands in a conciliatory motion. "Looking for something to help me with the knot. I don't have my knitting here, but—" She bit down on her lower lip and wrinkled her nose as she thought. The gesture was innocent, but also sexy and a fresh rush of lust puddled in Dave's gut. He closed his eyes and pressed his lips in a frown of disgust. Now was not the time to be ogling Lilly or thinking about how good she'd felt tucked against him last night.

"A fork!" Lilly said brightly.

The comment startled Dave from his musing, and he blinked his confusion at her.

"A fork?" Wayne said, his own countenance skeptical. "What d'you need a fork for?"

"I want a small pointed tip to help work the knot

loose. The tines of a fork would be perfect. Will you get me one from the kitchen?"

Wayne narrowed another suspicious glare at her, as if trying to guess what sort of ploy she was up to. He shook his head. "Nah. I ain't leaving you two alone with you untied. We all go."

Wrapping a hand around Lilly's arm, Wayne motioned with the gun for Dave to head out the door first. They all trooped down the hall to the kitchen, and as they went, Dave took a mental inventory of everything they passed. He'd been in Helen's house a hundred times or more. He knew it as well as he knew his own home, but he was seeing it through fresh eyes this time. Looking for anything he could use as a weapon. Looking for anything that would aid his and Lilly's escape. Did Wayne have a phone? What had been moved since Lilly started packing?

He must have been moving too slowly to suit his captor, because Wayne gave his back a hard push. "Move it, Hero. Remember, you try anything, you die."

Dave clenched his teeth, shoving down the urge to retaliate. He had to remember that as long as Wayne had the gun, he had the upper hand, and acting rashly could get Lilly hurt. Because he knew on some level that she wouldn't stand idly by and let Wayne shoot him. She'd try to intervene and would likely get herself shot in the process.

Damn it! Having her outside while he piddled with Wayne's car posed a complication he hadn't wanted.

Lilly went straight to the drawer that held Helen's utensils and took out a fork. "Okay, Dave, turn around."

He offered her his back and his bound hands while

his gaze swept the kitchen. *Remembering*. His heart twisted, shooting pain deep to his core. Being in this room, with the rooster decor and frilly white curtains, the copper pans hanging on the wall and the spice rack over the stove, filled him with a particularly keen grief. The kitchen had been where Helen thrived. She'd loved to try new recipes out for him. And she was damn good at it, too. He sighed sadly and whispered, "This room isn't the same without her in it. It seems…lonely. Fallow."

Lilly paused in her ministrations, and her silence, her stillness, spoke for her mood. "Yeah. That's a good word for it."

Wayne sat in a ladder-backed chair at the small oak table and waved the gun at them. "What are you talking about?"

"My sister. This kitchen. She loved to cook." Lilly tugged at the belt and began working again. "Just because we're talking to each other, doesn't mean we're conspiring."

"Yeah, well, I don't like it so…keep your trap shut."

Within a few minutes, Lilly had managed to untie the knots and free Dave's hands. While he rubbed his sore wrists, Lilly smoothed the belt out and set it carefully on the end of the kitchen table. "There. It's crumpled, but I think it will iron out and be just fine."

Wayne snorted. "What it will *be* is back on Hero's arms as soon as he gets my car running."

Dave rolled his aching shoulders, started toward the hall. "My turn in the bathroom."

"Freeze, pal." Wayne aimed the gun at him and shoved out of the chair, holding his side and wincing as he rose to his feet. "You're not going anywhere by yourself."

"Follow me then, but I am going to take a leak." He marched to the second bathroom off the hall and closed the door in Wayne's face.

As he did his business, he scoped out the bathroom for a weapon. If he had more time, he could have fashioned something out of the scant and innocuous items left following Lilly's packing. But he didn't want to leave Lilly alone with Wayne longer than needed, and he couldn't imagine a way to disarm or disable their captor using toilet paper, a hand towel and a travel-size bar of soap.

When he exited the bathroom, Wayne waved the gun, directing him back to the kitchen, where Lilly was eating a peanut butter sandwich.

"How is your wound this morning, Wayne?" Lilly asked and handed Dave a sandwich, as well. "I'll need to clean it again and change the dressing."

Wayne shrugged. "Later."

"Are you in pain?" Lilly asked.

Wayne twisted his mouth in an ugly frown. "Sweetheart, I'm always in pain these days, and I guess I *will be* in pain until I get the treatments for my cancer or until I die. Whichever comes first."

"What about taking more of your pain pills?" Dave suggested around a large bite of the sticky sandwich.

Wayne shot a dirty look at Dave. "Nice try, but since they make me sleepy, I won't take any more until I know you two are through helping me out there—" he hitched his head toward the back, where the junker was parked "—and are once again tied up nice and tight."

"How about something over-the-counter?" Lilly suggested.

"How about you both get yourselves outside and get my car running?" he snarled, then after a beat added, "Over-the-counter pills do nothing for me anymore."

"I'm sorry. If I could do something for you—"

"You can." Wayne waved the gun again. "You can help me get out of this Podunk town and out of the country. Now move it."

Dave's gut clenched. If he and Lilly helped Wayne escape, wouldn't they be accessories, or…something? Aiding and abetting? Except they were helping under duress. That had to count for something. Right?

He wasn't sure of all the legalities, but he knew cars, engines. And the truth was, he was unlikely to find anything wrong with Wayne's crap-mobile that he could fix without replacement parts. He could tweak things here and there, sure. But the list of problems he could repair or overhaul that would make any difference in the performance and long-term drivability of the junker was short. Very short. So his challenge became a choice. Stall as long as he could, fiddle with the engine to buy himself and Lilly some time, or…act quickly on his plan to disarm Wayne and discharge as many rounds from the Glock as he could. And then pray Wayne didn't have extra ammo stashed somewhere.

Neither option was good, but Wayne hadn't left him much choice.

With the Glock pointed at him, Dave stuffed the last of his peanut-butter-sandwich breakfast in his mouth and led the way outside. He tipped his face to the sky and inhaled the clean Rocky Mountain air. Today was the sort of beautiful day that made Dave long to be in a saddle, riding the range and working a herd.

His leg gave a twinge, or maybe he just imagined it did. He missed ranching like the dickens and would give anything to be back working with the McCalls.

But to get that life back, he first had to survive his current crisis. He gave Wayne a quick side glance, sizing up the man's grip of the weapon, his distance from his target and the likelihood that Lilly would be in the line of fire if anything went wrong. Did Lilly have a place to duck and cover?

"Come on," Wayne said, poking Dave in the back with the muzzle and guiding him to the parked jalopy. The thing really was a piece of junk. The seats inside were ripped. The paint job scratched, dinged and rusted. And without raising the hood, he knew the engine was likely in as bad of shape.

"You can sit there," Wayne called to Lilly, motioning to a pollen-dusted Adirondack chair by the back door. "But if you move a muscle to leave that chair, you get a bullet in your foot. You hear me?"

Lilly arched an eyebrow at Wayne and lifted a hand. "Okay. Mind if I scoot the chair out of the sun?" She pointed at a spot where the roofline made a small pool of shade.

"Whatever. Just...don't get any ideas." Wayne frowned as he cast his gaze back and forth between the two of them, as if realizing the folly of trying to keep both of his hostages under control without restraints. Gun or no gun, he was outnumbered.

Dave moved to the front of the beat-up sedan and popped the hood, propped it with the small attached iron bar. Leaned in to take a look. The nodules on the battery were corroded. He noticed that first. He could clean that up, but it wouldn't make any difference in the engine's performance. "Crank it up for me, would you? I need to listen to the motor," he called to Wayne.

His captor opened the driver's door and held his weapon pointed at Lilly while he turned the engine over. It sputtered to life, chugging and puffing black exhaust from the tailpipe.

When the car backfired, Lilly yelped and clapped a hand to her chest.

From behind the screen of the hood, Dave tried to make eye contact with Lilly, to send her a silent message about his intentions and her response to his actions when he put them in motion. She gave a nervous laugh over having jumped at the loud backfire and sent Dave an embarrassed half grin. He drilled a steady look on her that caught her attention. He moved his hand close to his chest and formed his fingers and thumb in the shape of a gun. *Fire the gun,* he mouthed.

Her brow dipped and he remembered her previous reservations and fears. He didn't have time to debate with her. He nailed a hard, stern look and jerked a quick nod, then called to Wayne, "Rev it again."

Wayne gave the engine gas, and the motor chugged loudly. Giving the engine a more genuine inspection, Dave saw a few problems immediately, and his ears detected what he was sure was an issue with the carburetor. "Okay, you can turn it off for now," he called over the rattling engine noise.

After cutting off the motor, Wayne moved back to the front of the car, where Dave braced his hands on the frame and stared into the aged assembly of parts. "Well?"

Dave sighed, calculating the best moment to catch Wayne off guard. He'd heard once that when a person was talking, their reflexes were slowed. And he needed every fraction-of-a-second advantage he could get.

"Here's the thing, man," Dave began in as friendly of a tone as he could muster. "Your hoses and belts look pretty worn. I can patch the hoses with some duct tape and that will hold you for a while, but eventually they'll give."

"And?"

"The carburetor's bad. It sounds like it needs replacing, and we don't have any parts to do that kind of repair."

Wayne frowned. "I only need it to get me outta town. Then I'll dump it and steal someth—"

Dave slammed his elbow into Wayne's solar plexus, followed immediately with a backward thrust of his fist into the guy's broken nose. Predictably, Wayne curled forward in defense of his injured gut and face. But he also swung the Glock toward Dave.

Ready for the move, Dave used his other hand to knock the muzzle up and grab for Wayne's wrist, driving his thumb into the tendons on the underside of his captor's wrist.

"Dave!" Lilly cried.

"You sonofabitch!" Wayne growled. "I warned you what—"

Tightening his grip on Wayne's wrist, Dave slammed his opponent's arm onto the car frame. Wayne howled in outrage and pain as the two grappled for possession of the gun. Wayne tried to turn the muzzle up, and when he had a slight angle, he fired.

The ear-shattering blast reverberated off the hood of the car, mingling with Lilly's scream.

One, Dave counted mentally, knowing he needed the Glock to be fired at least six times.

She rushed forward, grabbing at Wayne. "Stop! No!"

"Get back!" Dave yelled at her, while again slamming Wayne's wrist on the car. "Take cover!"

"I...will...kill...you...for this!" Wayne snarled as they continued wrestling for dominance and the Glock.

Finally, Dave wrenched the weapon away and used it to backhand Wayne in the nose. The robber moaned and cradled his nose as blood streamed from it.

Two, Dave counted as he fired into the dirt toward the back of the yard.

Wayne tackled him from behind, his captor's arms circling him and pinning his own arms at his sides as Wayne took him down. Dave clung to the Glock, firing over his head before Wayne grabbed at the gun. *Three.*

Again the two battled for the revolver. Dave knew if he lost possession of the weapon, one of the remaining rounds would be fired into his brain. And Lilly? Would Wayne's wrath extend to her as well?

Dave held the Glock with both hands, using his forehead to bash Wayne in his already injured nose. Dave bit his opponent's arm when it came within reach, and he tried to wrap his legs around Wayne's to subdue them as the two men struggled, rolling on the ground in a winner-take-all fight for their lives.

Wayne suddenly abandoned his battle for the gun and seized Dave by the front of his shirt. Lifted him a few inches from the ground and slammed him back on the hard earth. Once, twice…three times. Dave's head smacked against the gravel drive, and pain streaked through his skull like lightning. His breath whooshed from his lungs. He gasped like a landed fish. His vision blurred, and his ears rang. He fought to stay conscious…

Lilly…

Had to protect…

Wayne released his shirt. Grabbed for the gun.

Dave fought to maintain control of the revolver, but when his opponent slammed his wrist into the driveway, his grip on the Glock slipped.

Blinking, Dave tried to clear his vision. Tried to prepare for what came next.

Wayne pushed unsteadily to his knees, swiping at his swollen, bloody nose with his arm. "I told you not to do anything stupid."

Dave dragged in a rasping breath and swiped a hand toward the Glock. "Don't."

Wobbling as he rose to his feet, Wayne pointed the gun at Dave's chest. Center mass.

From his left, Lilly lunged at Wayne, shouting, "No-o-o-o!"

A blast of gunfire. Then…

For the briefest moment, silence. A slow-motion moment where it seemed the world held its breath. Or maybe it only seemed that way to Dave. His head felt heavy, his thoughts were sluggish. Was he shot? Dying? What?

He waited for the pain, but adrenaline numbed him.

Seeking proof of life, he focused on the thrum of his accelerated heartbeat thrashing his ribs.

And then the moment passed, and reality crashed down on him. A scalding pain ripped through the calf of his bad leg. A keening wail assaulted his ears, followed by the sound of a scuffle.

He craned his head in the direction of the noises. Lilly. Wayne. A tussle.

And then more gunfire.

Chapter 14

When Lilly saw Wayne aim the gun at Dave, a chill swept down her spine, and her heart stopped for a moment. In the next instant, something feral and protective swelled inside her. Without stopping to overthink it, she simply reacted, followed her gut. She'd plowed her shoulder in Wayne's side and swung her arms up to knock the gun away. She knew she'd made contact with something, because her hands stung and her shoulder ached.

But her ears rang, as well. Wayne had fired the gun.

Her heart in her throat, she spun to face Dave. He was lying motionless on the ground, his eyes wide and unblinking.

"Dave!" she screamed, fearing the worst. Beside her, Wayne was fumbling in the dirt near her feet. She dropped her gaze, stumbling back, when her foot hit something hard that nearly made her lose her balance. The gun. A jolt of awareness slammed through her. Wayne was reaching for the weapon.

He can't kill us if he's out of rounds. Reacting more than planning, she kicked the Glock. The gun spun across the packed dirt toward the gravel driveway. Wayne angled a dark glare at her and scrambled awkwardly toward it. Lilly hadn't played keep-away with her sister in more than twenty years, but the principle and strategies she'd learned remained.

Darting forward, she kicked the gun again, just before Wayne could grab it. Then she tackled him, shoving him face-first into the driveway before springing off him and diving for the weapon herself. Her move earned her scraped elbows and an oxygen-stealing thump to her lungs. But breath or not, she snatched up the Glock and gripped it between her hands.

She'd read enough spy thrillers to know there'd be recoil. Just the same, when she pointed the gun toward the edge of the yard and squeezed the trigger, the muzzle kicked up, and she rocked back on her bottom.

Wayne had clambered to his knees, and he crept toward her. "Give that to me, *Lilly*!" he grated through clenched teeth.

She needed to hold him off, empty the gun of ammunition…

Loosing a wild screech of adrenaline, fear and determination, she swung the muzzle near Wayne—she didn't want to kill him, just scare him away—and she fired again. Dirt and rocks near his feet flew up and pelted his legs.

Wayne danced back a step, his expression startled.

Her breath had returned and she panted in shallow, nervous gasps. *Fire again*, Dave's voice in her head said. *Keep firing.*

Her hands shook so hard she could barely hold the revolver straight.

"Lilly!" Wayne growled in warning, then he dove for the ground and crawled on his belly, military-style, toward her.

She aimed toward him, then, fearing she would, in fact, hit him, she pivoted to the side and fired near the rear of the old jalopy.

In her peripheral vision, she saw Wayne scramble to his feet. He snarled an ugly epithet at her as he stumbled toward her. She tensed, bracing for his attack, but he hit her with enough force that she lost her grip on the gun. Her heart sank as the weapon jarred from her sweaty hands.

Wayne snatched it up. Stiff-armed, he aimed it at her temple, fury twisting his face into an ugly mask.

A whimper escaped her throat as she stared down the muzzle. Drawing a tremulous breath, she shook her head and let tears fill her eyes. "Wayne, d-don't. I just wanted to—"

"Shut up!" he screamed at her. "I trusted you. I would have let you live, if you'd cooperated. But you betrayed me." He gritted his teeth.

As if someone had wrapped a comforting blanket around her shoulders, an odd peace filled Lilly as the certainty of her impending death settled in her core. Instead of spending her final moments begging for her life, a quiet acceptance flowed through her. Warmth chased the chill of dread and fear from her bones. She exhaled. Raised her eyes to Wayne's and whispered, "I forgive you."

Her statement clearly caught Wayne off guard. The muzzle wavered. He blinked, hesitated and swallowed hard before training the gun on her temple again. "No tricks, Lilly. I swear I'll—"

"No tricks," she said quietly and closed her eyes.

And she heard him pull the trigger.

Click.

He'd been shot.

Through the muzziness clouding his brain, Dave tried to orient himself. Head pounding, he managed to drag himself to a seated position. Assessed the damage. The stinging wound in his calf and blood spreading around the new rip in his jeans left no question where Wayne's shot had landed. Better his leg than his heart, but, damn, it hurt.

The sound of voices and gunfire jolted through him. Where was Lilly?

He pinched the bridge of his nose, needing to clear the fog. Despite the throbbing of his skull and calf, he clambered to his knees and struggled to his feet.

Across the yard, he spotted Lilly. Somehow she'd taken the gun from Wayne and was firing it at the ground. The way he'd told her to. His chest swelled with pride for an instant. He leaned heavily on the rusty sedan, knowing he needed to get to her. Protect her.

As Dave took his first stumbling steps toward Lilly, Wayne lunged at her. Snatched the gun.

A chill washed through Dave. How many rounds were left in the gun? He'd lost track when he blacked out, but even one was one too many. Gritting his teeth against the pain, he hobbled across the yard. Thanks to his injury, neither a swift nor silent approach was in the cards, but he made the most of a blind approach from behind Wayne.

With Wayne's focus on Lilly, Dave managed to get close, but—

His blood chilled as Wayne aimed the weapon at Lilly's head. Lilly went still, pale. She said something to Wayne that Dave couldn't hear over the buzz of adrenaline in his ears. He limped forward as fast as his injured leg allowed. But not fast enough.

Wayne pulled the trigger and—

Nothing.

A click.

Relief stole Dave's breath and weakened his legs. But he knew he couldn't waste the split-second opportunity presented to him. He seized Wayne from behind, throwing his full weight against their captor.

When they tumbled to the ground, Wayne gave a growl that was part fury, part agony. The robber twisted his body, rolling to his back, to face Dave's attack.

Dave wasted no time in grabbing the front of Wayne's shirt and treating his opponent to the same sort of head-jarring slams to the ground that had rattled Dave's senses earlier. He had to dodge Wayne's grasping, flailing hands, but each time he lifted and thrust Wayne against the hard dirt, the other man's efforts slackened. From his right, Lilly appeared to snatch the ammo-spent gun from Wayne's hand, and she cracked the butt of the gun against Wayne's temple.

The man's eyes rolled back, and he went limp under Dave's grip.

Lilly caught her breath, a look of horror crossing her face. "Did I kill him?"

Dave hesitated, watching for a trick, then slowly released their captor's shirt. "I don't think so."

She nudged him aside and placed a trembling hand on Wayne's throat, feeling for a pulse.

"He's alive."

She closed her eyes and expelled a relieved sigh.

Dave gulped a few deep breaths of his own, then recognized the situation for the opportunity it was. He took the gun from her and stashed it in his jeans at the small of his back. Grabbing Lilly's hand, he tugged her arm. "Let's go!"

Lilly stared at him blankly, obviously still overwhelmed by the shock of the last few minutes' events. "What?"

"We're free, and he's out. We have to go before he wakes up!" Dave shoved to his feet, grimacing and cursing when pain shot up his leg from his bleeding calf.

Worry dented Lilly's brow, and her gaze dipped to his bloody jeans. "Oh, my God! You were shot!"

"Flesh wound, I'm thinking…thanks to you knocking his aim off."

"I—I have to c-clean it." She blinked, stuttered, clearly still in shock. "W-we…should wrap it—"

"Later." He squeezed her hand. "Right now, we move. Hurry!"

She cast another concerned glance at Wayne, who was eerily still. "But if he's hurt—"

Trying to swallow his impatience, he tugged her arm

again. "Then I'm sure the sheriff will get him medical help. But only if we get out of here before he wakes up *and kills us*!"

She opened her mouth as if to protest, then snapped it close, her teeth clicking. "You're right, of course. I just—"

He helped her to her feet, and they headed down the driveway toward the narrow road that traversed the mountain. As his adrenaline waned, the lightning pain from his calf grew with every step. The warm trickle of blood that slid down inside his boot told him that, at the least, he needed to tie something around his calf to staunch the bleeding.

He stopped to lean against the side of the house and braced a hand on his good knee as he clenched his teeth in agony. Glancing back at Wayne's prone and motionless form, assuring himself the man hadn't revived, he growled, "Damn it, we're gonna have to wrap my leg. But quick."

Lilly nodded. "I have antibiotic spray inside."

He grabbed her forearm as she took a step toward the door. "Screw that."

"But it could get infected!"

Dave snatched his shirt off over his head and started ripping it into strips. "There'll be time for fighting infection later—" he handed her the strips "—once we are safely away from the maniac bank robber."

She sent another look over her shoulder toward Wayne, the battle between medical obligations and her own safety playing out on her face.

"Right," she said with clear reluctance. He knew everything about their current situation flew in the face of her nurse's training and instincts to render aid.

"When we get somewhere safe," he said, folding a T-shirt strip into a pad, "you can disinfect and stitch me to your heart's content."

He eased up one leg of his jeans, and Lilly made a sympathetic noise in her throat when the extent of the gash came into view. Perhaps a bit more than a flesh wound then.

Dave swallowed the bile that rose at the back of his throat. *Breathe.*

He remembered the instruction from when he'd broken this same leg a few months back. Erin McCall, his ex-boss's wife, had coached him through yoga breathing to keep him from passing out from the pain. Good advice. He inhaled purposefully through his nose and blew it out again slowly.

While he held the pad in place, she looped the strips of T-shirt around his calf, cinched it at his shin and stood again. "That'll have to do for now."

He jerked a nod, cast another glance to Wayne—still unmoving—and limped with a sort of hop-jog-hop-jog lope toward the road.

Lilly was at his side, matching his pace for several steps before she stopped and spun away.

Dave clenched his fists at his sides in frustration. "Lilly, come on! What are you doing?" She motioned to his crumpled truck, and Dave grumbled under his breath. Having reliable transportation had been one of the few things he had going for him as he looked for stopgap employment until his leg was well enough to start ranching again. Thanks to Wayne—that SOB—he no longer had even that much. Plus he now had another several weeks of hobbling around before he could even try to get his old job back.

She pulled her hand free of his and gasped, "Your phone!"

Dave's heart kicked at the fresh hope, only to sink again the next second, when the reality of the situation settled over him. After almost two days, his already low battery would doubtlessly be dead.

Lilly trotted to the truck, yanked open the driver's door and ducked her head inside the cab. When she didn't immediately emerge with the device, Dave got restless. The more pressing need was to get the hell away from the house before Wayne revived. They could have minutes…or mere seconds.

"Lil, come on! It's probably dead, anyway."

What seemed like eons passed before she backed out of the cab with his phone in hand and a frown twisting her lips. "Yep. Dead. Crud!"

She jogged to him, and they once again headed down the drive at a hasty clip. But some nagging sense of wrong plagued Dave. He tried to riddle out what was bothering him while hurrying away from the house and ignoring the shooting ache in his leg as best he could.

"Which way?" Lilly asked as they neared the road. "Are we headed toward town or a neighbor or—?"

And the nebulous sense crystalized. "Not the road." He took a step back. "We'll be too easy to track on the road if Wayne follows us. Besides, the road follows the shape of the mountain. The shortest path to the nearest neighbor is that way." He turned ninety degrees and pointed through the woods. "As the crow flies, I'm guessing it's about a mile, mile and a half." He gave her a hard look. "Can you handle a cross-country trek?"

She gave his leg a meaningful look. "Can *you*?"

None of this would be easy, his wound throbbing the way it was and his skull feeling like a bull had kicked him. But getting Lilly to safety was paramount. He pressed his lips in a grim line of determination. "I'll manage."

Putting a hand at her back, he steered her into the trees and tall weeds that surrounded Helen's house. The terrain was steep, dotted with boulders, deadfall and dense, tangled vegetation. Dave made slow progress, using saplings and low branches along the way for support. They batted limbs and vines out of the way and trudged uphill as fast as they could. Soon they were both huffing and panting for oxygen, but Dave didn't dare slow the pace.

When Lilly found a thick branch lying near the animal trail they were following, she fetched it for Dave to use as a makeshift crutch. Though he couldn't put his full weight on it, the hiking stick helped his balance.

Within a few minutes, the woods gave way to rocks and sharper inclines. In order to continue moving away from the house, they'd have to climb, scaling steep walls of sandstone where only scrub weeds grew through the cracks in the rocky terrain. Dave hesitated only a moment weighing the best route up. Leading with his good leg, Dave stepped, planted the branch hiking stick, then dragged his injured leg behind him. Over and again. Until the muscles of his good leg ached with fatigue.

"Dave," Lilly called from behind him, "I'm sorry. I have to rest. My leg muscles are quivering."

He leaned heavily on his crutch and surveyed their

position. They were exposed out on this stretch of rock face. He reached toward her, offering a hand up to the small shelf where he waited for her. "Can you make it another hundred feet or so? I know it's steep and tiring, but if we can get over this ridge, we won't be so exposed."

Lilly dragged herself onto the narrow ledge with him, and he wrapped his arm around her waist to steady her. Curling her fingers into his arms, she angled her head to gauge the distance to the top, then met his eyes. "I think so."

As she panted through her mouth, gulping air, her breath fanned his neck, and a yearning to taste her lips crashed into him, harder than Wayne's fists had. He swallowed hard and tried not to think about how much he wanted to kiss her.

"Sorry. I haven't been to the gym nearly enough lately, and having not eaten much in the last two days…" She licked her lips, then smacked her mouth dryly. They both needed hydration, but had nothing but the clothes they were wearing.

"Don't apologize. I'm not criticizing. You're doing great." He thumbed a trickle of sweat from her temple before it reached her eye. "Ready?"

When she nodded, his pride in her determination swelled. He couldn't help but press a quick kiss on her forehead. She flashed a grin and seemed to muster a second wind from his encouragement.

They climbed on, and all the while, Dave pictured Wayne rousing and, full of murderous wrath, tracking them through the woods, hot on their heels. He cast furtive glances behind them, keeping his ears perked for signs Wayne was approaching. A bird of prey riding the air currents over the valley below them screeched a lonely call. A loose stone Lilly had unsettled as she climbed rattled as it skittered down the sandstone slope. A light breeze rustled the trees below them. And his own pulse thudded in his ears. But he heard no indication of a pursuer. Just the same…

This hundred or so yards of climbing took twice as long as the first few hundred had. Fatigue and a steeper angle of ascent double-teamed them and slowed them to a crawl. Almost literally, seeing as they used their hands as much as their legs to climb.

At the top of the ridge, Dave followed Lilly to the dappled shade of the trees nearest them. She dropped weakly, her chest heaving as she gasped for breath. "Just give me…a minute."

He eased himself down beside her, grateful for the respite, but also antsy to move on. He wouldn't rest easy until they'd contacted the sheriff, and he knew Wayne was in custody and Lilly was safe.

Swiping his forehead with the back of his hand, he winced when he hit the tender spot where he'd been smacked with the Glock. Or maybe he had a new dent in his head thanks to Wayne. The tussle for the gun was a bit of a blur. Fists and thrashing and ruthless punches.

He rubbed a hand lightly over his ribs, registering the ache. His injuries were another reason to keep moving. The longer he sat still, the more his abused body would stiffen and throb. Better to stay loose, moving until this whole situation was resolved. He knew the only things keeping him going now were adrenaline and stubbornness.

He glanced at Lilly, who'd lain back on the ground and closed her eyes.

"Better now?"

"Some. I'd love to stay here for an hour or two and just…nap."

He made a humming noise of acknowledgment. "Me, too. But we gotta go. We'll be headed downhill now. That'll be easier," he said, mentally adding, *for you.* Because he knew with limited use of his bad leg, finding the traction and braking strength to control his descent would be as rough as the uphill. Maybe worse.

Firming her mouth, she sent him a knowing look, as if she could read his thoughts.

Lilly sat up with a sigh and glanced at the terrain ahead. Gasped quietly. "Look."

He glanced in the direction she was looking and saw nothing. "What?"

"The butterfly on those flowers. It's so beautiful."

He refocused his attention on the butterfly just as it flew from one blossom to another.

"A Melissa blue," she said. "See how the top of its wings are bluish and the underside is creamy with black spots? I think that means it's a male." She paused as the winged creature fluttered around the clump of wild-flowers, then flew their way. When it lit on her sleeve, Lilly's eyes rounded, and the pure joy in her face tugged deep in Dave's chest.

"I've loved butterflies since I was a kid," she said quietly, as if afraid to startle the one resting near her shoulder. "They kinda represent hope to me. The courage to keep going when times are tough." She paused to watch the butterfly's slow wing flap as it turned on her arm. "And love."

"That explains your choice for the tattoo." He gave her a teasing grin.

"Amongst others. I kinda collect them. My mom gave me my first butterfly trinket on a family vacation after my dad left us. That's where it started." She bit her bottom lip. "She got Helen a little stuffed bear with a pink heart embroidered on its chest."

He nodded. "I've seen it. She kept it on her dresser."

She gave a sad-sounding sigh. "I just packed it up with some of her other childhood mementos the other day."

With a silent flap of its wings, the butterfly flew away, disappearing behind a clump of weedy-looking yellow flowers. Lilly rolled her shoulders and shoved back to her feet. "Okay, I'm good to go."

He grunted in pain as he dragged himself up and steadied himself with the hiking stick. He hated the worried look she gave him, hated knowing his injuries could delay Wayne's capture. And Lilly's rescue. He caught her arm to gain her full attention.

"Getting word to the cops is our priority," he said. "If I slow you down, leave me."

She snorted derisively. "Yeah, right."

"I mean it, Lil. If I prove a hindrance, you go on without me. Keep going north, toward that valley you can see through those trees." He pointed in the direction he meant, but she fixed him with a stubborn frown.

"We're in this together, Dave. You didn't leave me when I was struggling going up the mountain, and I won't leave you as we go down."

"Lilly, I—"

She pressed a hand to his mouth to silence him. "I won't abandon a man with a head injury, so stop arguing."

He decided not to remind her she had left Wayne with a head injury. No point adding to her guilt over that.

She twisted her mouth and leaned closer. "Speaking of which, look at me. I need to check your pupils."

He grumbled his discontent. "We don't need any more delays."

"Five seconds, you obstinate cowboy." She pinned him with a steady gaze, staring deep into his eyes. For medical reasons. Because he could have a concussion. He knew that.

But the truth didn't stop his heart from bucking when he stared deeply into her green eyes. Green like the lakes that dotted the Colorado landscape, their waters clear and sparkling in the sun like jewels.

He knew he shouldn't feel anything remotely like the yearning that blossomed in his chest. Acknowledging his attraction to Lilly should feel like a betrayal to Helen. Instead it felt right. Real. Strong.

The five seconds she asked for passed, and she didn't look away. Dave swallowed hard, seeing the subtle change in her expression. Her all-business directness softened. Warmed.

Her breathing grew shallow and quick, matching his own. Dave canted toward her. Just an inch or so. Then closer. She didn't retreat. And so he brushed his lips over hers.

Chapter 15

Liquid heat streaked through Dave, making him forget the throbbing under his skull and the blazing sting in his calf.

The kiss was quick, barely a touch. Testing.

She inhaled sharply. Closed her eyes. But stayed where she was, her lips parting slightly.

Raising a hand to her cheek, he kissed her again. His lips clung to hers for a staggering heartbeat before he angled his mouth to capture hers more fully. She deepened the kiss, and he took the chance to explore the shape and feel of her lips moving against his. Pure heaven…and something they had no time for.

The crack of a twig snapped him from the blissful moment, yanking him back to the reality of the moment. To the criminal who could be pursuing them even now. He cast his gaze left and right, twisted to check behind them.

"Dave, what…?"

"Thought I heard something."

Now Lilly searched the area around them with an anxious look denting her brow.

With the help of his hiking stick for leverage, he turned full-circle, found nothing suspicious. But…

He held his hand out to her. "C'mon. We need to go."

She put her hand in his, and his chest tightened as he wrapped his fingers around hers.

The connection he felt with her shook him to his core. Tantalized him. Confused him.

Because what he felt for Lilly was truer than anything he'd known with Helen. With Lilly, the emotion that stole his breath and sank to his core felt more assuredly like love.

A short distance down the opposite side of the mountain, Lilly spotted a house with a wide porch. She'd almost missed it. Her thoughts had been so wrapped up in the kisses she'd shared with Dave that, had a flash of light not snagged her attention, she might have marched on through the woods, right past their salvation. A bird feeder with glass sides hung from the rafters on the home's porch and swung slightly in the breeze. As the feeder moved, the glass reflected the sun with a spark of brilliant light, likely what had caught her attention.

"Look!" She pointed out the home to Dave.

"Excellent. I'm not sure how much farther I'd have made it on this leg."

They adjusted their course to hike to the split-level

home, and he gripped her hand as they turned off the animal trail they'd been using.

Lilly's gaze dipped briefly to his injured calf as they ventured into the dense woods, the most direct path to the house. The strenuous hike couldn't be good for his wound. "As soon as we get a call in to the police, our next order of business is tending your leg. The sooner I disinfect and bind it up properly, the better."

He glanced her way, lifting a corner of his mouth. "No argument from me."

"Good."

And then they needed to have a serious conversation about what the hell had happened on the top of the mountain. Her lips tingled with the memory of his passionate kiss.

She sighed. Dwelling on the kiss wasn't helpful now and so, trying to refocus her thoughts, she added, "As it is, that bullet wound will probably leave a nasty scar."

He snorted. "What's one more? Years of ranch work and the surgery to rebuild my leg last December have already left me looking a bit like a road map."

She quickly squelched the niggle of curiosity about where the other scars might be. Not her concern. His body wasn't hers to discover, to explore and to savor. And yet, she couldn't deny there'd been something in that embrace, the look in his eyes…

Dave held a large branch out of her way, allowing her to lead the way around a rocky area and down a sharp incline.

"Watch your step. These rocks and loose dirt are tricky," he said.

True to his warning, small stones skittered and rolled

as she found the best path, careful to find purchase before moving forward. At the bottom of the slope, she waited as he inched his way down the incline sideways, using his good leg for support and the hiking stick for balance.

He hadn't said anything about the kiss as they hiked. Did that mean he'd dismissed it as nothing, or was he stewing over the implications, as she was? Maybe she was overthinking things. Maybe after all they'd been through together, the kiss was just an expression of friendship and relief that they were away from Wayne.

She mentally tested that theory, examining all the angles as they trudged through the dense underbrush, fanned away clouds of gnats and picked their way down the rugged terrain toward the isolated home. Would she have shared a friendly kiss with a man she wasn't attracted to? Her gut tightened. No, she admitted. She had an undeniable physical attraction to Dave. Her heart tripped thinking about the prickly heat and sensual hunger that had suffused her body when they'd kissed. Dave was a skilled kisser, no doubt. And she'd grown to appreciate him and his kindness, his protective instincts, his courage over the past two days.

But he was *Dave*. Helen's Dave. How could she entertain any notions of a relationship with her late sister's boyfriend? She scowled at the idea and, distracted by her conflicting thoughts, stumbled over a root.

Immediately, Dave had his hand at her elbow, steadying her. Because, damn it, that was the kind of helpful, considerate guy she was finding him to be. Despite her preconceived notions based on conversations with her venting sister.

"Thanks," she said, swiping a thin sheen of sweat from her forehead. As she turned to continue downhill toward the house, Dave caught her arm.

"Stop! Don't move," he said, his tone tense and his attention fixed on something just ahead of them in the rocks.

"What?" she asked, jerking her gaze around to search the path for a person, an animal… Then a movement on the ground caught her eye, as the perfectly camouflaged creature shook its tail. A rattlesnake.

Terror streaked through Lilly as she leaped back with a scream.

"Freeze!" Dave warned. "If we don't bother it, if we don't make it feel threatened, it will slither away." Then under his breath, he amended, "I hope."

"O-o-oh, God," she muttered, her voice trembling, "I hate snakes."

Dave slowly put a hand around hers and squeezed. "He's more scared of you than you are of him."

She snorted quietly. "That is the worst of clichés and does nothing to calm me down." She swallowed hard and shuddered, watching the reptile's tongue flick in and out. "Who even started that sorry line?"

He gave her side-eye. "I don't—" He sighed and adjusted his grip on his walking stick.

"Whatever. Just be still. They don't see well, but they detect motion and vibration. Once he settles down a bit, we're going to back slowly away."

Lilly held her breath and squeezed Dave's hand while her heart thrashed against her ribs. When the snake began to uncoil and slither out from under the rock, she whimpered. "It's coming toward us!"

"Easy," Dave said calmly, though she heard the undertone of gravity in his voice. "Both of you, stay calm…" He eased his walking stick toward the snake, slowly and gently redirecting the snake's course. The serpent stopped, scenting the stick with its tongue before moving in the other direction, into the rocks.

When it disappeared, Lilly released a tremulous breath. "Do you think it has friends around here?" She swept the area with a glance, her heart in her throat.

"Likely. The weather's warming up, and they're coming out of hibernation looking for a meal and a place to sun. Just watch your step. I'll lead."

Reluctantly, she released her grip on his hand so he could pick his way the rest of the distance down the slope to the house with the long porch.

Well, Lilly thought to herself, if nothing else, the snake helped redirect her circular and unresolved thoughts about the state of and future of her relationship with Dave. She paid careful attention to each footfall, each handhold, every step as they made their way to the porch.

"I don't see cars or a garage," Dave said as they crossed the yard of the mountain home.

"The bird feeder that caught my attention is empty, too. And there are no chairs on the porch. Who has a porch like this with that spectacular view and doesn't keep chairs outside?"

The wooden porch shook and their feet made hollow thumps as the crossed to the front door and knocked. Waited.

When no one answered their summons, Dave knocked again and called, "Hello? Anyone home?"

After another several disappointing seconds of silence, Lilly asked, "Do you suppose it's a vacation home? A rental or something?"

He lifted a shoulder. "Who knows?"

He tested the knob, which, naturally, didn't budge. "You're not going to break in, are you?"

He glanced at her, then stepped back, giving the solid, windowless door his scrutiny. "Long enough to use the phone to call the cops? Uh, yeah. Unless you have a better plan?"

"Let's look in a few windows, see if any are unlocked. You're not going to get far through that door." She waved a hand at the entry. "It's solid."

He tested the door again, giving another firm knock and shout while she strolled down the porch, tugging at windows. When she shielded her eyes and peeked in the dusty glass, she spotted the burglar bars reinforcing the window locks. The house was definitely locked up tight and prowler-proofed.

Sighing her disappointment and frustration, she braced her hands on her hips and moved to the porch rail at the back of the house to admire the panoramic view of the foothills to the Rockies.

"So pretty. And peaceful," she whispered.

Then her gaze snagged on a roof a short distance below and to the left.

Her pulse tripped. *Another house.*

"Dave!" She hurried back along the wraparound porch to the front of the vacant house. "We don't have to break in here. We have another option."

After another several minutes spent picking their way down the mountain toward the new house, they found a path that had obviously been beaten by the home's occupants as a trail through the scenic woods. Lilly kept a sharp eye for more snakes, not wanting a repeat of their earlier encounter.

"Do you see anyone? Any sign someone's home?" She studied the creek stone and rough-hewn wood house as they clambered down the trail to the side yard. Clothes were hung out to dry on a rope strung between two trees and a compact car was parked in the driveway. Both good signs.

"I think I can see the TV on through that front window," Dave replied. He pointed to a plate-glass window that faced the woods.

She paused as Dave hesitated at the edge of the trees and looked warily around the yard before crossing the grass. "What's wrong?"

"Maybe nothing," he replied and followed the stone walkway to the front stoop. Inside the television was blaring what sounded like a soap opera. Dave nodded toward the end of the driveway, where she spotted a paved street and a yellow mailbox. "But this house is close to the main road. If Wayne did wake up and follow the highway toward town, he could have seen this place and stopped in with his special brand of chaos."

"One way to find out," Lilly replied and knocked loudly on the front door.

The volume on the television lowered. Voices. The sound and vibration of footsteps approaching the door.

Lilly held her breath and bit her lip. *Please don't let it be Wayne. Please don't let it be—*

An older woman with steel-gray sausage curls and

wire-rimmed glasses opened the door and peered out, the security chain still fastened. "Yes?"

"I'm sorry to bother you, but we have an emergency and need to use your phone. May we, please?" Lilly asked.

The woman took one look at Dave's battered face and bleeding leg and blanched. "Heavenly days! What happened to you?"

"Long story," he said. "But we need your help."

"Clearly!" She pressed a hand to her mouth and glanced into the yard behind them as if considering her options. "I heard gunfire earlier. Was that—?"

"Yes," Lilly interrupted. She lifted a hand to stave off the woman's questions. "We'll explain everything. Right now, Dave needs medical attention, and we need to call the police right away. If we could just come in…"

The woman bobbed her head, making her gray pin curls bounce. "Just a moment." She closed the door and Lilly heard the chain being removed. When the older woman opened the door again, she said, "I already called the sheriff when I heard the gun shooting off." She took a step back and held the door open wider. "There's no hunting allowed in this part of town, and I hate to think of anyone shooting the deer and rabbits my husband and I enjoy seeing in our yard." She gave Dave a hooded, glowering look as if she believed he'd been hunting illegally.

"We weren't hunting," he explained as he hobbled into her living room. "In fact, you could say we were the prey."

The lady's brown eyes widened. "What in the world?"

An older man, presumably the husband the woman

had mentioned, appeared from the kitchen. "Who is it, Joanie?"

Dave offered the man his hand. "Dave Giblan, sir. We need to use your phone. Do you have a landline?"

"Henry Lee and my wife, Joanie. Help yourself." He waved a hand toward a rotary dial phone sitting by the couch.

Lilly blinked and suppressed a smile. Her grandmother had had a rotary dial phone, and she wished sometimes she'd saved the thing for nostalgic reasons. Dave started toward the phone, and she caught his arm. "Maybe you should go to the bathroom and wait for me." She sent a meaningful look to his bloody leg. "We don't want to get the Lees' carpet or furniture dirty."

Mrs. Lee gave Lilly a grateful smile. "Thank you, dear. You're welcome to the phone in the kitchen. And I can get first-aid things from the back for you."

"What in tarnation happened to you, young man?" Mr. Lee asked as he led them to the kitchen, where the sink was piled with dirty dishes and the air smelled of the freshly baked muffins that sat on the counter. Lilly's mouth watered, and her stomach growled. It had been hours since she'd eaten the peanut butter sandwich for breakfast, and the hike had left her thirsty and more ravenous than she'd been in a long time.

"In what way were you prey?" Mrs. Lee asked.

"Did you hear about the bank robbery two days ago at the First Bank of Boyd Valley?" Dave arched an eyebrow in query.

Mr. Lee's spine stiffened, and he put a hand on his wife's arm to pull her closer. "Yes, we heard. One of our best friends, Floyd Hanover, was killed." He narrowed a suspicious glare on them. "What do you two have to do with that?"

"We were both at the bank when it happened," Lilly said.

Mrs. Lee gasped and clapped a hand to her cheek. "Dear Lord!"

"Yeah, well, worse than that, the robber was hiding out at her house—" Dave seemed to be about to correct himself about the owner of the house but frowned and continued "—and he took us hostage when we showed up there."

"He's had us tied up in a bedroom ever since," Lilly finished when Dave paused, his jaw tightening with fury.

Mrs. Lee glanced at her husband then back at Lilly. "Where is your house, dear? You don't mean to tell me the robber has been on our mountain the whole time?"

Lilly nodded. "That's what I'm saying. And he still is. That's why we need to call the police."

Mrs. Lee paled again and snatched up the receiver of the wall phone—this one had a push-button dial pad—and shoved it toward Lilly. "By all means." Then to Dave and her husband, "Should we leave the house? Go into town somewhere until he's caught?" Her hand fluttered over her heart. "Good grief! A murderer loose on our mountain?"

While Lilly called 911, Dave sent Mr. Lee a hard look. "Do you own any guns? A handgun or hunting rifle?"

The older man shook his head. "No. Had my fill of weapons when I went to 'Nam, and I don't hunt. We've never felt the need to have any weapons here for home protection."

Mrs. Lee piped up. "We have bear spray. It's an old can. Haven't needed any in years."

Lilly and Dave exchanged a look, and Dave said, "Get it. It's better than nothing." Then rubbing a hand on his bare chest, he added, "And could I trouble you for a shirt? I ripped mine up for this. " He pointed to the improvised bandage on his leg.

Outside, the short *whoop* of a siren announced the arrival of a sheriff's deputy. Mr. Lee looked out the window over the kitchen sink. "They're probably here to talk to us about our earlier call about shots fired."

Lilly handed the phone to Mrs. Lee. "We still need an ambulance for Dave, but I want to talk to the sheriff. Will you finish with the operator, give them your address?"

With that, she, Dave and Mr. Lee headed out to meet the arriving deputy.

A bright light was shining in his eyes, and his head hurt like hell. Wayne cracked his eyes open and blinked, trying to place himself. Outside. The sun was baking him from a cloudless sky. Why was he—?

He sat up quickly, making his head spin and his abdomen ache. Damn it! He hated feeling this way, eaten up by the damn tumor. When he put his hand up to cradle his side where he felt the throbbing under his arm, a memory came down on him like a cloudburst. He'd been shot. The cowboy at the bank—

Barking a cuss word, he whipped his head left and right, scanning the yard where he sat. Gone. His hostages were gone. He bit out another foul word and pinched the bridge of his nose, which gave a throb of protest. Broken. The truck's airbag and Hero's head butt. A few deep breaths began to clear the cobwebs that muddled his thinking. He had to act. Make a new plan and quick.

Another search of the area told him the Glock was gone, as well. Stolen by Mr. Hero and the woman, no doubt. Lilly. Gritting his teeth, he shook his head and growled under his breath. He'd actually liked Lilly a little. She'd been easy on the eyes and cooperated with tending his wounds. Her insightfulness about what he'd been thinking unnerved him some, but...

But it had all been lies. His gut curled with anger. She'd never cared one bit about him or his cancer or what he was doing with his life. Acid puddled inside him. He'd given her too much leeway, and she'd betrayed him. Taken the gun from him and fired—

Grunting his rage and frustration, Wayne struggled to his feet and staggered toward the house where he'd holed up the last two days. His whole body hurt. If he'd ever thought he'd get used to the pain, he'd been wrong.

Of course, wrestling with that bastard cowboy hadn't helped. He dabbed at his lip and drew back bloody fingers. He thought of the bottle of painkillers inside. No way would he go anywhere without those. He wished he could take a couple now—hell, maybe he'd take the whole damn bottle and be done with it all—but pushed aside the notion. The pills would make him groggy, and he needed to be sharp enough to make a plan. Disappear.

As he stumbled past his old car, he grimaced. He

should have known the cowboy's promise of helping fix up the engine was a trick, damn it! He did a double take when his gaze passed the back tire. Flat as a pancake. And he had no spare. He braced a hand on the side panel and bent to take a closer look. The damn thing hadn't been flat earlier today, when they'd come out. How—?

He thought about Lilly firing off the gun, aiming at nothing particular…or had she? Maybe she'd shot out his tire on purpose. He gritted his teeth even harder. Fury boiled in him and made him sway on his feet. When he caught up to Lilly and Hero Boy—

Fisting his hands, he stalked into the house and down the hall to the bathroom to retrieve his pills. He spotted the pills on the back of the toilet, but before he got them, he also caught a glimpse of himself in the mirror.

His hair was disheveled, his shirt soiled and torn, his face and arms covered in sweat, dirt…and blood. His tussle with Hero had left his nose bleeding, a cut over his eye dripping and any number of scrapes on his arms and face welling droplets of blood. He remembered what Lilly had said about dirt in wounds, something called *sitsis* or *sepies* or something that could kill you if you didn't clean out wounds. He was pretty sure she'd just been trying to scare him, may have even been lying, but he figured he could spare thirty seconds to wash his face and arms. Just in case. All the bandages and antiseptics Lilly had used on his gunshot wound were still spread on the counter around the sink.

With a huff, he quickly removed his watch and laid it on the back of the toilet next to his pills. He filled the sink with water and began rinsing his arms and splashing his face before using a dab of the liquid soap to carefully wash the scrapes. He'd just cut off the water when, in the distance, he heard the whoop of a police siren.

His breath snagged in his lungs. Holy hell! Lilly and Hero had had a head start to get the police!

Why in blue blazes hadn't he thought of that sooner? His brain really was scrambled! God only knew how long he'd been blacked out, how much lead time Lilly and her boyfriend had. Instead of bitching and moaning about his aches and pains and flat tires, he had to get lost. And fast. He huffed through gritted teeth. But with his tire flat and Hero's truck wrecked—

He grabbed a towel and wiped his face with one pass, just enough to get the stinging, soapy water from around his eyes. Tossing the towel on the back of the toilet, he snagged his bottle of painkillers. Go, go, go!

He had to make tracks before the cops showed up.

He knew, as well as he knew what he'd do to Lilly and Hero if he ever saw them again, that the police were on their way to this hideout. They could be here in minutes. Seconds.

He'd have to go on foot. Would have to hide in the woods. Would have to travel light.

But most important, he had to clear out. *Now.*

Chapter 16

"Are we going to talk about it?" Lilly didn't look up from her work cleaning Dave's bullet wound. She wasn't sure what she would see in his face if she were to look at him now, but she also didn't know what her own eyes might betray, so she kept her head down, her hands busy.

The bullet had left a deep gash, but hadn't hit any major blood vessels, thank God. He'd need to go to the hospital for serious stitching as soon as possible. The emergency operator had promised an ambulance would come, but the two used by the nearest hospital were both out on more urgent calls.

She and Dave had talked to the sheriff's deputy who'd arrived at the Lees' house for a few minutes before Lilly had convinced everyone that her tending to

Dave's leg took precedence over a detailed recounting of the last three days. The authorities had the essentials regarding Wayne's identity, last known location and the highlights of their captivity. Deputy Strozier would be waiting to finish their interview and drive them to the hospital after Lilly finished disinfecting and rewrapping Dave's leg with supplies from Mrs. Lee's medicine cabinet and the deputy's patrol-car first-aid kit.

Dave sat on the closed toilet while she perched on the edge of the bathtub dabbing disinfectant on his gashed leg. He hadn't answered her question, so she flicked up her gaze. "Well?"

Mr. Lee had given him a basic white undershirt, which was just a tad too small and hugged Dave's broad shoulders.

"What is there to talk about?" he asked, but when he met her eyes briefly, she could tell he clearly knew what she meant.

She huffed, then couldn't mask the frustration in her tone. "Oh, I don't know. Maybe sports. Or politics. Or maybe the fact that we kissed about an hour ago."

He raised one eyebrow, and his expression remained nonplussed. "Mmm. Football's my favorite. Love the Broncos. Don't follow the Rockies too closely, but I'll catch a game here and there. And I generally avoid talking politics. You?"

She growled under her breath. "Dave…"

He chuckled as he sighed. "Why do women have to *talk* about *everything*. Analyzing and rehashing." He made a face, shook his head and fixed his gaze on hers. "Yeah, we kissed. And for the record, it was a pretty damn good kiss. A *great* kiss." He reached

for her cheek, and his fingertips sent sparks skittering through her veins. "A very meaningful, very...*hot*
kiss." He paused, his gaze widening as he stared into
her eyes. "Am I alone in thinking so?"

"Uh...no. It was..." His touch, his gentle gaze and
the memory of just how hot their kiss had been co-
alesced inside her. "But that's not the point. Helen—"

His jaw tightened, and his chin dropped as he averted
his eyes.

"How can we—?" she began, but he cut her off.

"Lilly..."

Her breath froze in her lungs as she watched his face
morph through guilt and regret to determination and
conviction. "I know you're going to think I'm the worst
of men for saying this, but... Helen is dead. I will never
forget her. She was special. But—" He inhaled and exhaled slowly, as if cleansing his grief from his body.
"The truth is, I never had with her, the kind of..." He
paused, his fingers waving in a way that told her he was
searching for the right word. "Chemistry? Heat? Connection? That I felt with you during that kiss."

Lilly's gut somersaulted. What did she do with that
admission? The woman in her, who had savored the kiss
as much as Dave had, wanted to exult that he shared
her feelings. The grieving sister wanted to take offense
at the slight to Helen. The wounded, abandoned little
girl, who'd grown to be a betrayed wife and divorcée
cautioned her to be skeptical and go slowly. She may
have seen some of Dave's best characteristics during
their ordeal together, but she couldn't discount Helen's
impressions of him as uncommitted so easily.

And what of Helen? How did she justify the feelings

she was forming for her late sister's boyfriend without sinking in a quagmire of guilt? She had no answers, so she did the only thing she knew to do. Retreat.

"I'm sorry if I misled you, Dave. I was emotional before...when we kissed." She swallowed hard. This would be so much easier if he weren't staring at her with his incisive eyes. His mahogany gaze pierced her, seemed to be able to read her deepest most private thoughts. All the more reason to put some distance between them.

He angled his head, and his expression darkened. "It's more than the kiss, Lil. The connection I feel with you started when—"

"Dave, stop." She sat taller and searched for the courage to do what she knew she must. "The kiss was a mistake. I was rash and impulsive to have kissed you back. It can't happen again."

"So that's it? We share a mind-blowing kiss that more than hints at amazing chemistry, and you can dismiss it as a mistake? Walk away without exploring the potential for—"

"You're my sister's fiancé!" she cried, louder than she intended. She cut a glance to the door, certain that the Lees and the waiting deputy had heard her.

"Not quite." A muscle in his jaw jumped as he clenched his teeth, his diamond-sharp gaze still cutting into her. "I never got the chance to propose—"

"A technicality."

"And Helen is gone. I'm sorry to keep being so blunt about—"

"I know she is. But it hasn't been that long." She tossed the wad of gauze she'd been cleaning his wound with in the trash with more force than necessary. A strange sensation, like flapping bird wings, battered her chest. The more he pressed her and shot down her arguments, the more the pulsing grew. She began to feel panicky and light-headed. "Doesn't propriety dictate something about not hooking up with your sister's boyfriend only five months after she dies? If not, it should! I can't do it!"

He turned up a palm. "The timing is awkward. But we aren't on a schedule. We can take—"

"No." She shook her head vehemently. She stood abruptly, and his foot, which had been on her lap, dropped to the floor with a jarring thump. "End of discussion." She scooted past him to get to the bathroom door.

He grunted in pain, or perhaps frustration, as he struggled to his feet. "Lilly!"

She glanced back at him, the sense of fluttery panic and confusion tightening her throat. "I'm sorry," she rasped. "I just can't."

Chapter 17

The not-so-distant sound of a siren whined briefly as Wayne stumbled through the house to collect a couple items before making tracks for the woods. His haul from the bank for starters.

He hadn't gone to this much trouble to get the cash, just to ditch it at the first sign of trouble. The first night at Lilly's house, he'd transferred the money to a small duffel bag that he could sling over his shoulder. He'd then stuffed the duffel in the washing machine as a temporary hiding place. Not the best choice but good enough at the time. At the top of the duffel he'd left room for a few more items, but the proximity of the siren left him no choice but to grab the bag and go.

As he passed through the kitchen from the utility room, headed for the back door, he snagged a banana, a butcher knife, a bag of raisin bread and a half-empty water bottle. He jammed the items in the duffel as he hurried down the back steps and sprinted, loping stiffly, toward the cover of the trees.

He knew he'd be leaving a trail of crushed grass and bent stems in his wake that a good tracker could follow, but he saw no recourse. He couldn't fly over the grass, and if he stayed put at the house, he'd be a sitting duck for the cops.

His best chance was to find a stream to hide his tracks, or perhaps walk in a few circles and retrace his steps to create false leads. That would all be time-consuming. Maybe his best move was just to go as far and fast as he could before the cops caught his scent.

Surely there were other homes on the mountain. He could steal a car and get the hell out of town.

He found what must have been a deer or elk trail. Besides the scat littering the ground, the tall grasses and scrub branches had been trampled and bent to make a path through the underbrush. He knew better than to hope that the pre-flattened grass and broken limbs would mask his progress, but the animal trail made for easier travel. He plowed his way into the woods, needing to move as far and as fast as he could. He kept his eyes open for a hollowed log, a cave, anything that might provide a hiding place. He quickly passed from woods to the rocky slope of the mountain, and his spirits lifted. His trail would be easier to mask on the rocks. But which way did he go? Better to be moving away from town than stumble blindly back into a populated area, where he could be spotted.

Grampa Moore had taught him how to use the sun and his analog watch as a compass—

He jerked his arm up and stared at his bare wrist with a sinking sensation in the pit of his stomach. Where was his watch? He'd last had it when—

Wayne spewed a litany of creative curses. He'd taken it off to wash up before he bolted from the house. In his head, his father's voice laughed at him. *Now who's a screwup?*

Urgency pounded in his brain. He needed that watch! He had little in this world that truly mattered to him, but that watch had meaning for him. Importance. Maybe he was a fool to give a damn about a family heirloom. His family hadn't valued him much, so why should he care about a stupid timepiece just because it had been his father's, his grandfather's before that?

He wanted to throw back his head and scream at the top of his lungs. The angry, frustrated, disgusted shout rose in his throat, choking him. But he stopped it. Gagged on it. Shoved it back down. Noise was his enemy just now. Venting his ire would draw the cops to him.

Instead, he focused the surging choler in his blood to fuel his battered body. He made his choice quickly. The path of least resistance. He headed down the hillside, picking his way as fast as he could, limping, staggering. He was down but not out.

And then he saw it. A cave. More a crack in a large rock really, but he could wedge himself in if he tried. He shove the duffel in first and after squeezing it through the initial narrow opening, the bag dropped. He blinked, worried for a moment that he'd lost the bank haul, then realized what had happened. If he could get through the slim crack, the space behind was wider.

Clenching his teeth against the pain, he wiggled his body through the fissure in the rock face. His skin scraped and his clothes snagged, but he made it through to the dank crevice about the size of a coffin. Shoving that disturbing image aside, he hunkered down. He wasn't sure how long the cops would search the mountain before they gave up. But Wayne would wait.

Lilly accompanied Dave to the hospital, even though he assured her she didn't need to. Where else was she supposed to go? Helen's house was off-limits while the sheriff's department combed through the debris of Wayne's time there, collecting evidence to be used against him when he was caught and brought to justice.

After all the hours she'd worked in the Denver ER, she should have felt more at home in the emergency room waiting area. But being on this side of the double doors, being the one waiting for news about someone she cared about, left her edgy and fretful. And, yes, she cared about Dave. But she wasn't prepared to give her feelings toward him any further name or definition at this point. She determinedly pushed the images of his expressive eyes and handsome, battered face from her thoughts while she paced the small waiting room.

A woman sitting in one of the hard chairs with her hand wrapped in a bloody bandage gave Lilly the stink eye as Lilly continued to restlessly pace.

"Do you mind?" the woman asked, nodding to the television opposite her. "You're blocking my view."

Lilly flashed a weak grin and dropped in the nearest chair. "Sorry."

She gave the muted television a cursory glance. The screen flashed images of Helen's house surrounded by patrol cars superimposed with a picture of Wayne in the corner of the screen. Her breath snagged as a fresh spike of adrenaline jarred her already ragged nerves.

"Can you turn the volume up?" she asked the woman.

"I don't have the remote. Ask at the desk."

After finding the control buttons on the TV taped over, Lilly hustled over to the reception desk to ask for a remote. But no one was behind the counter. Returning to the chairs, she tried to guess what was happening based on the changing images. No headlines scrolled at the bottom of the screen like her own local channel used. Frustration gnawed at her.

How had things gone down when the sheriff arrived at the house? Had Wayne still been unconscious in the backyard? Had he been in the house when the patrol cars arrived? Had he surrendered without a fight or was he taken down by force?

"Ms. Shaw?" a nurse called from the double swinging doors leading to the patient exam rooms. "You may come back now."

Lilly tore herself away from the mesmerizing images and hustled to follow the nurse. The nurse took her to an exam room, where Lilly found not only Dave, his leg wound wrapped with proper sterile dressing, but also the sheriff's deputy who had answered the call to the Lees' house.

Lilly pulled up when she saw Deputy Strozier and cast a worried look to Dave. "What's happened?"

"Just wanting to follow up with you, ma'am." Deputy Strozier motioned for Lilly to come in and have a seat. Once she was settled next to Dave, he closed the door and faced them with a stern expression.

"Well," the officer said, removing his hat long enough to scratch his head and pull his face in a hesitant frown, "there's good news and bad news."

Lilly's stomach bunched. "I've always hated that lead-in. Bad news is bad news no matter how you soften it with half-hearted positives."

He flashed a half smile of chagrin. "You're right. So here it is. We haven't located Wayne Moore yet."

Beside her, Dave sighed his frustration. "He couldn't have gone far without a vehicle."

"No. Not without a vehicle, but—"

Lilly groaned. "He stole a car somewhere?"

The deputy shook his head. "No evidence of that at this point. But it's a possibility we're pursuing."

"Do you have *any* leads on where he is?" Dave asked.

The deputy shook his head. "Nothing concrete. We've put out an APB for him and have searchers covering the area around your house." He divided a look between her and Dave, his expression growing more confident. "Look, it's just a matter of time. He won't get far before he's spotted, whether he's on foot or if he's found some wheels."

Dave put an arm around Lilly and drew her closer to his side. She didn't miss the fact that his instinct was to comfort her, even now that they were safe. And despite her rejection of him. His presence, as it had during their hours held hostage, reassured her, centered her.

"The thing is, we don't know what he's up to at the moment and what his plan is," Strozier continued.

Lilly angled her face toward Dave, and they exchanged a mutually concerned look. Wayne was still out there. Possibly still near the house.

Strozier's countenance firmed. "I know that's not the news you wanted to hear. But we will get him. He killed a security guard and robbed a bank, imprisoned the two of you…" He paused, squinting one eye as he pinned them with his gaze. "Trust me. Every law enforcement officer in the state is looking for him. He *will* be caught."

"Do you think he'll go back to Lilly's house?" Dave asked, and Lilly's breath whooshed from her lungs as if she'd been slammed by a wrestler. The notion had toyed at the back of her mind, but she'd been reluctant to give it voice, as if by speaking the horrid thought she might make it happen. Turning an expectant gaze toward Strozier, she bit her bottom lip.

The deputy twisted his mouth as he considered the question. "Doubtful. We searched the place top to bottom and didn't find the cash from the bank. He has to know the place will be watched." He shook his head. "No. I see no good reason why he would go back to your house, but we plan to post a man outside to watch your place, just in case."

She exhaled the breath it seemed she'd been holding since the ordeal began.

Pulling his shoulders back, Strozier brightened. "Which brings me to the good news. By tonight you should be clear to return to the house. I understand the forensics team was almost finished last time I talk to them. I'm afraid the team leaves a mess. Fingerprint dust and—"

She raised a hand. "That is the least of my worries. I was planning to hire a cleanup crew to scour it top to bottom before putting it on the market, anyway. I'll just pay the cleaners extra."

"Thank you, Deputy Strozier." Dave offered his hand to the man, and they shook before the deputy headed out of the exam room.

When they were alone again, Dave asked, "Are you going to head back to the house then?"

"I guess I am. After I replace my phone. I'm so ready for a hot shower and a good night's sleep."

Dave wrapped warm fingers around her elbow and turned her to face him. "You could have both at my place, if you wanted."

She wiggled loose from his hold and eyed him skeptically. "Thank you for the offer, but I need to feed Maddie. With all the strangers and noise in the house, she's bound to be a wreck and will need her person for comfort. Besides, I can't avoid the house forever."

His brow dipped in concern. "No, but you *can* avoid it until that bastard Wayne is caught. Bring Maddie to my place. Strozier might not think Wayne will be back, but I'm not willing to gamble on it. I'd feel better knowing you were safe from him."

A shiver slithered up her spine when she thought of going back in the house, full of reminders of the past few days. From the forensic team's mess to the discarded scraps of packing tape left from their escape attempts, the house would be full of bad memories.

Well, not all of the memories would be so awful.

She'd make herself focus on thoughts of the intimate and sometimes silly conversations she had with Dave. His kindness to Maddie. The first tantalizing hints of attraction as she'd fished blindly in his pocket for his keys.

She exhaled and firmed her resolve. That attraction was exactly why she needed to get away from Dave. She was too likely to give in to the pull that kept drawing her toward him. She may have told him "no" earlier, but something deep inside her whispered "yes!" She needed time and distance to quiet that voice before she made a colossal mistake.

Lilly cleared her throat and took a step back. "Deputy Strozier said they'd post a man to watch the house for the next couple of days. I'll be fine."

A nurse arrived in the room with a clipboard in one hand and a pair of crutches in the other. "All set. The doctor has signed your discharge papers. I just need your John Hancock and you are free to leave."

Lilly waited while the ER nurse went over Dave's orders for keeping his wound clean. The nurse also handed over the crutches and gave him prescriptions for an antibiotic and a painkiller. Once all the papers were signed and orders given, Lilly followed Dave out of the hospital to the parking lot, where they each waited for an Uber—hers to take her to her car at the bank and his to his home.

Dave leaned heavily on his crutches, his own fatigue and pain etched in his face. "I'm not giving up on you, Lilly. And I still think going back to the house is a bad ide—"

"Stop right there." She held up a hand to cut him

off. "I need to be alone tonight. I need to decompress. To think."

He lifted an eyebrow as if she'd just given him fresh hope. "You will think then? About us?"

"I doubt I'll think of much else," she admitted.

His lips tugged in a lopsided grin. "Good. Don't close your mind to it. Listen to your heart, Lil."

A small sedan pulled up, and the driver called, "You waiting for an Uber?"

"You take this one," he said, opening the car door for her.

Leaning in, he asked the driver for a pen. When he backed out, he took Lilly's hand and wrote a phone number on it. "Call if you change your mind or need *anything*."

She gave him a long last look, her gaze clinging to his dark chocolate eyes. In his gaze, she read his regrets, his longing…his affection. More affection than she'd known in years. Maybe in her life. Had Alan ever really loved her, even when they'd first married? She couldn't remember him ever looking at her with the pure emotion that Dave had in his eyes right now.

"Goodbye," she whispered. Something molecular seemed to ache at the thought of leaving him. Something deep in her soul felt like it was being ripped away. On impulse, she dropped a quick kiss on his lips, then hurried into the car before she changed her mind.

Two hours later, after mustering her courage on the front porch, Lilly entered the empty house. After leaving Dave at the hospital, she'd had her Uber driver drop her at the bank to retrieve her car. From the bank, she'd stopped to buy herself a new cell phone, because being alone in the house with no way to place an emergency call out just wasn't happening. She'd given the cellular company her account information, which allowed her to keep her old phone number, and the tech had been able to retrieve her pictures and contacts from the cloud. Whew!

As she stepped into the living room, her first thought was that Strozier had been right. The place was a disaster. She groaned knowing she'd have to tend to most of the mess herself, before the cleaning crew came. She couldn't live in the house, finish packing Helen's things and sorting them for charity with this much disruption and the fine black fingerprint dust on everything.

"Maddie? Maddie girl, where are you?" Making her way past the dirt and confusion of the living room, she headed straight for the bathroom. Cleaning was a problem she could tackle tomorrow. Tonight, she only wanted a hot shower and a bed. And her cat.

"Maddie?" She started stripping as she walked down the hall. Her muscles protested with a dull ache. The abuse and tension of the last two and a half days had taken a toll. She paused in the door of the bedroom and peered cautiously inside, as if expecting Wayne to be lurking there. Hiding in the shadows like he had been the day she'd returned from the bank, and he'd grabbed her, pointed the gun at her head and—

She shook her head to clear it of the memory. The room was vacant.

Except for Maddie, who peered out from under the bed and sneezed.

"Oh, Maddie! Thank goodness you're okay." She

grinned as she walked to the bed and knelt to pat her frightened cat. "I know it's kinda dusty around here. We'll get it sorted out tomorrow. Come on out, sweetie. It's safe now." *Please, God, let it be safe now!*

She sat on the bed and opened the new phone so it could charge while she was in the shower. When she crouched to plug the phone into the wall adapter, she stuck a hand under the bed to stroke Maddie's fur. "You okay, girl?"

Edging cautiously out from her hiding spot, her cat gave a soft "mew" and settled into a rumbling purr. Maddie bumped her hand, asking for more pats. Obviously she wasn't the only one glad to have the chaos of the last two days behind them. With a few last strokes of Maddie's long, soft fur, Lilly kicked off her shoes and strolled into the bathroom to let the shower water start heating up. Bracing a hand on the back of the toilet, she lifted her foot to kick off her slacks. When she straightened from the task, she heard a strange *clunk,* like something metal hitting the floor.

She bent at the waist to search for what had fallen. When she spied the object on the tiles behind the toilet, her heart lurched, and bile rose in her throat.

She crouched, and with a trembling hand, she picked up Wayne's prized possession. His grandfather's watch.

Deputy Strozier might not think Wayne would come back to the house, but Lilly was now certain he would.

Chapter 18

Lilly clutched the new phone, debating. Did she call Dave? She didn't want to be an alarmist. She had the deputy out front watching the house. But the empty house reverberated with frightening memories, too fresh in her mind to dismiss. The one thing that had helped her survive the past few days' ordeal without falling apart had been Dave's presence. Even tied up, as he was through most of it, his company, his courage, his level-headed thinking had been a balm. Sharing their grief over Helen had been healing, helpful.

Yes. She wanted him there with her, and she wouldn't examine too closely all the reasons why. She tapped in the phone number Dave had scribbled on her palm, then her finger stopped, hovering over the call icon.

No. She couldn't let herself be dependent on him or

any man. Men had let her down too many times in the past, and if Helen were to be believed, Dave was just as bad, just as unreliable. She had to cope on her own, no matter how difficult it was.

Besides, Dave was injured and needed time to sleep, to heal. She couldn't drag him back over here to be her security blanket. She had to figure out her future, find a way to cope the way she always had. Alone. She just wished *alone* wasn't so…lonely.

"Hello?" Dave's voice. As if conjured by her desperate wish that he were near.

She gasped and looked down at the phone. At some point while she'd been wishy-washing, her trembling finger had hit the green phone icon and completed the call. She pushed the disconnect icon quickly, embarrassment flushing her face. The phone rang within seconds. Dave calling back.

She could ignore his returned call and pretend she knew nothing about the hang-up. But as if by its own volition, her thumb nudged the screen to answer. Her heart thumped against her ribs as she lifted the phone to her ear. "Hi."

"Lilly? Is that you?"

"Yeah."

"Are you all right? What's happened?" He sounded anxious, and his concern touched her. When was the last time a man had cared about her well-being?

"I shouldn't have called. You need rest."

"If you need something, I'm happy to help. Tell me."

She said nothing, mentally fighting the urge to beg him to come over.

"Lilly?"

She heaved a deep sigh. "I'm all right. The house just felt so…empty. And—" She caught herself. If she told him about the watch, he'd take the choice from her and rush over. She knew he would, and she wanted him to. But…

"And what? Damn it, Lilly. Talk to me!" he said, not unkindly. His tone was pleading, sympathetic.

Tears prickled her eyes and stung her sinuses. "He left his watch."

"What?"

She cleared the emotion from her throat and explained how she'd found the watch before her shower. "I took it out to the officer watching the house. It's evidence. But—"

"You said he freaked when you tried to move it while you treated his wound. We know it's a prized possession."

"Yeah."

Dave was only quiet for a couple seconds, but she knew where his thoughts were traveling even before he said, "I'm coming over."

Dave borrowed his elderly neighbor's car, citing an emergency and promising to have the vehicle back in the morning after he picked up a rental. He hightailed it to Lilly's and identified himself to the officer in the patrol car sitting at the end of her driveway.

She was watching for him and met him on the porch as he labored up the stairs with his crutches. He'd no more than topped the last step before she fell against him, hugging him. Trembling. Her breath shuddering.

He dropped his crutches to hold her, realizing he

needed her close as badly as she seemed to need him. "It's okay, Lil. I've got you."

Her hair was damp, and she smelled of floral shampoo and clean pajamas. Like a bit of heaven. Like *home*.

His breath snagged when the thought flitted through his mind. As much as he liked Helen, enjoyed her company, he'd never experienced the sense of belonging, the absolute *rightness* with her that he felt with Lilly. Was that what his gut had been telling him all along with Helen, the reason he'd been so slow to commit to her? Helen hadn't been his destiny, and deep down his soul had known it.

"I didn't want to call you. I hit the call button by accident," Lilly rasped.

He angled her back to peer at her freshly scrubbed face in the porch light. "And the other numbers? Did they dial themselves?"

She scowled at him, a pink flush staining her cheeks. "Of course not. But… I shouldn't have called. I shouldn't have…wanted you here."

He dipped his eyebrows as he studied her. "But you do. So when are you going to quit beating yourself up for the way you feel?"

She pulled free of his embrace and turned away. "Please, let's not rehash this. I didn't call you so that we could argue."

He sighed and bent to retrieve his crutches. "I don't want to fight with you either, Lil. Far from it. And if you'd listen to what I know your instincts are telling you, we'd never have to have this discussion again."

She opened her mouth, her expression conflicted, but said nothing as her internal battle played out on her face.

"Lil, I could see your indecision when you left the hospital. You kissed me because your heart told you it was right." When she shook her head, he placed a hand on her arm. "Okay. For now we'll agree to disagree, because I'm not going anywhere. Not when we both know Wayne will be back to get that watch. You may have turned it over to the cops, but *he* doesn't know that."

He saw the shiver that chased through her. While he'd rather believe she wanted him there for *him*, he'd settle for being her protection. Staying bought him time to figure out how to reach past her defenses and destroy the wall that stood between them.

Finally Lilly gave a small nod and led the way inside. She stopped in the middle of the living room floor, hugging herself and casting her gaze around at the clutter Wayne and the police had left. Crumbs, beer bottles, dirty dishes, wadded wrappers and, over it all, a fine layer of black powder. The man was a pig and had left behind a sty. The fingerprint powder only doused the trash, reminders of their ordeal, with a dark sense of macabre.

She sighed and pinched the bridge of her nose. "I decided to leave this to clean later. I can't stand to even look at it right now."

"So don't." He hobbled closer and raised a hand to her shoulder. "Let's go to another room."

She sent him a sad look. "The kitchen's just as bad. The only room that doesn't give me the heebie-jeebies at the moment is the guest bedroom, and only because I have no memories of him there."

He bobbed a nod. "Then that's where we'll go." He

started down the hall and paused at the bedroom door, when he noticed she hadn't followed. "Lilly?"

She grunted and stalked past him into the room, her bare feet silent on the hardwood floor. "I can't sell this house fast enough. It's a morass of bad or bittersweet memories."

"You have none that are good?" he asked, and she gave a dismissive shrug.

A parade of his own good memories in the house with Helen walked through his brain, leaving his heart feeling bruised for the loss. Yet for all the time he'd spent here with Helen, his thoughts zeroed in on the most recent moments spent here, especially of huddling against Lilly on the bed so she could sleep without choking. They'd shared confidences, exchanged dry humor and bolstered each other during the long hours of captivity.

"Truth is, I rarely visited Helen here. She usually came to my place. There's more to do in Denver." Lilly hugged herself and stared blankly at the floor, her expression bereft. Weary.

Dave squeezed the foam handgrips of the crutches, knowing he had a choice to make. He could risk looking like a reprobate and fight for the woman he'd fallen for, despite his history with Helen…or be discreet and walk away, forever wondering what could have been.

A cold disquiet settled in his bones. He hadn't been able to do anything about losing his job due to his injury last December. Hadn't been able to do anything about losing Helen. Had spent excruciating hours tied up and unable to do anything to stop Wayne's reign of terror. But he'd be damned if he'd let Lilly slip through his fingers, when he wanted her more than his next breath. He was through with feeling helpless, with being unable to change the crap that kept coming at him. He firmed his jaw and set his mind. But…

He also needed Lilly to want him. He wouldn't shove his way into her life if she had any regrets or reservations. Helen had left him with a reputation for being unfeeling, unavailable, uncommitted, despite his best efforts to make her happy. Was that why Lilly fought her feelings for him? Because he could see her confusion and tangled emotions as clear as day when she looked at him. Her attraction to him was in her kiss, and her appreciation for him in her smiles. But doubts still lurked in her haunted eyes.

"Lilly, we both need sleep. Come to bed." Sighing his fatigue and consternation, he sank down on the guest bed, which he could tell Lilly had recently remade with clean sheets. The fact that a cell phone was plugged in charging on the nightstand gave further credence to his theory she'd already planned to spend the night in this room. Setting his crutches aside, he propped his injured leg at an angle on the mattress, and within seconds, Maddie jumped up next to him and head-butted Dave's hand.

Dave scratched the cat's cheek and stroked her back. "Hey, Maddie. Glad to see you survived unscathed."

Lilly began pacing, her fingers twining and untwining as she fidgeted restlessly.

Dave stroked the cat, sending loose tufts of her long fur flying, but kept a keen eye on Lilly for the next couple of minutes. When it became clear she wasn't about to quit pacing and fretting, he nudged the cat aside and patted the mattress. "Lilly, come on. Sit. Talk to me."

She faced him but shook her head. "Dave, I'm just… tired of talk."

"Then we won't talk. We'll sleep. I know I'm exhausted." He pulled back the sheets, and after taking off his shoes, he carefully moved his injured leg under the covers. He wasn't lying about his fatigue. While at his house, he'd cleaned up, brushed his teeth and shaved, then dressed in comfortable athletic shorts and a T-shirt in preparation for bed before her call came in. Now the comfy mattress and fluffy pillow beckoned to him.

She gaped at him. "You're sleeping in here?"

"The better to protect you, my dear," he said in his best Big Bad Wolf voice.

Her scowl and lifted eyebrow challenged him. "Mmm-hmm, and who is supposed to protect me from you?"

He gave her a mock-startled gasp. "Wha—little old me? Why, I wouldn't hurt a fly."

She crossed her arms over her chest. "You know what I mean."

Setting aside the teasing, he narrowed his eyes on her. "Lilly, nothing is going to happen in this bed that you don't want. If all you want is sleep, then we'll sleep." When she continued to stare at him with a conflicted expression, he added, "We've done it before. We slept next to each other the other night without it turning sexual."

He didn't add that just because he hadn't made any sexual overtures toward her the night she slept propped against him didn't mean he hadn't entertained erotic thoughts about her. Her scent, her softness and her breath on his skin had been a sensual feast that teased his imagination.

She scoffed. "The other night, our hands were shackled. That hardly counts."

He opened his mouth to counter her argument, but snapped it closed again when she flipped off the lights and returned to the bed. Whipping back the sheets, she climbed into the bed and sent a waft of air to him that smelled deliciously of fresh sheets, floral shampoo and toothpaste. Normal domestic scents that made him think of building a home with Lilly and being surrounded by her sweet aroma every day.

Whoa, wrangler! he scolded silently. He was really getting ahead of himself there. But it didn't escape his notice that he'd never had those sorts of daydreams and longings with Helen.

Lilly cut a side glance to him. "We sleep," she said firmly as she settled and drew the covers up to her chin.

"We sleep," he confirmed. "Good night, Lilly."

"'Night." She rolled onto her side, her back to him, and Maddie crawled up to sleep atop the covers in the bend of her legs, still purring.

Dave lay on his back, staring at the ceiling, one arm folded behind his head. Sleep dragged at him, but he kept an ear tuned for strange noises in the house that might indicate a prowler. *Wayne.* His gut roiled knowing their captor was still out there.

He wasn't usually a heavy sleeper, but as tired as he was tonight, he feared he might fall into a deep slumber and not hear trouble. He debated his options, even as his eyes drifted closed and his limbs relaxed.

He woke again some undetermined time later to a subtle noise. He tensed, immediately wide awake, and strained to listen for a repeat of the muffled sound that had roused him.

When the quiet noise came again, it wasn't what he expected. Not a thump of footsteps or creak of a door, but a sniff. A tiny sigh. A tremulous indrawn breath.

Lilly was crying.

Chapter 19

"Lil?"

Lilly stilled when she heard Dave's voice. She held her breath, certain she couldn't exhale without him hearing her tears. Or had he already heard her? She'd been sure he was asleep, but—

"What's wrong, sweetheart? Why are you crying?" His sympathetic tone crumbled what little reserves she had left.

"I don't know," she said honestly. She wiped her nose and gave an indelicate sniff. Now that she'd been discovered, she saw no point in being discreet.

She felt the bed jostle as he turned to her and pulled the hair back from her face. "Please, Lil. Talk to me. What's upset you?"

"I don't know. Truly. Nothing…and everything.

Stress and relief. Helen, Wayne, you, Alan... Everything kind of boiled up all at once, and I couldn't stop the tears." She pressed the heels of her hands into her eyes and groaned. "I'm sorry I woke you."

"Don't apologize. I understand. It's a lot to process." He rubbed her arm, and his kindness dug deeper into her raw soul.

A fresh wave of tears filled her eyes. "Yeah."

"It's my recent understanding that sometimes crying can simply be for the catharsis. Is that it?"

She blinked damply, surprised at his insight. "How—?" She stopped herself. Helen. Of course.

"I paid attention, even if she said I didn't."

Lilly believed him. She was seeing a man who might not always get things right, but he always tried. Her sister had sold him short.

He stroked her hair and spoke quietly. "Can I do anything for you?"

"No. I—" Her voice cracked. Damn it, why did he have to be so kind? He only made it harder to push him away.

Dave tugged on her shoulder, turning her onto her back. Her movement rousted Maddie from her position against Lilly's legs, and the cat jumped down from the bed.

Braced on one arm to lean over her, Dave dried her cheeks with his fingers. "You've been a rock the last few days. You deserve a good catharsis. Don't shove it down on my account."

A pale sliver of moonlight filtered in through the window over the bed and lit his chiseled face. Even with the bruising from his scrap with Wayne, he looked so handsome, it made her heart hurt. Lord help her...

"Go back to sleep." She patted his chest near his shoulder. "I'm okay."

He tipped his head, peering at her with a skeptical frown. Putting his arms around her, he drew her close as he settle back against his pillow. "C'mere."

"Dave, I—"

"Shh. Close your eyes and relax. I'm just going to hold you."

She should have used the hand she had against his chest as leverage to push him away. But as he snuggled her close and began massaging the muscles at the base of her skull, her tension dissolved, along with her resolve. Her loneliness and fear evaporated. Her tears dried.

The comfort he offered was a welcome balm that easily lulled her into a state of anoetic bliss.

Her achy limbs relaxed. Her scampering pulse slowed. And the lethargy she'd been fighting for days, as she'd needed to stay alert to dangerous shifts in her situation, permeated every cell.

Until...

Dave moved his massaging fingers from her nape to her shoulders, then let his palm stroke along her spine. As his hand traveled down her back, his touch, intended to soothe, sent sparks of heat crackling through her veins. He gave the small of her back a deep rub, and a sweet hum radiated along her nerves like plucked guitar strings. Her body sang with every caress as he trailed his fingers back up to her neck, where he buried his fingers in her hair and massaged her scalp. She heard a soft moan, and when Dave's attentions stilled, she realized the erotic sound had come from her own throat.

Tipping her head back, she met his eyes. In the beam of moonlight, his dark brown gaze was alive with glimmers of desire. All of the calm repose she'd known briefly scattered, but the surge of sensation fueling her now had a different source. Longing. Curiosity. Recklessness.

But leading the charge was a pure and primitive hunger.

Lilly curled one hand around the back of his head and captured his mouth with a quick but resounding kiss. Beneath her hand, which still rested on his chest, she felt the tremor that raced through him. His fingers curled more firmly against her skull, and his gaze searched hers, delving deeply, reaching into her soul. "Lilly?"

She kissed him again, this time lingering to explore and arouse. When, after several moments, he drew his head back, his breath fanned her face with shallow pants similar to her own. He whispered her name again, stroking her cheek with his thumb. "Is this really what you want? I need to hear you say it. I want you to be sure."

"Yes," she said, before she could change her mind. For once she wanted to follow her heart instead of always listening to the voices of reason or doubt that filled her head. She'd earned a night of escape, hadn't she? And she couldn't deny the near feverish yearning that pounded in her veins. Her desires had been dormant for months, and now awakened, they roared and paced, clawing at her for release. "Oh, yes," she repeated and tugged him close for another kiss.

Dave wrapped his arms around her, rolling to his

back so that her body stretched along the length of him. She closed her eyes, savoring the feeling of being held against the strength and sinew of his taut frame. She pleasured in the evidence of his arousal, wiggling her hips to entice him more. He answered with a low growl and squeezed her bottom with both hands, pulling her closer still. Careful not to bump his injured leg, she slid her foot up his good calf. She teased him with her toes while her tongue delved into his mouth with sensual strokes.

Ripples of sweet sensation flowed through her with each kiss, each caress of his hands against her eager skin. When he skimmed his touch up, beneath her nightshirt, the calluses on his palm scraped lightly along her spine, sending fresh sparks shooting through her. His hands continued up until he was coaxing the nightshirt over her head.

She levered up, helping him with her bedclothes, and with a quick flick of her wrist, she discarded it on the floor. She hovered over him, her breasts bare and peaked. He cupped one breast and rolled the nipple with his thumb, while his thirsty gaze drank in her nakedness. "So beautiful," he murmured.

"Now you." She sat up, straddling him, and tugged his T-shirt off over his head and let it drop on the floor next to hers. Smoothing her hands over his chest, she admired the sculpted muscles he'd acquired through strenuous ranch work. He may not have been on the job in recent months, but the firm ridges and plains of his pecs and abs reflected years of conditioning.

When she reclined against him again, her sensitized breasts tingled as she pressed her body, skin to skin with his. He shifted her to her back and fitted himself between her legs.

Lilly explored him with her fingers, her lips, learning what he liked, what made erotic rumbles vibrate in his throat. They took turns discovering each other, hands roaming, teeth teasing and tongues seducing. When he hooked his thumbs in her panties, she raised her hips and slipped out of them while anticipation thrummed to her core. Removing his shorts and briefs took more care, so that they didn't disturb his injury. Then he opened the drawer of the nightstand and took out one of the condoms there.

"How did you know there were—?" She swallowed the rest of the sentence, the obvious answer coming to her as soon as she spoke.

Dave lifted one eyebrow as if asking, *Do you really have to ask?*

She recalled finding condoms in other places throughout the house as she'd packed drawers and closets. She shoved all the implications of that from her mind and focused on Dave as he sheathed himself and turned back to her.

Lilly cradled Dave in the *V* of her legs and raised her hips to welcome him. Heat clambered inside her and coiled low in her belly as he joined their bodies with a long, slow thrust.

She clung to him, knowing that something more profound was happening between them than sex for escape. As good as he felt, moving inside her, her arousal coiling tighter with every stroke, the most intense sensation centered behind her ribs.

Without meaning to, against every warning she'd

given herself, she'd allowed her heart to become involved with what was happening between her and Dave. Not just in a physical way, either. A spiritual one. Dave had recognized the link and begged her to surrender her feelings from their first kiss on the top of the mountain.

She was even more certain she'd developed a fragile bond with Dave when, in the moments after they'd each climaxed, he propped on his elbows to hover over her and gave her the most beatific smile. Warmth filled her to bursting, seeing the joy and affection that lit his face. She couldn't contain the returned smile that sprang from deep within her.

And she knew she was in big trouble.

Wayne woke from a restless sleep, shivering, aching, disoriented. Where was he? Darkness swallowed him. Fecund, nauseating scents filled his nose. He tried to shift, to get comfortable, but was wedged in a narrow space. The walls scraped him. The surface below him jabbed with sharp angles and hard lumps. When he moved, something near him moved, too. He heard the scratching, the flapping, the squeak. A bat? Why—?

Another shudder rolled through him. He was hot. And cold. And his side throbbed.

His mouth felt dry, but he couldn't form any spit.

He wiggled an arm up to his side, and when he touched the place that pulsed painfully, a sharp jolt of agony streaked through him. He groaned and cursed and gritted his teeth.

Taking shallow breaths, because breathing deeply made his side hurt worse, he tried to clear his mind. He had pain pills…somewhere. But his tumor had never hurt like this before.

Focusing, remembering, took effort, and his confusion was unsettling.

First things first. He turned his hand to feel the rough wall beside him. Rock. He was in some kind of narrow cave. Hiding. Police. Gunshot wound.

One blurry memory led to another. The next racking chill felt like last year's flu. The fever. The aches. His hand skimmed up to his tender, pulsing side. The wound was hot. Infection.

The woman had warned him. Lilly.

He was ill. Maybe dying. Lilly could help him. But he was tired. So tired. Another chill rolled through his stiff muscles, and he closed his eyes. Just a little more sleep.

Dave slept hard for several hours until Lilly's restless tossing finally dragged him out of his slumber. He rubbed his eyes and stretched when he realized Lilly had climbed out of bed. Peering toward the foot of the bed, he found her pulling on her undies and nightshirt. "Hey, you all right?"

She lifted a startled gaze. "Sorry. Didn't mean to wake you."

"Couldn't you sleep?"

"I did, but then I had a bad dream."

"Understandable. About Wayne?"

She frowned. "No."

"Then what?"

She hesitated and shook her head. "You don't want to know."

"I do. Especially if talking about it will help."

"I'll be back in a sec." She left the bedroom, and he heard the hall bathroom door close.

He threw back the sheets, swung his legs off the bed and clicked on the bedside lamp. A glance at the alarm clock told him the sun wouldn't be up for a couple more hours. He gathered his own clothes off the floor and was donning his shorts when Maddie jumped up on the bed and trotted over to him.

"Breakfast?" the cat inquired with a meow.

"Sorry, girl. Still sleep time."

Maddie bumped his arm with her head. *"Pats then?"* her purr asked.

Dave rubbed the feline's cheek and yawned. "Go back to sleep now, okay?"

"What?" Lilly asked as she returned.

"Just telling Maddie that it wasn't really morning and to go back to bed."

Lilly chuckled, but the laugh sounded forced. Something was definitely wrong. As she slid under the covers, she worked her legs around Maddie, who'd settled down in a crouch. When Lilly rolled over to sleep on her back, folding the sheet across her chest and closing her eyes, Maddie snuggled against her hip with a purr.

Dave searched for a way to lighten the mood, cheer Lilly up. "I found the tattoo, by the way. Lower back, center. Base of your spine."

She angled a quick half grin at him. "Yep. See? Never say never. You saw it after all."

"So…a butterfly. Because it represents hope to you? And…love, you said?"

Her smile brightened, and she patted his chest. "Very good."

"Hey, I do listen."

Lilly rolled her head to face him. "When my mom gave me my first butterfly—that key chain from Dollywood—"

"Yeah?"

"She said she wanted it to remind me that even though our dad had gone—he'd left just a few months before that trip—she'd always love me and knew I had lots of good things to look forward to in life." She chuckled softly. "And then she said, 'Every lily needs a butterfly.' I know it's corny, but...that's why they're sentimental for me. Why I started collecting butterflies."

"And your mom died a few years back?" he asked.

She heaved a sigh. "Like six...no, seven years now. I'm the last Shaw." She curled her fingers against his shirt and narrowed a curious glance at him. "What about your family? Are they still alive?"

"Dad is. He's in Laramie. And I have a brother in the army. Not sure exactly where he is. Army won't say."

"Are you close?"

He hesitated. "I love my family. But... I don't know what defines *close*. We talk every now and then. We're on good terms, but we don't call unless we have news to report."

Her expression dimmed, and she lowered her gaze. "Don't take them for granted, Dave."

He hummed an acknowledgment, regretting that her dark mood was back.

He didn't need to search too hard to know what, if

not Wayne, had upset her. "Want to talk about your bad dream?"

"No." She shifted slightly, giving him part of her back without rousing Maddie, and grew silent.

Seeing how easily Lilly had closed him out stung. He twisted his lips and rubbed his chin. "It's time we addressed the elephant in the room."

A wariness filled her eyes, and she angled her head to stare at him. He could see her pulse flutter in the hollow of her throat. After wetting her lips, she whispered, "Helen."

"Helen," Dave confirmed, and Lilly felt a stab of grief in her chest.

Damn it, she'd wanted to avoid this, wanted to pretend her feelings for him were just the result of shared trauma. That once they both returned to their regular lives, they'd put these past few days behind them. But then they'd made love, and she'd felt more alive than she had in years. Something real had developed between them. Something wonderful and terrifying. Something that felt a lot like a betrayal to her sister. So how did they traverse these dangerous waters?

Lilly spread her hands and shook her head. "I've been trying to decide what to say to you about this, and… I. Just. Don't. Know."

"Lilly, we are the two people in the world who loved and respected Helen the most."

"Exactly!" She angled a sharp glance at him. "Which is why *nothing* should have happened between us!" She swallowed the knot in her throat, digging deep for the courage to ask the hard question. "How do I know I'm not just a replacement for her? Are you sure I'm not just filling her shoes? Her sister the convenient stand-in?" His expression said he was galled, but she plunged on. "A rebound to ease your grief or guilt? Because that's what my dream was about. She was so mad when she found out we'd slept together. So hurt." Lilly wound the sheet around her fingers. "Dave, I'm sorry, but… making love was wrong."

"Absolutely, unequivocally, no. To all of the above. You are not a stand-in for Helen." Sitting on the edge of the bed, he exhaled a frustrated-sounding huff and shifted to face her. "And if making love was wrong, then why did it feel so *right* to me?"

His question kicked her in the chest, stealing her breath. Because, in so many ways, it had felt right to her, too. She bit the inside of her cheek and rasped, "Don't say that."

His eyebrows dipped in consternation, and his dark umber eyes grew sad. He took her hand and laced their fingers. "It's the truth, Lilly. Not talking about it doesn't make it go away."

She shook her head, trying to process the tumult in her head. "How can it *ever* be right when Helen—"

"Helen is gone."

She grunted at his bluntness and pulled her hand from his.

He dropped his chin to his chest, contorting his face with misery. "I miss her, too, Lil." A beat later, he raised eyes bright with passion to hers. "But how can I ignore the fact that I've felt truer, deeper feelings for you in the last three days than I felt with her in all the months we were dating?"

She squeezed the sheet in her fists and shook her head. "Don't put that on me."

He blinked and jerked his chin up. "Put what? I'm just telling you how I feel. I thought that was what women wanted!" Then, mumbling, he added, "Geez, I can't win."

Sympathy plucked her heart. She understood his confusion. Shared in it. Sitting up, she raked the hair back from her face. "I'm just saying... I don't *want* you to feel more for me than her. It only adds to the guilt—"

He seized her hand again, clinging to it when she tried to retract it. "I'm not trying to make you feel guilty. But we need to deal with whatever it is that's happening between us."

She straightened her back, determined to make him accept her position. "*No.* We need to put a stop to whatever is happening. We can't pursue this."

He flipped one palm up, his expression stunned. "That's your answer? Ignore what we have together? Pretend there isn't enough chemistry here to open a biotech lab?"

Pain swelled in her chest. Regret brought tears to her eyes. "I know we have chemistry, Dave. Tonight proved that in spades. But my head keeps telling me that no amount of chemistry or emotional connection is enough to overcome the—" she swallowed the lump in her throat "—betrayal it would be."

"Betrayal?"

She nodded. "Helen was my sister. She loved you."

He nodded slowly. "And I don't want to sound insensitive, but...we can't build our lives around loyalty to someone who's not here anymore."

"Are you saying loyalty means nothing to you?"

"No! You're twisting my words," he said, aiming a finger at her. Flattening his hand on his chest, he added, "Loyalty is *very* important to me. Do you really think I haven't thought about Helen these last few days?"

She shook her head.

After a moment, he took a slow breath and said quietly, "It's not like you came busting into town and seduced me away from her while she was alive. I don't see any betrayal here." He reached over to scratch Maddie's cheek as the cat resettled after being jostled by Lilly's restless movement. "The fact that you're worried about Helen's posthumous feelings only confirms that. That's all that your dream meant."

Lilly ran a finger under her eyelashes to dry the moisture that had leaked onto her cheek. She flopped back on the pillow again and heaved a sigh. "I don't know, Dave."

"I do know, Lilly." He brushed her hair back from her cheek and traced the line of her jaw with a knuckle. "And the fact that you love your sister so much and are still protective of her all these months after she was taken from us just…makes me love you more."

She darted a stunned gaze to his. "Love?"

"Yeah. That's what I'd call it."

She released a shuddering breath. "Oh, Dave. I'm…scared."

His brow furrowed in confusion. "Why does it scare you to hear me say I'm falling in love with you?"

"Because I have feelings for you, too, and it just makes it harder to do what I have to. And because I know how much losing this—" she waved a hand between them "—is going to hurt. It already does."

"Don't do this, Lil. We can figure it out." The heartache in his tone ripped at her soul.

"I'm sorry, Dave, but my mind is made up." She climbed out of the bed and aimed a finger at him. "I'm going to the other room. Don't follow me."

Wayne woke again, bathed in sweat and as miserable as he'd been in days. The chill was gone, and he knew that meant a brief reprieve from the building fever. The cave was dark. Still night then, but surely it was getting near morning. He figured searchers would start looking for him again at daybreak. He'd heard the helicopters, the voices on the mountain yesterday. If he was going to get help from Lilly for his wound, he needed to get moving before daylight.

And when Lilly had finished treating his infection, he'd take his revenge.

To his credit, Dave gave her the space she asked for. It was Lilly, an hour later, staring at the ceiling and imagining every rustle and creak outside was Wayne returning, who chose to go back to the guest bedroom. Dave's deep, even breathing assured her that he was asleep, Maddie beside him. Feeling like a coward, she crawled under the covers and turned her back to him. Just being in the same room with him made her feel so much safer she wanted to cry. How was she going to face the months to come without him? How had she fallen so far so fast with someone so wrong—and at the same time so right—for her?

Maddie eased across the bed to cuddle with Lilly, her purr a balm to Lilly's restless heart. Closing her eyes, Lilly searched for sleep. She'd managed a drowsy lethargy when Maddie's head popped up, and she stared at the door to the hall. Lilly hadn't heard anything, but the fine hairs on her nape stood up.

Chapter 20

Lilly nudged Dave, waking him, and pointed to Maddie, her expression conveying the alarm her silence didn't. As they watched, the cat jumped down from the bed and crawled underneath it. Whether Lilly had heard anything or not, her cat had, and that was good enough for Lilly.

"Stay here," Dave mouthed, his face grim. He tossed back the covers and reached for his crutches.

Lilly grabbed his arm and shook her head. "You're hardly stealthy on those," she whispered, her volume barely a breath, and she aimed her chin toward the crutches. "Stay with me. We'll call the deputy outside. He gave me his number. It's saved in my phone."

Lilly picked up her new cell, and with a few quick finger wipes and taps, she called the deputy's personal cell. The deputy had told her he would be on duty until eight in the morning, at which time he'd text her the cell number for his relief.

Dave scowled and cast an expectant glance toward the hall. Clearly he was champing at the bit to personally take on Wayne, crutches be damned.

Over the sound of the deputy's cell ringing through her phone, she heard a light scuffing noise. Dave heard it, too, and he turned to her with an impatient glare. "Hide," he said in a hushed tone. "Get under the bed or in a closet or—"

He stopped, jerking his gaze toward the door again when the loose floorboard in the hall squeaked. Pressing his mouth into a taut line, she saw the decision in his eyes without him saying a word. Dave wasn't waiting for the deputy.

She held up a finger, her expression beseeching him to wait just a few moments, even as the deputy's phone clicked over to voice mail. Puzzled and frustrated that the deputy wasn't answering, she eased up on the bed to peer out at the front yard. The first rays of morning sun shone down on the cruiser parked at the end of her driveway. And revealed a nightmare. The driver's door was open, and a wide red gash crossed the deputy's throat. The windshield was covered in a spray of crimson.

Lilly gasped loudly. Covering her mouth both to muffle the scream that swelled in her throat and fight the urge to vomit, she sank down on the mattress again and turned a wide-eyed look to Dave.

Seeing her reaction, Dave sidled closer and rose to

kneel on his good leg as he looked out into the yard. He mumbled a vile curse under his breath.

"That's right," a chilling voice from the door said. "The cop is dead. Nobody will be running in to save you."

Lilly whirled toward Wayne, terror crawling up her spine. He held a bloody knife in his hand, one from Helen's professional chef collection. Despite the cool morning, Wayne's face was beaded with sweat, and his eyes held a disturbing sheen, a glassiness she recognized as febrile. "We have unfinished business."

Dave shoved to his feet and grabbed a crutch, raising it like a lance and wielding it as a weapon. "Stay back, you sonofabitch. If you touch Lilly, I'll pummel you within an inch of your life."

Lilly glanced down at the phone still in her hand. While Dave held Wayne's attention, she thumbed her phone app and called 911.

The emergency operator answered, and she blurted, "Wayne Moore is at my house! He's armed, and he murdered the cop out front. Send help, please!"

"Hey! Hang that up!" Wayne bellowed, aiming the bloody blade at her.

Instead she rattled off the address.

With a growl, Wayne charged. She yelped in fear, scrambling to the far side of the bed. Dave swung the crutch, smacking Wayne with it, but Wayne kept coming. Blocking the crutch with one arm, he raised the knife and slashed at Dave. When Dave juked away from the blade, Wayne grabbed the end of the crutch and yanked.

Dave toppled off balance and lost his grip. With a

growl, Wayne threw the crutch toward the hall and came at Dave again, knife up.

Although unsteady without the support of his crutches, Dave sidestepped, ducked and feinted as Wayne jabbed with the blade again and again.

Leaving the line to the emergency operator open, Lilly tossed the phone in the corner behind her, freeing her hands for combat. She was scared to the bone, certain Wayne would not hesitate to kill them this time, but she wouldn't go down without a fight. She and Dave weren't tied up now, and they had a two-to-one advantage. Fueled by adrenaline and a conviction that Wayne had to be stopped, she dove into the action.

Grabbing a pillow as protection from his blade, Lilly surged at Wayne. As shields went, the pillow was pitiful, but it was better than nothing. Wayne turned his attention to her and slashed her foam-and-cotton defense. As hoped, her distraction bought Dave a few critical seconds.

From her peripheral vision, she saw Dave snatch up the second crutch. He swung it at Wayne's knife arm, just as Wayne raised the blade over his head. The crutch smashed into Wayne's side, and he emitted a pained howl as he staggered back a couple steps.

Lilly shifted her gaze to the blood-soaked shirt Wayne wore, and through a tear in the fabric, she saw that the gunshot wound she'd been treating for him had grown angry and infected. His feverish eyes and sweaty face made more sense now.

"Wayne, stop this!" she said in a firm voice that belied her fear. Wayne and Dave locked glares, crouched in attack-ready poses, but she continued. "I know you're here for your father's watch, but I don't have it."

His focus riveted on Dave, Wayne shook his head and through teeth gritted in pain, he snarled, "It *is* here. I left it here."

"I found it and gave it to the police," Lilly countered. "It's not here anymore."

Dave remained poised, his focus glued on Wayne, ready for the next attack and using both legs despite his injury.

Wayne furrowed his brow, panting for a breath, and sent her another quick side glance before returning his glare to Dave. "Lies. It's here somewhere, and I'll get it." He inhaled deeply, and his nostrils flared. "But the watch ain't all I came for."

She nodded and aimed a finger at his side. "Your wound. It's infected. I see that." She raised both hands. "If you'll put down that knife, I'll do what I can to clean the wound. I promise. But only if you'll promise that—"

He scoffed. "Too late for bargaining, Lilly."

"No, it's not. It's never too late to turn this whole thing around. You can get medical help, surrender to the police and make a deal that—"

"Make a deal?" His lip curled in disdain. "To do what? Die in prison? Spend the next year or so in pain, wasting away. Screw that."

"You'll receive the medical treatment you need in prison."

Wayne snorted his derision. "Oh, yeah. I'm sure the state pen is a regular Mayo Clinic." He shook his head. "No. If I can't get out of the country, get treatment somewhere where there's no extradition, then I might as well eat a bullet here and now."

Dave shifted his gaze briefly to Lilly, and Wayne chuckled dryly. "Don't get excited, Hero. If I do go down, I'm taking you both with me."

"I've got a better idea," Dave said. "You walk out now, before the cops come, and no one gets hurt."

Wayne motioned to his side. "A little late for that, too, Hero. Even if I did want to make a run for it, this bullet scratch you gave me is dragging me down. Way down." He winced and pressed a hand over his wound.

Dave flipped up a palm. "So then how do you see this ending? What's your endgame now?"

"Hell if I know." Wayne glowered at Dave. "I had a plan. I had a good plan for gettin' out of town and using the loot from the bank to get well. But you screwed that up for me when you played hero and shot me, you bastard." A muscle in Wayne's jaw ticked. "Now everything's gone to hell, and I hold you responsible. That's why you have to die."

With that, Wayne lunged at Dave.

Dave swung the crutch in an upward arc, hitting Wayne's knife hand, then striking his cheek.

While Wayne fumbled to regain a firm grip on the knife, Dave tossed the crutch aside and took Wayne on hand-to-hand. Leading with his shoulder, Dave knocked Wayne back and grappled for possession of the knife.

Lilly watched in a haze of horror. What could she do that wouldn't make matters worse for Dave? She glanced at the second bed pillow. The distraction had worked last time, so…

Dave feinted left then right, avoiding the thrusts of

the blade, and aiming blows at Wayne's ribs and face. When Dave landed a blow on Wayne's injured nose, Wayne cradled his face and loosed a loud, bone-chilling howl of rage and pain. Staggered back a step. Two.

His roar spooked Maddie from her under-the-bed hiding place, and she darted for the hall, right behind Wayne's unsteady feet. Wayne tripped over Lilly's fleeing cat and toppled backward onto his butt, his head thumping hard against the wood-plank floor.

Dave seized his chance. He landed on Wayne and pinned his opponent's wrists to the floor. Tossing the pillow aside, Lilly scuttled over to help Dave pin Wayne to the floor. She grabbed Wayne by the hair and yanked his head back, earning another yowl of agony and his fiery glare. Her move allowed Dave to grip their opponent's knife hand with both of his and slam Wayne's wrist against the floor. Once. Twice. The third time the knife skittered loose and clunked on the hardwood planks.

Lilly seized the knife and aimed it at Wayne's eye. "Be still, or I'll blind you!"

Panting from exertion, Dave straddled Wayne's legs and sat back to pin them to the floor. He extended his injured leg with a groan, and Lilly saw the blood blossoming on the bandages. He'd reopened his gunshot wound in the struggle.

Wayne stopped struggling, his breathing ragged and his glower murderous. "Do it, Lilly. I dare you."

Lilly used her knees and body weight to trap his arms. She continued to point the blade at his face, her hand shaking as adrenaline and fear continued to ravage her.

"I hope you both burn in hell," Wayne snarled, vitriol his only weapon now. His words hit their mark. Pain lanced her chest, along with a strange sympathy for the man who'd imprisoned them, taunted them, terrified them for days. Feeling the shiver that racked his body, she pressed a hand to his perspiration-dampened brow. His skin was frighteningly hot.

"Wayne," she said, her voice rasping, "you need a doctor."

"Get your hand...off me."

She swallowed hard, trying to unclog the emotion in her throat. "I never wanted things to end like this. I wanted to help you." She felt Dave's curious gaze on her as she continued. "I tried to be your friend, to tend your wound. I'd have helped you negotiate a surrender with the police that would have given you—"

His eyes snapped to meet hers, narrowing with contempt. "Surrender? That will never, *ever* happen."

As if to prove his point, he jerked futilely against their hold on him. He had surprising strength for someone so clearly ravaged with fever and pain.

Raising her gaze to Dave, he stared back at her with a peculiar look on his face.

A few minutes later, Lilly heard car engines outside, voices, the squeak and static crackle of a bullhorn. "Wayne Moore, this is the sheriff. We have the house surrounded. Lay down any weapons and come out with your hands up."

Dave raised his eyes to meet hers, relief permeating his expression.

"Can you manage him long enough for me to go out and talk to the cavalry?" she asked Dave.

He jerked a nod. "Go on."

She waited until Dave held Wayne's wrists before she stood up. Still reluctant to leave Dave alone with Wayne, even for a few minutes.

Outside, the sheriff deputy repeated the bullhorn call for Wayne to surrender. Lilly hurried to the front door, put her hands out so the deputies could see she was unarmed and headed down the porch steps.

A deputy met her at the base of the steps. "Ma'am, are you all right? We had a call that Wayne Moore was here."

She nodded. "Yes to both. Dave Giblan is inside with him. First bedroom on the left."

As she filled him in on how they'd subdued Wayne and the knife he'd had, the deputy gave a signal. Two more deputies rushed forward, guns drawn.

"We need an ambulance, too," she said. "Wayne's hurt and Dave's leg was bleeding."

"An ambulance is on the way." The deputy pointed to her arm. "You're bleeding, too."

She dropped a puzzled gaze to the cut on her arm, the blood that trickled down her forearm toward her wrist. She'd been so caught up in battling Wayne, so pumped with adrenaline, she hadn't noticed the cut, probably from when she'd charged Wayne with the pillow.

Through the front door the deputies had left open, she heard shouted commands as the officers took control of the fugitive. A couple of minutes later, the deputies appeared again, one on either side of Wayne, whose hands were cuffed behind him, as they escorted him to the waiting patrol car.

Wayne gave Lilly a chilling look as he was marched past her, and he muttered, "Never."

An uneasy prickle ran up her spine. What had he meant by that?

Her muscles remained taut, her nerves jumping until Dave came through the front door, hobbling on his crutches. She rushed to him and caught him in a bear hug as he reached the bottom step of the porch.

When the sheriff's deputy she'd been speaking to approached, she and Dave parted only enough to face the deputy. Dave kept his arm wrapped around her shoulders as if afraid she'd disappear if he didn't keep a grip on her, and she tucked her arm around his waist.

"After your injuries have been treated, we'll need to interview you both about what happened this morning," the deputy said. "I'm sure you're—"

A shout from one of the other officers cut him off.

Startled by the commotion, Lilly jerked her attention to the yard. To Wayne and the officers flanking him.

Wayne's legs seemed to have given out, and he sagged toward the ground. As the deputies bent to drag him to his feet, Wayne twisted, raising his cuffed hands toward the utility belt of the officer on his left.

"Wayne, no!" Lilly shouted.

But her captor grabbed the deputy's gun. Fired a random shot.

The other two deputies drew. More gunfire.

Lilly flinched at the loud bangs. Screamed.

Wayne's body jerked then went limp. Didn't move.

Lilly stared in disbelief as the deputy beside them reached for his shoulder radio and rattled off a litany of codes to the dispatcher.

Her legs trembled, and Dave wrapped her in a tight hold, the only thing keeping her upright. Her gut swam in acid. But as the shock wore off, her duty reared its head, and she fought to free herself from Dave's arms.

"Lilly, no! Don't. It's over." Dave tried to restrain her, and she slapped at his hands.

"Let me go! I'm a nurse. I have to at least try to help him!" She wrenched free and staggered over to Wayne. The deputies also tried to keep her back, but she wouldn't hear it. "I'm a nurse! Let me help him!"

She watched the deputies numbly as they checked Wayne for a pulse, then stepped back, shoulders drooping and faces grim.

"Ma'am, it's too late. He's gone," the officer who'd checked Wayne's pulse said.

Never, Wayne had said. *Surrender? That will never, ever happen.*

As badly as Wayne had treated her and Dave, she valued every life, and it tore at her soul that Wayne saw no out other than death. Her muscles turned to jelly, and she slumped to the ground.

"Oh, Wayne," she murmured, "no."

"Suicide by cop" she'd heard it called. A quick death for a man who saw only cancer, suffering and imprisonment in his future.

Dave sank onto the grass beside her, pulling her into his arms. One of the deputies who'd fired on Wayne staggered away and threw up.

Lilly shook from head to toe, a bittersweet regret welling inside her, but Dave's solid presence gave her a measure of comfort she desperately needed.

"I didn't want it to end like this," she said softly, more

to herself, to Wayne, than to anyone else. "He was a jerk to us, but I never wanted him to die."

Dave squeezed her tighter and kissed the top of her head. "I know. But at least it's all over now. You're safe."

"Safe," she muttered, the concept feeling foreign to her. Her fingers curled into Dave's shirt as a disturbing thought occurred to her. If their ordeal was over, where did that leave her association with Dave?

She might be safe from physical harm from Wayne now, but she still felt vulnerable, as if perched on the precipice of a cliff. She glanced up into Dave's eyes and knew why. Last night, when she'd given Dave a piece of her heart.

And betrayed Helen.

The only way she saw to redeem herself was to cut Dave completely out of her life.

Chapter 21

Time lost all meaning for Lilly as the police processed the scene, took their statements for the third time in four days and finally released them to leave the scene.

But where to go? Helen's house echoed with bad memories, was swathed in police tape and marred with bloodstains. She could go to a motel. There was a decent one in Boyd Valley, but the thought of being alone scared her. Well, maybe not entirely alone. With Dave's help, she'd gotten her terrified cat out from under the bed in the master bedroom and put Maddie in her travel carrier.

"Poor girl," she cooed quietly, reaching through the open door of the carrier to pat her cat's head. "It's gonna be okay, Maddie-cakes."

"Maddie," Dave said, peering over Lilly's shoulder,

"I take back every bad thing I said about you not helping. That was one well-timed bolt. Lassie would be proud."

Lilly lifted the corner of her mouth. "She definitely earned a handful of treats and several days of complete silence and recovery."

"I think we all have." Dave placed a hand on Lilly's shoulder and gave her muscles a deep rub. Rather than relaxing her, she tensed.

She moved away from his massage and faced him with a knit in her brow. "Dave, I need time, too." She cleared her throat. "Away from you."

He leaned on his crutches and frowned. "I see."

She let her shoulders droop. "Do you?"

"No." He exhaled harshly. "At least Helen would tell me what I was doing wrong, what I needed to change."

The mention of her sister knotted Lilly's gut. "Dave..."

His hangdog expression bore to her marrow. "I don't want to lose you, Lilly."

She shook her head, moisture filling her eyes. "It's not about anything you did or didn't do. The fact is nothing can happen between us. It's wrong!"

His expression hardened, and his dark eyes drilled into her. "Something has already happened between us, Lilly. You know that."

"Sleeping with you was foolish of me. I was vulnerable and scared and—"

"I'm not talking about sex. I've fallen in love with you, Lilly. And I think if you are honest with yourself, you'll admit you have feelings for me, too."

A tremor rolled through her, and she mentally

blocked his assertion. Shaking her head, she turned and picked up Maddie's carrier. "It doesn't matter what either of us feels."

"What?" His voice sharpened in disbelief. "How can love not matter? It's the only thing that matters!"

"Not if it's *wrong*. I can't betray Helen like that!" Hugging Maddie's carrier close, she staggered out to her car and loaded her cat on the front passenger seat, buckling the seat belt around the carrier.

Dave on his crutches caught up to her as she flung open the driver's side door. "Lilly, I can't make you love me, but know this—the love I feel for you is truer than anything I ever felt for Helen. I *tried* to love her, but with you, it comes naturally. Denying that would mean betraying my heart."

Pain lanced her chest, stole her breath. "Goodbye, Dave," she rasped as she climbed in her car and closed her door.

As she drove away, Maddie gave a sad mewl from her carrier.

"I know, Maddie. I'll miss him, too."

Lilly more than missed Dave. She ached for him. He filled her thoughts, even when she returned to work at the emergency room in Denver. Between patients, she'd wonder how his leg was healing and long for his company.

Alone in her bed at night, her body yearned for his touch, the warmth and assurance of his arms around her. Even Maddie's gentle purr didn't ease the hollow pain in her heart as she stared into the lonely darkness.

She'd felt alone before. After her father left. After

her divorce. After Helen died. So why did this loss feel so much bleaker? She tried to tell herself she was doing the right thing for Helen, but that postulate was cold comfort as one colorless day stretched into the next.

One Sunday afternoon as she was sorting the last of Helen's possessions—finally—deciding what to donate to charity, she came across the small stuffed bear with the pink heart on its chest that their mother had given Helen that long-ago day at Dollywood. She stared at the bear with a heavy heart and heaved a wistful sigh, wondering what words of encouragement and comfort their mother had given Helen along with her new treasure. Had her stuffed bear been a symbol of hope for Helen the way the butterfly key chain had been for Lilly?

They'd never talked much about their personal grief after their father left, wanting to shield and protect their mother when it became clear how fragile their mom's mental health was.

Even after their mother's death, she and Helen had avoided talking about the past, as if by a silent agreement not to open old wounds regarding their father.

Lilly sank down on the floor with her sister's bear, remembering what Dave had told her. Helen had never stopped wondering where their father had gone. She'd looked for him. Found him.

She said knowing he was happy, even if it wasn't with her, gave her a little peace.

Lilly stilled, her breath stuck in her lungs. When was the last time *she'd* known real peace?

From the day of her parents' divorce, her hurt over her father's desertion and her mother's manic depression had made her childhood a struggle. Her own divorce had made her feel unloved and unwanted. Helen's death had left her restless and grieved to her marrow.

But she had known peace. Comfort. Security.

With Dave.

She'd known a special calm and happiness when they'd rested on the top of the mountain before he kissed her. She'd experienced a deep sense of belonging and renewal when they'd made love. And even with Wayne down the hall, posing a threat to them, even bound as they'd been, she'd felt safe having Dave beside her. Because having him with her felt…right.

Lilly tucked Helen's bear against her chest and whispered, "What do I do?"

An old conversation with her sister filtered through her memory. Helen had taken a long weekend away with Dave one December after the McCall's herd had gone to auction. They'd had snow, a fireplace, a hot tub and hours of time to relax together for a change. Yet Helen had returned from the trip unhappy. At the time, Lilly had blamed Dave, wondering why he couldn't get things right for Helen. But in hindsight, now, Lilly focused on a particular statement Helen had made.

"He's like a new pair of shoes," Helen had explained. "They look great, they're your size, they match your outfit and maybe you even got them on sale. They seem perfect for you in every way and you *want* to love them…but they just don't feel right on your feet. They pinch your toe or rub your heel or…whatever. So I keep wearing those shoes, Lil, hoping to break them in and make them more comfortable, but they still hurt my feet."

Lilly's heart beat seemed to slow.

"I *tried* to love her," Dave had said, "but with you, it comes naturally. Denying that would mean betraying my heart."

Lilly pressed a hand to her mouth and blinked back tears as the truth crystalized. *Helen and Dave hadn't fit.*

But she and Dave did. Dave had seen it right away, but she'd fought it. Out of guilt. Because wouldn't Helen have been angry? Hurt?

Again, Dave's voice echoed in her head, recounting Helen's search for their father. *She wouldn't begrudge him the love he'd found with his new family.*

Helen, it seemed, had been far more forgiving and openhearted than Lilly had given her credit for. Had been more forgiving than Lilly had been.

Lilly frowned and stuck Helen's bear in the "keep" box. The next item out of the "sort" box was a family picture. Lilly, Helen, their mom and their dad. The colors in the photo had faded, but not the smiles. Her chest ached with a twenty-year-old hurt as she examined her father's face. She hadn't forgiven her father, had maybe dragged a bit of her baggage into her marriage with Alan. Another man she needed to forgive in order to move on.

Forgiving is about giving yourself a chance to heal. It's not for them. It's something you have to do, for yourself.

Damn it. Dave's wisdom was spot on. She saw it now. Along with how foolish she'd been to push away the first man to make her feel whole, and happy, and… at peace. With Dave she'd experienced real love. And she'd thrown it away.

Her breath escaped her in a whoosh, left her winded and dumbstruck. She and Dave *fit.* After weeks of missing him, mulling their time together, agonizing over Helen, the truth had finally clicked. She'd needed time, and he'd given her the space to figure out what he already knew. She took Helen's bear back out of the storage box and stroked the worn fuzz. She also liked to think Helen had helped her see how to come to terms with the pain from her past. How to forgive and move forward with a healthy, loving relationship. With Dave.

"What have I done?" Lilly shoved to her feet and placed Helen's stuffed bear on the pillow of her bed. "Maddie," she called as she grabbed her purse and jammed her feet into her shoes, "I'm going out. I have to fix a mistake."

Lilly had almost reached her car in the parking lot of her apartment complex when she spotted her neighbor, standing near the bank of mailboxes talking to a tall guy in a black cowboy hat. Her heart jolted. The cowboy hat made her think of Dave. *It's a sign.*

Lilly laughed at herself as she opened her car door. Everything made her think of Dave, so why should that cowboy and his hat be any different? A sign? No. More like excitement.

She tossed her purse on the passenger seat and gave the cowboy another glance as she slid behind the wheel. And then the cowboy turned.

She blinked. Took off her sunglasses. Gasped.

Dave! Was here. Outside her apartment…and—

She climbed out of her car on trembling knees and clung to the car door for support. "Dave?"

He approached, a small bundle of flowers in his hand, and gave her an awkward smile. "Hi."

"What—?"

"I know. I promised to give you space. Time, but…" He drew a deep breath. "I got good news today and wanted to share it with…someone." He sighed and twisted his mouth. "No. Not someone. With you. I got good news and the only person I wanted to share it with was you."

"Oh, Dave…"

He raised a hand in a what-are-you-gonna-do? gesture. "Thing is, I want to share more than just my good news with you. I want to share *everything* with you. I need you in my life, Lilly."

When she only stared at him with tears in her eyes and emotion choking her, he added, "Oh, and these are for you." He held the flowers out to her. "Lilies." He cleared his throat. "You know…because—"

He rolled his eyes. "Corny, I know, but…"

She shook her head and took the flowers, her hand trembling. "No. Perfect."

A sob broke from her chest as she stumbled into his arms and threw her arms around his neck. "Dave, I'm sorry. You were right."

He pulled back from her embrace and finger-combed the hair back from her eyes. "Um, what?"

"You were right about us. My heart knew it, but I wouldn't let myself see it."

He thumbed away a tear that tracked down her cheek. "Just so I know we're on the same wavelength—"

"You don't pinch my toes, Dave. You're the shoes I want to wear every day."

"Um, thanks?"

She laughed. "That's my way of saying I love you."

She framed his handsome face with her palms. "It took a lot of thinking to work through what my heart was saying. I had some clutter to clear, but I want to be with you, Dave."

His smile lit his face. "Really?"

She nodded. "I'm sorry it took so long for me to recognize it and that I pushed you away. I still have work to do, things to come to terms with before I can make any plans for the future."

"Things like…?"

"Old relationships. I was hiding behind Helen, using her as an excuse, when the truth was I was scared. My track record with men is pretty pitiful. Our dad left. My husband cheated. I felt like I wasn't enough for them."

He pulled a face that told her he wanted to contradict her, and she silenced him by placing her fingers on his lips. "And…when I met you, I viewed you through the distorted lens I had of men. That, and…I judged you based on all the negative stuff Helen had to say when she was upset about your relationship."

He arched an eyebrow and pressed a kiss to the fingers she still had over his mouth.

"I believed everything bad she told me," she said, "because it fit the narrative I'd created about my dad leaving. About Alan cheating. I'd been hurt, and I couldn't see past my heartache and anger to give you a fair shake."

He scrunched his nose, and said sheepishly, "Helen was probably right about some of what she told you. I've made my share of mistakes. I have flaws."

She scoffed. "We all do. But I'd like to decide for myself what yours are. I want to discover all the layers that make you the kind and courageous man I got to know while we were held hostage."

"*All* of my layers?" He gave her a teasing grin. "That could take some time."

She looped her arms around his neck and rose on her toes to kiss him. "I'm not going anywhere. We have all the time in the world."

Epilogue

Twenty-two months later

"Happy Valentine's Day," Dave said, squatting to place a bouquet of pink carnations on Helen's snow-covered grave. "I didn't forget." The pang he felt today was gentler than the harsh grief he'd known for months following Helen's death, but the guilt he'd harbored had healed, in large part because of the woman by his side.

Lilly stepped forward, kissed her gloved hand and put it on the face of her sister's grave marker. "I hope you know you are still loved so, so much, sis. And missed. That will never change."

Dave steadied Lilly as she stepped back on the icy ground, slipping his arm around her waist and drawing her close. "Do you think she sees us? That she's happy?"

No sooner had he asked the question than a sunbeam slipped through a gap in the gray clouds overhead and shone down on the mountain range in the distance. Lilly noticed the glowing beam as well and smiled. "I think we can assume so."

Even if he didn't believe in signs, Lilly had noticed enough "coincidences" over the past months that he'd almost changed his mind about whether Helen was sending messages from beyond. A butterfly that lit on Lilly when they visited the cemetery together last fall. A rainbow that decorated the sky on Helen's birthday. And the bird's nest built in a tree outside his kitchen window by a family of cardinals this spring.

"Cardinals are messengers from deceased loved ones you know," Lilly had said when they first spied the birds roosting in the nest. "Saying they love you."

At the time, he'd rolled his eyes at Lilly's belief in the wives' tale, but he'd taken comfort in the birds and grinned each time he heard them singing outside his window.

Now, as he savored the view of the golden sunlight shining on the mountains Helen had loved, he could almost believe it was Helen's radiant smile.

Lilly angled her head to look up at him. "Ready to go?"

He inhaled the crisp winter air and nodded. "Probably should. Our dinner reservation is in fifty minutes, and we have one more stop to make."

"Another stop? Where?" she asked, falling in step beside him as they crunched through the snow to his new truck.

"You'll see." He gave her a mysterious grin and

helped her climb up to the passenger seat. Once behind the wheel, he cranked the heater. Although he'd completed his physical therapy and had full use of his injured leg again, on chilly days, the pins in his shin reminded him of his old injury with a dull ache. He didn't begrudge the occasional twinge in his calf. Reminders of what he'd survived only made his current happiness all the sweeter.

The McCalls had kept their word to reemploy him when his leg healed. The Double M Ranch was doing so well, he'd even been given a sizable bonus, back pay for his loyalty and hard work during the McCall family's past financial difficulties.

Lilly shot him a curious glance as he turned in the opposite direction of the restaurant when he left the cemetery. "Do I get a hint where you're taking me?"

He squeezed her hand and lifted it to brush a kiss on her knuckles. "Nope."

About twenty minutes later, he pulled in the driveway to the Butterfly Pavilion in Westminster, where he'd taken her on their first official date twenty-two months ago. She gasped her excitement and gaped at him with pure joy in her eyes. "Do we really have time for this? I thought you said we needed to be at dinner in another half an hour."

He shrugged as if missing their reservation was no big deal. "If they give our table away, we'll go somewhere else."

She glanced around the empty parking lot and her shoulders drooped. "Oh, Dave, I don't think they're open."

He cut the engine and opened his door. "Let's just check."

He circled the front fender and held the passenger door while she climbed out, his heart beating a giddy tattoo against his ribs. The front door opened as they approached, and they were greeted by a woman with a clipboard who said, "Hello! Happy Valentine's Day! Mr. Giblan?"

"Yes. And this is my girlfriend, Lilly."

Lilly shook the woman's hand and shot Dave a suspicious look. "You prearranged for us to come after hours?"

His grin was unrepentant. "I did."

"I believe you said the Wings of the Tropics exhibit was where your particular interest was?" the docent asked.

Lilly's eyes brightened. "Butterflies are special to me. Yes."

The woman nodded and waved toward the back of the center. "This way then."

Dave laced his fingers with Lilly's as they followed the woman through the special doors into the building where tropical plants grew year round. Sharing the warm conservatory with the tropical flora were butterflies of every imaginable color. More than sixteen hundred of them.

Lilly laughed as she stepped onto the path that lead through the lush greenery, bright flowers and thousands of fluttering wings. She tipped her head back and turned 360 degrees, grinning as she admired the winged creatures. "They're so beautiful. I love this place!"

"You're the one who's beautiful," he said, "and I love *you*."

His comment drew her attention and an appreciative smile. "Thank you, Dave. I love you, too."

"In that case—" Heart thumping with anticipation, he dropped to one knee and reached in his pocket. Pulling out the folded bandana he had stashed there, he unfolded it and lifted the ring he'd brought for this moment. "Will you do me the honor of becoming my wife?"

Lilly clapped a hand to her mouth, and her eyes grew damp. "Oh, Dave. I—" She laughed again, the sound choked with happy tears. When she leaned in for a closer look at the ring, she dabbed at her eyes and croaked, "It's so pretty!"

He reached for her hand and slipped the ring on her finger. For another moment, she admired the ring, turning her hand to watch the jewels shimmer. A slim oval diamond in the center with a round sapphire on each side.

One of the many butterflies flapping around them lit on her hand, and she giggled joyfully. "Look! I'm not the only one who thinks so! Hi, lovely."

He put his finger in front of a butterfly resting on a bloom near him, and the winged insect crawled on his finger. Carefully he moved his hand so the yellow-winged creature could crawl onto Lilly's nose. She sputtered a laugh and looked at the butterfly with crossing eyes.

When the butterfly fluttered off her nose to another blossoming plant, Lilly studied the ring again. She raised shining eyes to his. "You know, this configuration kinda looks like the Melissa blue that we—"

"Yeah. On purpose."

She caught her breath, and her chin wobbled as fresh tears filled her eyes. "Oh, Dave…"

His gut tightened as he realized she hadn't answered him.

For the past two years, he'd kept his promise not to push her. He'd given her all the time and space she needed when she asked. In recent months, however, she hadn't wanted time away. She'd moved closer, gotten a job at the Boyd Valley Health Clinic, shared every free minute away from their jobs with him. They spent hours talking. Laughing. Making love. She'd seemed happy. He knew he had been as happy as he'd ever been. Helen still came up now and then, but as a happy memory, not as a guilt-soaked wedge between them.

Had he read Lilly wrong after all these months? Had he rushed her with his proposal, bringing back painful memories?

He climbed to his feet—still thankful he could after weeks in recovery—and framed her face with his hands. "Aw, Lilly, did I mess up? I promised not to rush you, I know. And we don't have to set a date, but I thought… I mean, it's Valentine's Day, and I wanted to do something special and romantic and—"

"You did," she said, nodding and gripping his sleeves. Tears still slipped down her cheeks. "This is all so sweet and so…perfect!" She drew a shuddering breath and wiped her face. "How Helen could have ever complained about you, I'll never know. You've been nothing but a gentleman to me. I mean, you're sweet and thoughtful and attentive…" She sniffed and shook her head.

His stomach knotted as he sensed something dreadful in her hesitation. "But?"

Her brow dipped, her expression confused. "But what?"

"I thought I heard a *but*." He knuckled away a tear on her cheek. "And you haven't answered me. Do you want to marry me?"

Her eyes widened with surprise. "I didn't? You thought that—" She chuckled and pressed a kiss on his mouth. "I'm sorry. I guess with all this—" she motioned around them to the many fluttering wings "—I'm kinda like a kid in a candy store." Stepping closer, she cupped the back of his head and peered deeply into his eyes. "I love you, too, and I do want to marry you, Dave. Yes, yes, yes!"

* * * * *

*Don't miss other books in Beth Cornelison's
McCall Adventure Ranch miniseries:*

Rancher's Covert Christmas
Rancher's Deadly Reunion
Rancher's High-Stakes Rescue

*Available now wherever
Harlequin Romantic Suspense books
and ebooks are sold!*

SPECIAL EXCERPT FROM

H HARLEQUIN®

ROMANTIC suspense

*Paramedic Remo DeLuca finds Celia Poller on the side
of the road after a car accident. Severely injured,
Celia has short-term memory loss and the only thing
she's sure of is that she has a son—and that someone
is threatening both their lives!*

*Read on for a sneak preview of
Melinda Di Lorenzo's next thrilling romance,*
First Responder on Call.

Remo took a very slow, very careful look up and down
the alley. The side closest to them was clear. But the
other? Not so much. Just outside Remo's mom's place,
the man Celia had so cleverly distracted was engaged in
a visibly heated discussion with another guy, presumably
the one from the car his mother had noted.

Remo drew his head back into the yard and hazarded
a whisper. "Company's still out there. We can wait and
see what happens, or we can slip out and make a run for
it. Move low and quick along the outside of the fence."

Celia met his eyes, and he expected her to pick the
former. Instead, she said, "On the count of three?"

He couldn't keep the surprise from his voice. "Really?"

She answered in a quick, sure voice. "I know it's
risky, but it's not like staying here is totally safe, either. A
neighbor will eventually notice us and give us away. Or
call the police and give Teller a legitimate reason to chase
us. And at least this way, those guys out there don't know

that we know they're here. Right now, they're trying to flush us out quietly."

"As long as you're sure."

"I'm sure."

He put a hand on Xavier's back. "You want to ride with me, buddy?"

The kid turned and stretched out his arms, and Remo took him from his mom and settled him against his hip, then reached for Celia's hand.

"One," he said softly.

"Two," she replied.

"Three," piped up Xavier in his own little whisper.

And they went for it.

Don't miss
First Responder on Call *by Melinda Di Lorenzo,*
available August 2019 wherever
Harlequin® Romantic Suspense books
and ebooks are sold.

www.Harlequin.com